# STRANGE
# BEDFELLOWS

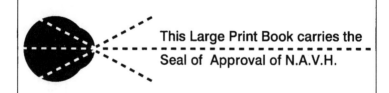

This Large Print Book carries the
Seal of Approval of N.A.V.H.

# STRANGE BEDFELLOWS

*A Jacob Burns Mystery*

## Matt Witten

**Thorndike Press • Thorndike, Maine**

Published in 2001 by arrangement with
NAL Signet, a division of Penguin Putnam Inc.

Thorndike Press Large Print Mystery Series.

The tree indicium is a trademark of Thorndike Press.

The text of this Large Print edition is unabridged.
Other aspects of the book may vary from the original edition.

Set in 16 pt. Plantin by Minnie B. Raven.

Printed in the United States on permanent paper.

**Library of Congress Cataloging-in-Publication Data**

Witten, Matthew.
    Strange bedfellows : a Jacob Burns mystery / Matt Witten.
        p.  cm.
    ISBN 0-7862-3214-5 (lg. print : hc : alk. paper)
    1. Campaign management — Fiction.  2. New York (State) — Fiction.  3. Elections — Fiction.  4. Large type books.  I. Title.
PS3573.I919 S77    2001
    813′.54—dc21                                    00-068287

*For my father*

# ACKNOWLEDGMENTS

I would like to thank my literary agent, Jimmy Vines; my editor, Joe Pittman; and the folks who helped me along the way: Carmen Bassin-Beumer, Betsy Blaustein, Nancy Butcher, Navorn Johnson, Leslie Schwartz, Larry Shuman, Benson Silverman, Matt Solo, Robert Tompkins, Jeffrey Wait, Justin Wilcox, Celia Witten, and everybody at Malice Domestic, the Creative Bloc, and the late, lamented Madeline's Espresso Bar.

I wish to express special gratitude to Jean Bordewich for running for Congress from the 22nd District and giving the voters a good choice.

Finally, many thanks to Nancy Seid, who is not only my wife and girlfriend, but also a darn fierce editor.

**Warning:** This book is fiction! The people aren't real! Nothing in it ever happened!

# 1

When longtime congressman Mortimer "Mo" Wilson died suddenly last spring after eating some bad sushi, my old pal Will called me that same night. "Jake," he boomed excitedly, "I'm considering running for Congress. What do you think?"

"I think, take two aspirin and a pint of José Cuervo and call me in the morning."

"Come on, this district is ready for a change. It's a whole new millennium —"

"Make that a quart."

I mean, who was he trying to kid? Our district in the wilds of upstate New York hadn't elected a Democrat since the Great Depression. It hadn't *ever* elected someone of the Hebraic persuasion. And Will was both.

Not only that, he was saddled with the unfortunate last name of Shmuckler. Tell me, would *you* vote for some guy named Will *Shmuckler?*

But Will ignored my advice. After the governor called a special election to fill the vacant seat, Will won the Democratic primary, running unopposed — no one else bothered. Now he was going head to head against the Republican, an empty suit named Jack "the Hack" Tamarack. The Hack had kissed high-powered GOP butt for two decades, most recently as legal counsel to the Republican State Senate Majority, and he was finally getting his reward: the safest seat in the entire U.S. House of Representatives.

Technically speaking, the Republicans had a primary, too. But the party mucky-mucks funneled enough TV ad money to the Hack so he could bury any dreamers foolish enough to oppose him. And once he had the GOP nomination . . . well, in the 22nd District, if you ran Robert Redford as a Democrat and a ringtail monkey as a Republican, the monkey would win — as long as he was against gun control.

So with the special election fast approaching and Will calling me frantically ten times a day to pass out leaflets, host candidate's coffees, and so on, I had no trouble whatever restraining my nonexistent enthusiasm. Years ago, as a wee young sprat, I had been "clean for Gene" McCarthy, canvassed for George McGovern, and spent the winter of 1975–76 tramping the snows of New Hampshire for Morris Udall, the best one-eyed candidate ever to run for president. Now, though, I was forty-one, with two kids in elementary school. I was way too old and way too busy for romantic lost causes.

And yet, somehow I did end up passing out those leaflets and hosting those coffees. I had no choice. See, the Shmuck (my affectionate nickname for him) was my freshman-year college roommate. We chased Holyoke girls and Smithies together, discussed The Meaning of Life in our dorm bathroom together, and one memorable Saturday night even puked our guts out from the same bottle of Mr. Boston Blackberry Brandy.

These days Will lived way down at the southern end of the 22nd District, over an hour away, so we hardly ever saw each other. Our lives had diverged in other ways, too: he'd stayed in the political sphere as an environmental lawyer, while I got into the writing biz. But the old ties between us still remained strong, like an old Bob Dylan song that stirs your innards even twenty-five years later.

So I did what Will asked. Eventually I found myself practically running the Saratoga County part of his campaign. My modest three-bedroom home in the town of Saratoga Springs turned into his local headquarters. By the beginning of September I could hardly wait until the big vote, two

11

weeks away, so I could get my life back. And get all those darn leaflets off my dining room table.

The final straw came when he awakened me from a deep sleep on the night before my kids' first day of school. He barely had a chance to get out "Hi, it's me," before I interrupted him.

"Shmuck, it's past midnight. I don't want to talk about your campaign —"

"That's not why I'm calling."

I heard a hubbub of background noises and an intercom. It sounded like a train station — or a hospital. "Where are you?" I asked in alarm. "You okay?"

"Not exactly. I'm in jail."

He sounded strangely calm. "*Jail?* What for?" I shouted.

Now his fake *sangfroid* gave way to a desperate cry. "I swear to God, I didn't kill him!"

"Kill *who?!*"

"The Hack," he said. "Somebody shot the Hack."

# 2

Early the next morning, my wife and I took our sons Derek Jeter and Bernie Williams to the bus stop for their first day of school. Their real names are Daniel and Nathan, but when they became rabid New York Yankee fans, they changed their monikers. (For those of you who never crack the sports pages, the original Derek J. and Bernie W. are Yankees who've won the World Series more often than I can count.)

Our boys used to call themselves Babe Ruth and Wayne Gretzky, and then Leonardo and Raphael — after the Ninja Turtles of course, not the painters. As Andrea and I waved good-bye to them through the bus window that morning, we both had tears in our eyes. Kids are such *weeds*. How long would our sweet little boys stay Derek and Bernie? By this time next year, would they be Hulk Hogan and Macho Man, or Shaquille and Kobe, or Pikachu and Charizard?

Derek was in second grade already, an old pro at this whole school bus thing, but Bernie was just a kindergartner. He clutched his older brother's hand and tried to look brave, but it was obvious he was churning inside.

Maybe it was fortunate that I didn't have time to dwell on my own muddled emotions that morning. I was on my way down south to Troy, to try to help Will beat his murder rap.

Why me? you may ask. Well, oddly enough, I had developed something of a reputation as a guy who could solve murders. I'd gotten mixed up in a couple of them — through no fault of my own, I hasten to add. So it made sense that when Will was accused of shooting someone, he'd come to me for help. And it made sense that I'd say yes.

No question about it, Will Shmuckler had his flaws. He was too much of a starry-eyed idealist for my increasingly curmudgeonly and middle-aged tastes. He was also way too much of a Boston Red Sox fan, a condition that I'm convinced leads to insanity. But despite that, I was pretty sure he wouldn't kill anyone — even someone who probably deserved it, like Jack the Hack.

I had to admit, though, the circumstantial evidence I'd read that morning in the *Daily Saratogian* sounded awfully damning. Will had better come up with some good explanations, I thought, as I pulled into the

Rensselaer County Jail where he was being held —

Only he wasn't there anymore. Not even eleven-thirty yet, but he was already out on bail. I guess that's one perk to being a lawyer: when you get in trouble yourself, you know which strings to pull.

I got back in my car and drove out to Will's home outside Coxsackie, down below Albany. Coxsackie isn't the world's most happening town; in fact, the state prison is their main employer. But Will's house itself is charming, a rambling old Victorian on a hill overlooking the Hudson River. It's the perfect place to put your feet up in front of a crackling fire and read an old P.G. Wodehouse novel.

Not that Will ever did that. He was a Type A guy to the max, who threw himself into his work the same way he was now throwing himself into his political campaign. As the lone in-house attorney for the Hudson-Adirondack Preservation Society, the region's premier environmental organization, he was fully capable of busting his tail eighteen hours a day for seven months straight in order to save some obscure subspecies of dung beetle.

Any time he had left over from work he spent fixing up his house. He was single now, his most recent girlfriend having left him several months ago. He always dated nice women, good marriage material, but they always ended up leaving him. "Going out with Will is like going out with Alvin the Chipmunk on speed," one of them complained to Andrea once.

When I showed up that morning, Will was in the kitchen guzzling coffee and worrying about how much his bail would cost. He'd had to put up his house as collateral to the bail bondsman.

"I spend ten years working on this place," he complained as he waved me inside. "And now that I finally get it like I want it, I'll have to *sell* it and go live in some God-awful studio apartment."

It seemed strange that Will would be so preoccupied with his house when he had a murder accusation hanging over his head. But I guess this was his way to avoid dealing with it. I eyed him closely. Like me, Will was six feet tall and slender with curly black hair, plus the traditional Jewish nose. Often when we were out in public together, someone would mistake us for brothers. "You think I look like this ugly *shnook?*" I'd say huffily to the waitress or whomever, and Will would do the same.

Hopefully we didn't look too alike right

now, though, because Will was a total mess. His right cheek gave intermittent involuntary twitches. Half of his hair seemed to be heading toward Oshkosh, while the other half was going to Zanzibar. The bags under his eyes were so big, you could have carried legal briefs in them.

For the past month or two, he'd looked more and more frazzled each time I saw him. At my candidate's coffees, he would toss back three cups of high-test in twenty minutes. Now he looked worse than ever, like the Wild Man of Borneo with a monster hangover. Or like Alvin on 'ludes.

"How you feeling, buddy?" I asked. "How was your night in jail?"

His right cheek twitched again. "Wonderful. My cellmate was Republican. Thinks the Democrats are too soft on crime."

"I hope he'll vote for you anyhow."

"Doubt he'll get the chance. Seems he has this little problem with robbing liquor stores."

"You know such interesting people."

"Yeah, right. If I get convicted, I'll write a book."

We headed for Will's living room, with its bookcases made of sweet-smelling cherry wood and a big bay window revealing the sunny, sparkling river. The walls were covered with nature photos, which Will shot himself while climbing the forty-six high peaks of the Adirondacks. In his typical headstrong way, it wasn't enough for Will to casually take up weekend hiking — he had to nail every single one of those forty-six peaks.

This morning he and I were feeling our way through a different kind of wilderness, a potentially much more dangerous one. "Will," I said, "you want to tell me what happened last night?"

He groaned. "I'm sure you read all about it on the front page, along with every other voter in the district."

"I'd like to hear it from you."

"Yeah, okay." He gulped down the dregs of his sixteen-ounce mug and began. "Last night I was supposed to do that half-hour debate with the Hack — oh God, now that he's dead, I shouldn't call him the Hack anymore."

"Don't worry about it."

"It's so horrible." He gave two more quick twitches. "See, the debate was supposed to start at nine. But you know how I like to get places early, so I was there by eight-thirty —"

"At the radio station?"

"Right. WTRO."

I nodded. I had resolutely ignored all the debate hype last night, so I could focus on the kids and getting them ready for school, but I knew the story behind the debate. Will had challenged the Hack to debate him, and the Hack felt politically obligated to accept. But he didn't want to risk debating on TV, where a large number of people might actually be watching. Instead he insisted on WTRO, the public radio station down in Troy. That way, even if he screwed up hardly anyone would hear it, since NPR is not exactly the favorite of the masses. Especially in upstate New York.

Will continued. "When I got there, they put me in the green room — you know, the waiting room — and then they left. A few minutes later they brought in the Hack — I mean Jack — and then left again. So me and Jack were stuck alone together."

"Didn't either of you bring campaign workers along?"

"*I* didn't. I like having quiet time before a speech or whatever to gather my thoughts. Maybe Jack was the same way, because there we were, just the two of us. It kind of made me sick. Here we were making small talk, but this was a guy that I wanted to beat his brains out." Will flushed. "I mean in the debate, not literally."

"I understand."

"So I went in the bathroom, just off the green room. I figured I'd sit on the toilet for ten minutes and review my notes. Which is what I was doing when I sort of became vaguely aware of conversation in the other room. Jack was saying something like, 'Hi, how you doing?' Then he made this surprised little squeak, like *'Aah!'* And then all of a sudden . . . there was a gunshot."

Will shuddered. "I was afraid they'd come in the bathroom and shoot me next. It's lucky I had my pants down, because I got the shit scared out of me for real. But then I heard footsteps running away, and I figured it was safe to come out. So I opened the door a crack — and Jack was lying on the sofa with his head blown off.

"That's how the radio people found me and Jack when they came running in. And they found the gun, too, just lying there. If only the killer took it away with him, then at least I'd have something to back up my story."

"But that's good news. The cops will be able to trace the gun."

Will rubbed his eyes, looking suddenly exhausted. "I heard some cop say the serial numbers were filed off."

"Maybe they'll find fingerprints," I said

brightly, trying to cheer him up.

It didn't work. "Yeah, that would be nice," he said gloomily. "But the gun was wiped clean, or else the guy was wearing gloves. That's what the D.A. said at my arraignment when he was outlining their preliminary evidence."

I had a flash of inspiration. "Gunpowder residue," I said, snapping my fingers. "They must've checked your hand for residue."

"They did."

"And they didn't find any, right? So that proves you're innocent."

He shook his head ruefully. "That's what I thought. But it turns out the stuff, the antimony or barium or whatever, can just wash off. Or even rub off. So its absence doesn't prove anything, especially with a sink in the next room."

How aggravating — with all the advances in scientific crime stuff, none of it seemed to be helping Will . . . at least not yet, anyway. Will's mopiness was catching. I fought it off. "Is it possible someone's trying to frame you?"

"Can't imagine who."

I tried another tack. "Did anyone at the station see somebody running away?"

Will shook his head. "And no one heard anybody, either."

"How about a car? Anyone see a car drive off?"

"Not that I know of."

This didn't sound good. My face must have shown it. "You've got to help me," Will pleaded, "you've *got* to. If they send me back to that jail, I'll stick my finger in a light socket!"

I patted him on the shoulder. "Don't worry, Shmuck," I reassured him, with much more confidence than I felt. "We'll get this squared away in no time."

And if you believe that, I've got an Internet stock to sell you.

From Will's house I drove to the scene of the crime. I'd been to WTRO once before, when they interviewed me about my movie.

Ah yes, my movie. I should explain about that, and why I was free to traipse around that morning playing Colombo instead of commuting off to some j.o.b. somewhere.

It's like this. After I escaped from grad school at age twenty-four (with an M.F.A. in Playwriting, of all the ridiculous degrees), I spent fifteen years writing artsy, *avant-garde* screenplays that never got produced and artsy, *avant-garde* stage plays that *did* get produced — off-off-Broadway, for audiences of about four people, including me.

But then one day, while sitting at my old pockmarked desk and debating which bills to pay and which to put off, I somehow took it into my head to write an incredibly dumb disaster movie about deadly gas seeping out of the ground after an earthquake and threatening to destroy the entire population of San Francisco. *The Gas that Ate San Francisco* took five weeks to write, it was the worst piece of junk I'd ever done . . . and it made me a million dollars.

Even after the agents, managers, producers, lawyers, tax men, and other bloodsuckers drank their fill, I still wound up with 300K, free and clear. It was so much money, I decided to take some time off and figure out What I Wanted to Do Next with My Life.

That was almost two years ago now, and I still hadn't figured it out. But hey, between a bull stock market and Andrea's salary as a community college professor, that 300K was holding steady. And my extended sabbatical gave me plenty of time to pursue my other interests, like hanging out at the local espresso bar, teaching Creative Writing at the local state prison, and playing *a lot* of baseball with Derek and Bernie.

I had also, much to my surprise, decided to become a Capitalist Landlord. Six months ago I bought the decrepit house next door and began the long process of tearing things down and building them back up again. After a decade and a half of being a brain-driven writer, I thoroughly enjoyed getting down and dirty. I rented the house out last week to three Skidmore College students, and I gave them such an enthusiastic blow-by-blow description of the rehab process that they almost fell asleep standing on their feet. Now whenever they saw me coming they scurried away like rabbits, afraid I'd shower them with yet more vital information about dry rot.

My movie — actually, after all the rewriting and editing they did, it wasn't quite "my movie" anymore — opened last Christmas and earned the studio enough green stuff to make my million bucks look like chickenfeed. My agent called me with all kinds of lucrative offers to write all kinds of inane movies. My personal favorite was an action-adventure pic about a gang of evil Micronesian terrorists setting loose a thousand cloned grizzly bears in New York City.

But I said no to all offers. Maybe it was writer's block, or maybe I was just being ornery, or maybe in my heart of hearts I still wanted to write the artsy stuff. All I knew for sure was, the idea of sitting alone in my study and wrestling with adjectives and dangling participles from dawn to dusk, coming up with such deathless lines as "Oh, no! It's the bears!", made me want to scream. I'd rather rehab another house.

In fact, I was thinking about buying a HUD foreclosure down the street that was going up for auction next month. What the heck, I told myself, if this was a midlife crisis, then it was a darn painless one.

As I drove up to the radio station, I recalled that the guy who'd interviewed me last year, Charlie Noll, had been going through similar What To Do Next questions about his own life. I'd given him a bunch of tips about getting into freelance writing. I hoped he would remember that and help me out today.

Parking outside the WTRO building, I was disconcerted by how *normal* it looked. There was only one cop car out there, and no yellow tape. I went inside and gave my name to the twenty-something, bleached blonde receptionist at the front desk. She recognized my name as belonging to a famous local screenwriter — in upstate New York, I'm a big fish in a small pond — and batted her eyes at me. She batted them for so long, I got nervous she was about to ask me to read a screenplay she wrote. You'd be amazed how often that happens.

But it didn't happen this time. Maybe she batted her eyes at everyone, just to keep in practice. She escorted me back to the big boss and left us.

He was a big boss, all right. A burly man in a red flannel shirt, Charlie Noll looked more like a lumberjack than an effete NPR-type intellectual. But he'd been running the station for twenty years now, doing everything from political commentary to DJ'ing to fixing the boiler. When I came in, he put down his thick cigar, rose from his chair, and grabbed my hand heartily. "It's the movie man," he greeted me.

"Good to see you, Charlie. How's the freelance writing business?"

He waved my query away. "Don't ask. I'm gonna be married to this station until death do us part. So what brings you here — as if I didn't know. You're helping out your old pal Shmuckler, aren't you?"

"How'd you know we were pals?"

"Hey, nothing gets past old Charlie. I gotta tell you, I'll bet my right ball Shmuckler did it. I'm the one found the body, you know. Talk about gross. And Shmuckler was standing right there. I asked him straight off, I said, 'Did you kill him?' And he didn't deny it, just stood there."

"He was probably in shock."

"Yeah, I would be too, if I just finished killing somebody."

"Okay, so we won't call you as a defense witness. You wanna show me where it happened?"

He checked his watch. "Sure, I got a few minutes 'til air time. We're doing a special on filberts."

"On *what?*" I asked, as we walked down the hallway.

"You know, the nut. Studies show, if you eat at least a quarter pound of filberts per day, it reduces your chances of prostate cancer by thirty-eight percent."

"I'll keep that in mind." Actually, I'd try to forget it immediately. *Filberts?* What would they think of next? Besides, I was planning to put off thinking about prostate cancer for at least another twenty years.

We came to the end of the hallway and started up another one, and finally I saw the yellow crime scene tape I'd been expecting. It was blocking the entrance to the infamous green room. Actually the room was painted blue, but why quibble.

I leaned over the tape to look in there — and immediately regretted it. That blue green room had way too much red. One sofa was decorated with large scarlet splotches, and there was a sea of dried blood on the floor nearby.

On the wall behind the sofa and slightly above it, the cops had drawn a circle in white chalk. In the middle of the circle was a small hole, with more blood splattered all around it. It looked like someone had shot a bullet through the Hack's head and into the wall, and parts of his head had burst open.

I doubled over and tried to breathe. It's a good thing I hadn't eaten lunch yet, or I would have lost it.

"Sorry, I should've warned you," Charlie said. "I figured what with you being an experienced murder investigator and all . . ."

Yeah, some murder investigator. The truth is, I'm such a wimp about blood I faint when I get a tetanus shot. But I steeled myself. "Can we go in?" I asked.

"Read the tape. 'Do Not Cross.' They got a cop guarding the place."

"Yeah? What, is he invisible?"

"No, he just went out for a bite to eat."

"Sounds like our big chance. Come on, Charlie, I won't tell anyone if you won't."

Without waiting for a reply, I lifted my leg and went over the tape. Charlie didn't argue. In fact, he went over the tape right behind me. "I've been wanting to do this all morning," he said.

Keeping my eyes away from the gore, I crossed the room and headed for the bathroom. "Do me a favor," I asked Charlie. "After I go in the john and close the door, could you say, in a regular voice, 'Hi, how you doing?' "

Charlie looked puzzled, but nodded. I closed the door and sat on the toilet. Then I heard Charlie saying, "Hi, how you doing?" from the other room. It was muffled, but I heard it. Well, at least that part of Will's story checked out.

I rejoined Charlie in the green room, still averting my eyes from all things crimson. "Did anyone here at the station have any connection with the Hack?"

"That's what the cops asked. Answer's no. Besides, there were only five of us in the station when the Hack was killed, and four of us were in the recording studio together."

"How about the fifth?"

"That was the receptionist, and she doesn't seem like a killer to me."

She did have killer eyelashes, but still, I had to agree with Charlie. Well, maybe the shooter came from outside. I stepped to the window. The sidewalk was only a few feet away, and just beyond it was a row of two-hour parking spots.

WTRO was plopped down amidst a strip-mall wasteland, surrounded by vacant storefronts featuring peeling FOR RENT signs. The booming national economy was bypassing Troy with a vengeance. I wondered how many Troy residents — what do they call themselves anyway, Trojans? — were walking around outside the WTRO building at the time of the crime, 8:45 p.m. on Labor Day.

Not many, I guessed. And it was already dark by then. Perfect circumstances for a getaway.

But how could the killer make it into the building unseen in the first place? Unless that twenty-something blonde was off somewhere touching up her eyeshadow, she would have spotted any intruders.

I turned to Charlie. "What if somebody parked outside, looked through this window, and saw the Hack sitting all by himself in the green room? Could they sneak into the building, and into this room, with no one from the station seeing them?"

"Fat chance," Charlie declared. "They'd have to come through the front door, and they'd never make it."

"You must have another door to the building."

"Emergency exit. Locks automatically. You can't come in through there."

"Let's go check it out."

Charlie rolled his eyes, but took me out to the hall. The emergency exit door was a mere five steps farther down. We went outside and let the door close behind us. Then we tested it.

*Presto.* "Automatic lock" notwithstanding, the door opened instantly.

Presumably the lock was just as "automatic" last night, too. I was feeling pretty proud of my P.I. skills — and more important, Will's story was suddenly looking a lot more believable.

"Still, *someone* at the station would've seen or heard *something*," Charlie said defensively as we headed back toward the front of the building.

"But you were all either in the recording studio or at the front desk. And they're both at least a hallway and a half away from the murder, right?"

"I guess so, yeah. But —"

"You gotta remember, this debate was public knowledge. Killer could've been anyone. He could've shown up here early and waited for just the right moment to kill the Hack."

By now we had reached the lobby. Charlie leaned against the receptionist's desk, and she batted her eyes at him. Maybe it was just that her contacts needed cleaning.

"Jacob," Charlie said thoughtfully, "how well do you really know Will Shmuckler? What makes you so sure he didn't do it?"

"Because he didn't."

"Fact is, your guy had this pathetic dream of becoming a congressman. But he didn't have a snowball's chance in hell — unless he did something drastic."

"Killing the Hack wouldn't have been *drastic,* it would've been *suicidal.* I mean, look what's happening now that he's accused of murder. He won't get a single vote."

Charlie shrugged. "Okay, so it was an act of passion. The Hack stuck out his tongue and said, 'Nyah, nyah, I'm gonna beat you,' and Shmuckler couldn't take it. Pulled out his gun and shot him."

"Will doesn't *have* a gun. He's for gun control."

Charlie snorted with disgust. "I know, and he's against capital punishment. For a politician who wants to get elected, that's pretty suicidal right there. You may call it principled politics, but I call it wasting your time. Speaking of which, I better run," he said, shaking my hand and hurrying off. "My show's about to start. Filberts are calling me."

I watched him go. He was right about capital punishment, of course; taking a stand against it in this conservative era is futile. But agreeing with him made me feel sad. I still longed for the old days, when I thought my generation *stood* for something. Now it seemed like all we stood for was filberts.

Meanwhile the receptionist was gazing up at me. Her newly painted lips were parted, and her eyes were setting the world's record for most bats per minute. "Mr. Burns," she said breathily, "I'm a screenwriter, too."

Oh no, here it comes. "That's great," I said, and made a mad dash out of the building before she could thrust a screenplay in my hands.

Outside the afternoon sun was shining brightly, but I felt murky. As I fished my sunglasses out of my pocket, I tried to imagine what I would do next if I were Sam Spade.

My guess is, old Sam would have fired up a cigarette, guzzled some whiskey from a hip flask, and swaggered back inside to interview the WTRO employees — especially the eye-batter. Then he would have taken the eye-batter home with him and taught her all about screenwriting and a few other things, too.

But for better or worse, I *wasn't* Sam

Spade. I had two kids, it was two o'clock already, and I knew exactly what I had to do next — hurry back to Saratoga, so I'd be in time to pick up my sons at their bus stop. Now that I was hitting Dreaded Middle Age, that's what *I* stood for: Derek and Bernie. Whoever killed the Hack, it sure was inconsiderate of him to do it during my kids' first week of school.

But maybe the killer didn't have time to wait. Maybe, I reflected as I got onto I-87 north, he had to get rid of the Hack *now*, before the election.

But why? Who else besides Will would benefit from the Hack not getting elected?

Or was I barking up the wrong shrub entirely?

# 3

While the kids were having their afternoon Wheaties and discussing who was the best shortstop of all time, I called Will and told him the rather skimpy results of my day's sleuthing. That's when I learned he was plugging on with his campaign for Congress.

The New York State Board of Elections had ruled earlier in the day that the special election must go on as planned, even though one of the candidates on the ballot was dead. The Board was adhering strictly to state law, which declares that if a candidate dies within three weeks of an election, the voting proceeds without interruption and any votes for the dead guy simply get tossed out. The Hack had been killed exactly fifteen days before show time.

There was no law against suspected murderers running for Congress, but still, I had trouble believing Will really wanted to persevere. "You're joking, right?" I said, incredulous. "You'll embarrass yourself. The Republicans will pick a write-in candidate, and he'll kill you. You'll get fewer votes than Elvis Presley."

"Not if you can prove I'm innocent before the election."

"That's just two weeks from now. I'm not God. I'm not even Kinsey Millhone."

"Look, I refuse to let this stupid thing stop me!" Will shouted hotly. "I'm *innocent*. Why should I quit? That would be admitting guilt!"

I didn't have an answer to that, and I agreed to meet him at a campaign event that night and give him moral support. The event was a candidates' forum sponsored by the Student Political Alliance at Skidmore College, Saratoga's one lonely bastion of liberalism. The forum was scheduled a month ago. The Hack had declined to attend, so the organizers had planned to have Will sitting alongside an empty seat.

It seemed odd that the event wasn't canceled out of respect for the man who'd died the night before. But the Student Political Alliance decided to stick with it, apparently on the theory that the death made their event much more noteworthy. Maybe they'd even get on TV.

Ordinarily, of course, watching a politician sitting next to an empty seat would not be a huge draw. But thanks to Will's new-found notoriety as a killer, the three-hundred-seat auditorium was already jam-packed with students and media people when I arrived there at 6:45. I had to stand in the back. I noticed several policemen in the auditorium, too.

At seven o'clock, Will came onstage and sat in his chair. There was an eerie silence. No one knew whether to cheer or hiss. His gray suit was disheveled, and he looked very small and shaky up there. I saw the inevitable cup of java in his hand, and wondered how much caffeine he'd consumed today.

Will was accompanied by the moderator, a Skidmore student wearing a red flannel shirt and a ponytail. He came to the microphone and asked for a moment of silence for Jack Tamarack. Will and the rest of us all bowed our heads — except for the media photographers, who ignored the solemn moment and instead noisily shot Will with his head bowed.

Then the moderator gave a truly surreal introduction of Will. "I would like to remind people that we are all innocent until proven guilty. So please, everyone keep an open mind as I now introduce to you the Democratic candidate for United States congressman, William Shmuckler."

Once again the hall was weirdly silent, since no one knew how to react as Will stood up and began speaking. "I would like to express my heartfelt sympathy to Jack Tamarack's family," he said, and spoke for a couple of minutes in a stilted, clichéd way about having respected his opponent, and how democracy requires us all to respect our opponents. Then he segued awkwardly into his standard stump speech about protecting the environment. What did this have to do with Jack Tamarack's death? The crowd began shifting restlessly.

Will was speaking haltingly, losing his place, stuttering. It was clear he had no business being on stage that day. He was still in shock. I felt bad that I hadn't protested harder against his going through with this.

Fortunately, Will realized pretty fast that his standard stump speech was inappropriate today. So he quickly brought the speech to a close with a second, stumbling expression of sympathy for the Tamarack family.

When he finally finished talking — it was only four or five minutes, but it felt like an eternity — the moderator stood up. "Mr. Shmuckler will now take questions," he said. "Please stand in line at the microphone in the middle aisle."

Thirty people, most of them media, instantly jumped up and raced each other in a frenzy for the microphone. There was pushing, shoving, screaming. "People, please! Calm down!" the moderator called out, but no one listened. Several students standing in the way of the media got knocked down. They pushed back. The cops jumped in and began shoving people around. It had all the makings of a full-scale riot. Will stood up at the front looking stricken.

Eventually the pandemonium died down, and the questions started pouring in. "Did you kill Jack Tamarack?" was the first.

"No," Will said.

"Where were you at the time of the murder?" came the follow-up.

"For legal reasons I can't answer," said Will.

Flash bulbs were popping, TV cameramen were angling for position. "Where'd you get the gun?" the next questioner asked.

"For legal reasons I can't answer any questions about the murder. I'm sorry," Will said.

But the questions kept on coming. "Why'd you kill him?" "Were you upset that you were going to lose the election?" "Don't you think it will be seen as outrageous that you're still running?"

Finally Will couldn't take it anymore. He mumbled, "Thank you. Good night," and edged off the stage.

I hurried out the back of the auditorium and dashed to the side door to meet him. I found him in the hallway, scurrying away from me.

"Hey, Will!" I called out. He turned toward me, and his eyes widened. He seemed to be looking over my shoulder. Then he took off like a bat out of hell. Behind me I heard people running and shouting Will's name. I turned around to see ten or fifteen media people bearing down on me, chasing after Will. How could I stop these people from torturing my friend? There was nothing I could do . . .

But then, without thinking, I reached out my arms and grabbed the first reporter in the pack, a tall, thin man with red hair and glasses. He gave me a puzzled look as I shoved him in the way of reporter number two, a muscular woman with a camera that fell to the floor but luckily didn't break. Reporter number three stopped in her tracks, to make sure she didn't run into the camera. Behind her, a short man with unwieldy TV equipment had to stop, too.

I threw my arms around a cute woman reporter who was trying to make it around the pileup. She stomped me in the foot with a high heel, and that was the end of that maneuver. But by the time the media people got going again, Will had successfully made his escape. A couple of minutes later, when I stood in front of the building looking around for Will, the fourth estate was out there too, doing the same thing I was and cursing their luck.

Later that night, my phone rang. It was Will. "I made an ass of myself tonight, didn't I?" he said.

"I'm afraid so," I replied.

"But I'm not giving up," he said, and when I tried to convince him to at least take a few days off, he hung up on me. When I called him back, his phone was off the hook.

The Hack's funeral was scheduled for the very next day, which surprised me; usually, the only folks that bury their dead that quick are Jewish people and Kennedys. I felt like a sleazeball attending the funeral, since I'd never even met the man — and from what I knew, I didn't like him.

But most of the two hundred other mourners in this huge, impersonal chapel probably didn't like the dead man all that much either. My guess was, they were here because they had to be. I didn't see too many tears, that's for sure. Of course, maybe Republicans don't cry as much as other people.

I recognized the mayor of Saratoga and three or four other local politicos, but no one else. These weren't the type of folks I usually hung out with, and anyway, I tend to have a sievelike memory for faces. Yet another bad trait for a murder investigator. Ah, well.

The unctuous, bushy-eyebrowed minister droned through a long routine about what a great man the Hack had been. If you bought his *shpiel*, the Hack was a loving son, husband, and father who went to church every Sunday and devoted his life to serving others. He always obeyed the speed limit, put fallen baby birds back in their nests, and never picked his nose in public.

Okay, maybe the minister didn't quite say *all* of that, but he came darn close. He was from the Henry James school of literature, never using one word when one hundred would do the job just as well. Even worse, he had a habit of lingering over the "s" sound when it came at the end of a syllable, so a word like "consciousness" took him about ten seconds to spit out. *"Consciousssss-nesssss."* It was excruciating. When he sputtered to a halt at last, and the organ churned out a sad ditty, all of us "mournerssss" hightailed it out of the church as fast as we politely could.

I decided to skip the cemetery, out of fear that the minister might show up with new gas in his linguistic tank. Instead I went to my home away from home, Madeline's Espresso Bar on Broadway, for a cappuccino. Thus fortified, I then crashed the wake at the Hack's house.

The Hack had lived right in Saratoga Springs, like myself. But whereas I lived in a small colonial in a working-class neighborhood, he lived in a two-story brick affair on Fifth Avenue, one of Saratoga's priciest streets. As I stepped past the Corinthian pillars on the porch and opened the solid oak front door, I felt utterly out of place, like I always do in fancy houses. I got rich so suddenly, even now I don't *feel* rich. I still pick up dirty pennies from the sidewalk.

The Hack's living room was full of forty-something white men wearing suits and ties — in other words, guys who looked just like me. But still, to my eyes they were creatures from another planet. I wonder, do other men feel like they're donning some bizarre alien raiment when they put on a suit and tie, or is it just me?

When I'm ill at ease socially I always gravitate toward the other misfits, and that's what I did now. I ambled over to the one guy who stuck out like a Tibetan lama at a

Burger King. He looked about eighty-five, by far the oldest guy there. His suit hung too loose, and was probably three times cheaper than any other suit in the room — even mine, and that's saying something.

Most striking of all, the man had the grizzled, careworn face, rough, calloused hands, and sinewy arms that shouted, "blue collar." No one else at the wake had any of these characteristics.

Nor did anyone else have anything resembling his facial expression. It was an unfocused sneer, like he was disgusted with something but wasn't quite sure what.

His sneer was so off-putting that I paused before reaching him, planning to turn back. But then he glanced up and saw me, and I couldn't figure out a graceful way to retreat. "Hi," I said nervously.

He nodded suspiciously. Who was this strange old bird? Maybe the Hack's lawn care guy or something.

"It's a sad day, huh? Were you a friend of Jack's?" I ventured.

"Not exactly," he rasped in a scratchy voice. "I'm his father."

I gulped with surprise. Nothing about this man's blue-collar look or edgy attitude reminded me of the smooth, dull politico I knew as the Hack.

The old man's eyes crinkled with bitter amusement. "What's the matter, I don't look the part?"

"No, you do," I stuttered. "Actually, you look just like him."

"Bullshit," he snarled. But then, out of nowhere, he started to cry. That got him coughing, and soon his whole body was racked by a ferocious coughing spasm.

"Are you okay?" I asked, rather stupidly, because he obviously *wasn't* okay. "Can I get you something?" But he was coughing and shaking so hard, he couldn't answer.

I looked around the room for help, but none of the suit-and-tie guys were paying any attention at all to Hack Sr.'s noisy health crisis. They were wrapped up in their conversations about real estate, politics, and golf. It was as if they had signed a secret pact to ignore the old man.

Hack Sr.'s hacking was getting so explosive I half-expected him to have some kind of seizure. Should I call 911? Get him some whiskey? Or just ease on out of the house and let someone else deal with it?

Just then a little boy about Derek Jeter's age came into the room. He ran up to the old man and threw his arms around him. "Grandpa," he said.

The old man's killer coughs gradually

subsided, replaced by gasps. Finally even those receded into ordinary breaths. Hack Sr. tenderly ruffled his grandson's hair and held him close.

Feeling guilty for having brought on this fierce attack, I slipped out of the room. I walked toward the kitchen, which beckoned me with welcoming food smells and the gentleness of women's voices.

There must have been a good twenty-five women in that kitchen, and I swear to God, *every single one of them* was holding a casserole dish. Additional casseroles were overflowing the counters, heating up in the oven, and cooling off in the refrigerator. Why is it that when someone dies, all the women who knew him feel compelled to cook casseroles?

Well, no doubt the widow would be grateful for all that chicken pot pie in the lonely weeks ahead. Speaking of which, where *was* the widow?

Maybe right here in the kitchen. I searched the room for a female specimen who looked more stricken with grief, and less preoccupied with casseroles, than the rest.

But these specimens all looked equally bland. No grief here. I moved on.

I wandered down a hallway toward the bedrooms. At first I thought they were all deserted, but then I heard voices seeping from behind one of the closed doors. It sounded like they were arguing — quite heatedly, in fact. I put my ear to the door, but was confounded by all the competing noise from the kitchen and living room. On an impulse, I opened the door and walked in.

All six people in the room immediately shut up and looked my way. There were three frowning middle-aged men sitting beside each other on the edge of the bed, reminding me somehow of the Three Stooges. Standing in front of them were a man and a woman, both in their thirties, and both of them red-faced and angry. Meanwhile a bald man with an ironic expression stood apart from everyone else, leaning against a wall. He tapped his foot impatiently, waiting for me to leave.

The polite thing would have been to say, "Excuse me," and close the door quietly behind me. But instead I stared back at them, trying to remember where I'd seen them before. In particular, I was trying to place that angry thirty-something man with the square jaw and piercing blue eyes — Pierce, that was his name, Robert Pierce, the state assemblyman from Wilton.

Pierce was only about five-foot-seven but

he was definitely on the rise, a star in local GOP politics, their new fair-haired boy. Everyone had expected him to be chosen as the next congressman when Mo Wilson was laid low. But the party bosses fooled everyone by picking the Hack instead, and Pierce was said to have swallowed his pride and accepted their verdict.

Now, though, with the Hack out of the way, it looked like Pierce would get his big chance after all. According to the newspapers I'd read that morning at Madeline's, the local Republican big cheeses — the county chairmen of the 22nd District — were about to endorse someone as their official, party-approved write-in candidate. All the pundits were predicting that they would select Pierce, who would of course go on to clobber his opponent, the Jewish liberal suspected murderer, in the election.

The lone woman in the room broke into my thoughts. "Looking for someone?" she asked, trying to soften her irritation with a hint of a smile.

She was too waif-like for my tastes, but attractive in an Ally McBealish sort of way. Though she looked more exasperated than grief-stricken, I finally recognized her anyway: she was the Hack's widow. I'd seen her mug on the back of his campaign brochures, gazing up at him adoringly.

What argument had I interrupted? And who were all the other men in the room? Unfortunately I didn't have time to figure it out. "Excuse me," I said belatedly and withdrew, closing the door behind me.

The quarrel instantly started up again — but quieter this time. They were trying to be discreet. All I could hear was an occasional "Screw you!" or "The hell with that!"

Disappointed, I started back down the hallway. But then I noticed an open bathroom to my left, immediately next door to the bedroom in question. Even better, there was a connecting door, now closed, between the two rooms.

*Carpeing* the *diem,* I snuck into the bathroom and shut the door to the hall. The noises from the living room and kitchen fell away. I tiptoed to the connecting door, dropped down to the floor, and put my ear as close as it could go to the crack under the door.

The voices began leaking through. "If you think I'm gonna lie down and let you fuck me," a man was saying, "dream on."

"Damn it, Pierce," another man growled, "if the widow goes through with it, and you two split the vote, that asshole Shmuckler could *win.*"

"Give it a rest," the first speaker — Pierce — said. "Shmuckler'll be lucky to get five percent."

"We don't know that," a third voice whined. "What if people get some sick kick out of voting for a murderer? We can't risk it."

"So you're gonna let this bitch scare you into doing what she wants?" Pierce yelled, outraged.

Then there was a sudden silence. What was going on in there? I wriggled even closer to the door, putting my ear right up against the crack —

And the door burst open.

I looked up from the floor. The bald guy was standing there with his hands on his hips, glowering down at me. Behind him, five other pairs of eyes glowered down at me too.

Feeling like a poor excuse for a worm, something too low to even use as fish bait, I scrambled awkwardly to my feet. "Excuse me," I mumbled for the second time in two minutes, grinning inanely, and got the hell out of there.

My wife laughed her head off later that day, when I told her how I'd been caught in the act. "Hey, it wasn't funny," I complained.

"I'm sure it wasn't," she said, and laughed even harder.

I didn't get too riled at her, though. I knew this was just Andrea's way of releasing nervous tension. She had gone along with my decision to help Will beat his murder rap, since she'd become friends with him too over the years. But she wasn't too thrilled about the whole thing. She still maintained — with some justification, I must admit — that the only reason I'd escaped my previous Sam Spade impersonations alive was because I got lucky as hell.

Finally she got her guffaws under control. "So what were these people quarreling about?" she asked.

I'd had plenty of time to cogitate about that quarrel, with its allusions to "splitting the vote" and "letting this bitch scare you." "I think the other men in that room were Republican county chairmen," I said. "Pierce and the widow were both asking them for the party endorsement. And the widow was threatening to run anyway, even if they didn't endorse her — and even if that meant the Republican vote would be split."

Andrea whistled. "She's acting pretty ballsy for someone who just lost her husband."

"Yeah. And she didn't seem too horribly

51

broken up about his death, either."

"I'll have to ask Rosalyn about her."

Rosalyn was Andrea's friend, a fellow English prof at her community college. "Why Rosalyn?"

Andrea frowned at me. "I thought I told you. The Hack's wife took a course from her."

"Oh, right, I remember." Actually, I didn't. Yet another symptom of the alarming forgetfulness I'd been having lately. Dreaded middle age strikes again.

Any further discussion of Rosalyn and the widow was halted by my two sons, who suddenly raced into the room whooping with joy. "Daddy, guess what?" Derek shouted. "We found the Yankees' web page!"

"It's so cool!" his little brother, Bernie, exclaimed. "It tells you everything about Bernie Williams. *Everything!*"

Three months ago we bought the kids a fancy new computer, and now that machine gave both of them their reason for living. We limited them to an hour apiece of computer time per day, but that hour was the absolute high point of their existence. The hard drive went on the fritz for two days last month, and Bernie was still having nightmares about it.

We bought the computer because we felt

guilty that All the Other Kids Had Them, and maybe we weren't preparing our own children sufficiently for the computer age. In retrospect, I have doubts about our purchase. Okay, it wasn't nearly as foolish as the Stairmaster that's rusting away in our basement. But Derek and Bernie were just as happy — and more creative — doing the stuff they used to do before the computer came, like reading, playing catch, and drawing pictures of baseball players.

Even worse, now I was stuck listening to endless anecdotes about their computer experiences. Myself, I find computers incredibly uninteresting.

Although in truth, maybe my real problem was jealousy. How could my seven-year-old — heck, even my five-year-old — understand computers better than I did? Every time I try to get information from the Internet, I end up with a headache.

Eager to change the subject from computers, I asked, "So how was school today, guys?"

"Fine," they answered in unison. Then they hurried back to their beloved machine, which had completely taken over Andrea's study — or as it was now called, "the computer room."

*"Fine."* School was only two days old, and

already they were totally blasé about it.

Ah well, at least school wasn't traumatizing them, I comforted myself as I picked up the phone book and looked for Rosalyn's number. I doubted she'd be at home, though. She was probably at her boyfriend Sam's house, locked into some heavy discussion about Commitment and Children and "Are We Ready?" Sometimes it seemed like half of Andrea's unmarried friends were having that exact same discussion with their boyfriends, which Andrea and I privately called the "Marry me, asshole" conversation. After marriage, of course, it's replaced by the ever popular "You never tell me I'm pretty anymore."

But I guess Rosalyn and Sam were taking a break from the deep stuff, because she was home when I called. "Sure, I had Susan Tamarack," Rosalyn said. "She was in my Comp 102 class this summer. Why?"

"What was she like?"

"Don't know. She was pretty quiet, one of those students that always sit in the back. So you must feel pretty bad about your friend killing Susan's husband."

"I'm not so sure he did it. Listen, why was Susan Tamarack taking a community college course? Seems like an odd thing to do, when your husband is in the middle of a huge political campaign."

"Doesn't seem odd to me. Maybe she wanted to try a new thing, you know, something just for herself. I remember on the first day of class, when I had the students interview each other, she said she hadn't been working or going to school for ten years."

And now she wanted to get elected to Congress. Not a bad entry-level position. "She ever say anything about her marriage?"

"Like what?"

"I don't know. Anything."

There was a brief silence, then Rosalyn said, "I think she felt pretty fried, trying to take care of her kid and get her schoolwork done at the same time she was doing the whole politician's wife routine. But nothing really sticks out."

"How about in her writing? Anything stick out there?"

"Hey, I had *thirty students* in that dumb course, just about ruined my summer. I was in such a hurry to grade those papers, I could've had J. D. Salinger himself in my class and I wouldn't have noticed it."

She was exaggerating, I knew; Rosalyn was actually a painfully committed teacher who marked every misplaced comma and obsessed over whether to give an A- or B+.

"Are Comp 102 students still required to do portfolios?" I asked.

I knew about these portfolios — or, as I always thought of them, "port*follyos*" — from my pre-Hollywood millionaire days, when I used to teach Comp 102 at the community college as an adjunct. At the end of the semester, I'd have to gather together five of each student's best essays for two other profs in the department to read. The profs could then fail the student, even if his actual teacher — in this case, me — had passed him.

In theory, this was supposed to introduce accountability to the grading process. But in reality, the portfolios had absolutely zilch impact, because no professors had ever had the social gaucherie to overrule their colleagues. The whole setup was just typical academic folly.

"Yeah, we still have portfolios," Rosalyn said. "Which reminds me, I have to get my summer portfolios to the committee."

"I'd like to take a look at what Susan Tamarack wrote," I said.

No answer.

"Rosalyn?"

"I can't do that," she finally responded.

"Why not?"

"Wouldn't be ethical. Some of these students write pretty personal stuff. I promise them at the beginning of the semester, no one will ever see what they write except for me."

"And two other professors."

"Well, yeah."

"Come on, Roz."

"Hey, it's a privacy issue. Would you want random people reading *your* personal stuff?"

"If it might help solve a murder and keep an innocent man out of jail, then sure. No problem."

"I really don't see how Susan's portfolio could help you."

In all honesty, I wasn't so sure it could help me either. But I had no idea where else to start my investigation and I was getting desperate, so I kept my doubts to myself. "She was married to the man. Maybe she knew something. Maybe she *did* something."

"I'm sorry, Jake —"

"Get real, will you? These aren't exactly privileged communications. You're an English professor grading papers, not a Catholic priest taking a confession."

"You'd be surprised. Sometimes there's not much difference."

We went around in circles for another ten minutes before we hung up, mutually aggravated. I had half a mind to call up Sam and advise him to avoid commitment with this woman at all costs. She was too darn scrupulous. If they got married, she'd probably get on his case all the time about how he held his fork.

Rosalyn did have a point, though: Comp students do write highly personal stuff. It always used to shock me how open they'd be. But I guess if your teacher assigns you an essay about, say, "An Important Event in My Life," or "My Most Embarrassing Moment," then you don't really have much choice about being open. Especially if you want an A.

So who knows what I might find in Susan Tamarack's portfolio? Maybe I'd hit the jackpot and come up with something entitled, "Why I'm Planning to Kill My Husband."

Unfortunately, without Rosalyn's help I wouldn't come up with *anything*.

Or would I? Maybe I could convince Andrea to sneak into Rosalyn's office at school and get the goods.

I broached the idea to her that night, during a moment of postcoital tenderness. But the tender moment died quickly, when it turned out Andrea shared her friend's scruples.

"Come on, honey," I wheedled, "snatching the portfolio will be *fun*. Don't you want to be a private dick, too?"

She touched me in the obvious place. "No, that's your job."

"Seriously."

She withdrew her hand. "I can't do it. If I broke into Rosalyn's office, I'd feel like I was betraying her."

"The person you're betraying here is *Will*." I was pissed. It was lucky we'd already made love, because our argument was getting hot enough that it would have created some serious *coitus interruptus*.

Just then the phone rang, giving us a welcome *argumentus interruptus*. I picked up. "Hello, Shmuck-dude," I said.

"How'd you know it was me?"

"Who else calls here at midnight? I tried to reach you before, but your phone was busy all night."

"It was off the hook. I managed to sleep for three whole hours. First time I've slept in days. So what have you found out?"

"Not much, I'm afraid."

Will exploded. "What do you mean, 'not much'? Damn it, this is no time to get all California laid-back!"

"Hey, I'm working on it, trust me," I said, and proceeded to tell him about the impromptu bedroom conference that I'd crashed at the funeral.

I could feel Will's excitement pouring through the phone line. "Of course! Why didn't *I* think of that?"

"Think of what?"

"Robert Pierce! He's the most power hungry sonufabitch in the world. I heard that when the party endorsed the Hack instead of him, he got so mad he punched somebody out. The guy's mentally unstable. I'll bet he killed the Hack!"

I thought Will was really reaching, but I didn't argue. I'd already done way too much arguing for one night. "I'll look into it," I said.

But Will read me perfectly. "You think I'm nuts, don't you?"

"Not at all —"

"Jake, you gotta nail this guy. My life is turning into a bad Kafka novel. I had to cancel all my campaign appearances and hide in my house with the curtains down. The reporters are waiting on my front lawn with TV vans and antennas and stuff. And meanwhile I left messages for my volunteers and nobody's even calling me back. I'll bet they've all stopped passing out leaflets."

How could he think about leaflets at a time like this? Didn't he realize his campaign was deader than Milli Vanilli's career? Must be more of that avoidance thing. "Listen, it's good you're staying home. I'm sure your lawyer would tell you —"

"Lawyer? Who has money for a lawyer?"

"Don't be stupid. You need a —"

"Why? I'm innocent. No way I'm gonna pay a lawyer and lose this house."

"I'll be glad to lend you the money —"

"Enough already. Look, the election's only thirteen days away. If you can't clear my name before then, I'll *never* get elected!"

It was so late, and I was so burned out, that I said exactly what I was thinking — always a dangerous policy. "Buddy, save your breath. Forget the election. Even if I do clear your name, you don't have the ghost of a ghost of a chance —"

"Are you kidding? This is my golden opportunity. The Republicans are stuck with a write-in campaign, and most people are too dumb and lazy to figure out how to write someone in. The Hack's death was an incredibly lucky break!"

I sighed. "Glad to hear it. But since that's a murder motive, you might not want to spread it around too much," I said, and hung up.

# 4

I lay awake half the night trying to dream up an organized plan of attack, but came up empty. The next morning, as soon as we got the kids off to the bus, I went down to the newsstand on Broadway and checked the front pages of all the upstate newspapers.

The papers were filled with speculation about who would get the endorsement — smart money was still on Pierce — but nobody had anything fresh on the murder. Apparently the cops hadn't found any new evidence. Furthermore, the Troy police chief confirmed that the murder weapon's serial numbers were filed off and the gun was untraceable. Of course, none of this bothered the editorial writers in the slightest. They all simply assumed Will was guilty.

Did the filed off serial numbers indicate some sort of hardened criminal was involved?

Badly in need of a pick-me-up, I grabbed some morning caffeine at Madeline's, where I ran into my old friend Dave Mackerel. Thanks to my tireless matchmaking efforts,

Dave was now dating Madeline herself. The two of them had hosted a coffee for Will after I twisted their arms, and Dave wasted no time giving me grief about it.

"Hey, Jake," he started in, "next time you ask me to throw a party for someone, make sure he's not a homicidal maniac, okay?"

"He's not. He was framed."

"Oh no, you don't," he said, standing up. "You're not getting me involved in this. No way." Dave was a cop, and he'd helped me solve a murder once — and almost lost his job and pension because of it. "Madeline and I are taking a mini-vacation, and nothing's gonna stop us."

I got Dave to sit back down and listen, but I couldn't convince him of Will's innocence. No doubt Will's other campaign volunteers would feel the same as Dave. I couldn't count on any support from them.

But so what? Did Sam Spade ever get support?

After Dave left me, I squared my shoulders and headed off to the Hack's campaign headquarters. The Republican county chairmen had a press conference scheduled there for eleven, to announce who they were endorsing for Congress.

The Hack's HQ was right on Broadway, in a storefront that used to be a Papa Gorilla's restaurant before it went out of business. I'd looked into renting it for Will, but the price was way out of his league. Only a Republican could afford a place like that. The Hack probably got more donations from tobacco companies alone than Will got from all of his contributors put together.

The windows were still poignantly plastered with "Tamarack for Congress" posters. Well, that was one good reason for the chairmen to endorse Susan Tamarack: they wouldn't have to go to the trouble of making up new posters.

Looking through the window, I saw a long row of eleven men seated solemnly behind two tables at the far end of the room. There were cameras trained on them from all five local television stations. Newspaper reporters, their ball points, spiral notebooks, and laptop computers poised, filled several rows of folding chairs. The big press conference was about to commence.

I hurried through the front door, but was immediately stopped by a large, surly, twenty-something black man with an elephant-shaped tie clip. "Who are you with?" he demanded.

Good question. For close to twenty years I'd been a freelancer who was basically with *nobody*, and I always got stumped whenever people asked me this difficult query. But finally I'd developed a stock reply, which I employed now. "I'm with the madmen and the dreamers," I told the black Republican bouncer. *Black Republican* — what an oxymoron. Kind of like Jews for Jesus.

The surly oxymoron was as unimpressed with me as I was with him. "If you're not a member of the media," he said, "you'll have to exit the premises."

"But —"

"Ladies and gentlemen, welcome," proclaimed a deep-voiced man standing at the front table. It was the same bald guy who'd opened the bathroom door on me yesterday and turned me into a worm.

"Sir, please leave," Oxymoron said, crowding me backward toward the door. Several reporters turned to watch me get thrown out. I was being wormed yet again.

But then I spotted Judy Demarest in the back row. Besides being my wife's bowling buddy, Judy was also editor-in-chief of the *Daily Saratogian.* "I'm covering this for the *Saratogian,*" I told Oxymoron, and gestured toward Judy.

After she got over her surprise, she gave Oxymoron an amused nod. His nostrils flared with annoyance, showing off a healthy cluster of nose hairs, but there was nothing he could do. He stepped out of my way and I walked past him.

I grabbed the last empty seat in the room, right next to Judy. "Who's the bald guy?" I whispered out of the side of my mouth.

She raised her eyebrow, acting shocked at my ignorance. "Senator Ducky, of course," she whispered back. "Some reporter you are."

"So fire me," I said, then looked back at Senator Donald "Ducky" Medwick. I hadn't recognized him, but I knew who he was, all right.

Like my two sons, Ducky Medwick had the same name as a famous baseball star, the original Ducky M. having pounded out home runs for the St. Louis Browns back in the 30s. But any similarities between Senator Ducky and my sons ended right there. My sons had a lot more hair, whereas Ducky had a lot more power. As the majority leader of the New York State Senate, he had successfully stymied progressive legislation in New York for over a decade.

Ducky was also, as he pointed out now in his speech, the Hack's last boss before he died. When the Hack worked as legal counsel to the Senate Majority, Ducky was the man he reported to.

"On both a professional and personal

level," Ducky intoned, "I had tremendous love and respect for Jack Tamarack." Oh phooey, not another eulogy. I tuned him out and eyed the eleven suits at the front table. I recognized three of them as the Three Stooges who were sitting on the widow's bed yesterday. The other eight stooges were probably fellow county chairmen from the 22nd District. Who had they finally decided to endorse? I looked all around the room, but neither Robert Pierce nor the widow was anywhere to be seen.

Senator Ducky ended his blarney at last, then stepped aside for Phil Rogers, the GOP chairman for Saratoga County. The whiny voice in the widow's bedroom yesterday had been his, and it was equally whiny today.

"Folks," he said in his grating, high-pitched tone, "since we want this announcement to make the twelve o'clock news, I'm going to do it without further ado. We've selected the candidate who we believe is best qualified to carry on Jack Tamarack's legacy. The candidate who shares Jack's views on cutting taxes, fighting crime, and standing up for family values. And that candidate is . . . Susan Tamarack!"

On cue, the widow appeared from the back room dressed all in black, with perfect makeup highlighting her high cheekbones and dark soulful eyes. She looked stunning. I half-expected to hear Bert Parks strike up the Miss America theme song. Senator Ducky and his men all stood up and applauded. I almost applauded myself. Widows are such sympathetic figures, especially when they're waif-like and beautiful. It was a touching moment —

Until some wild-eyed lunatic ruined it.

Oxymoron must have let down his guard, distracted by the widow's gorgeousness. Otherwise the short, scruffy old man with the long beard and frayed, patched jacket would never have made it past him. Now Mr. Scruffy was racing up to the front of the room, screaming, "This is a travesty! A travesty, I tell you! Where is the spirit of our beloved forefathers? Why are we letting these filthy rich plutocrats tell us who to vote for?"

He was skinny and frail-looking and couldn't have weighed more than a hundred pounds, but he managed to shove a stunned Phil Rogers out of his way. Then he turned and faced the press, waving his arms and shouting, "I ask you, what makes this woman *qualified?* She's no more qualified than her ninnyhammer husband was! They're tools of the Gateses and the Rockefellers, all of them!"

Meanwhile Oxymoron was hurrying to the front, moving quickly for such a large man. He lifted up the thin-chested intruder, threw him over his shoulder like a sack of potatoes, and carried him away.

Mr. Scruffy didn't even resist. I guess he'd known it was coming, and it didn't seem to bother him in the slightest. He kept up his diatribe while still being held upside down in Oxymoron's arms. "I'm the last real Republican alive! We're supposed to be the party of Abraham Lincoln, standing for freedom, and now look at us! You people better watch your step, because I won't let you get away with this! Jack Tamarack got what he deserved, and so will all of you!"

Somebody opened the door, and Oxymoron literally threw Mr. Scruffy outside, then shut the door and locked it. In the ensuing silence, you could hear everyone in the room let out a sigh of relief. At the front, Senator Ducky gave a dry laugh. Pretty soon everybody else was laughing too.

Everybody but me, that is. Mr. Scruffy's parting words had sounded awfully ominous. Maybe they were just figures of speech, but . . .

"Let's try this a second time," Rogers whined. "I am proud to introduce the next congressperson from the 22nd District . . .

Susan Tamarack!"

As the eleven stooges dutifully applauded all over again, I turned to Judy and asked, "Who was that masked man?"

"Yancy Huggins."

"Who's he?"

She threw me another of her raised-eyebrow, how-can-you-be-so-ignorant looks, but before she could give me a hard time, I said, "Oh, right, it's all coming back to me." It actually was, middle-aged forgetfulness notwithstanding. Yancy H. was a gadfly from Stony Creek, way up north, who ran against the Hack in the Republican primary and got two percent of the vote. Most of that two percent were probably people who meant to vote for the Hack, but pulled the wrong lever by mistake.

I peered out the window past the "Tamarack for Congress" posters, but Huggins was gone. Meanwhile the widow was at the podium now.

She stood there woodenly, her body too tense to move. When she began speaking she used a frozen monotone, reading off lame platitudes from a prepared speech. I'd heard my share of lousy speeches in the past couple of days, but this one took the cake. It was so amateurish I felt bad for her. My five year old could read with more expression.

And my seven year old could write a better speech. If this was what she learned in Rosalyn's Comp 102 class, she deserved her money back.

Enough of this. I was tired of hanging out with stooges in suits and the women who love them. It was time to get with the madmen and the dreamers. I jumped up and bolted out the door in search of Yancy Huggins, the last real Republican.

The man who believed that Jack Tamarack got exactly what he deserved.

I didn't have far to look. Huggins was holding forth at the corner of Broadway and Phila, standing on a soapbox — yes, an honest to God soapbox, marked "Alamud Soap" and at least a century old. I had to hand it to the guy, at least he had style.

"My fellow countrymen," he was shouting, "the Visigoths are on the march! They're taking away our freedom to hunt deer, to go fishing and swimming in our lakes, to think for ourselves!" Meanwhile the pedestrians stepped around him, avoiding eye contact and going on about their business. Sometimes a passer-by paused long enough to throw a giggle his way. Robert Pierce was a veritable giant compared to this fellow. Huggins was four-eleven max, and he looked pretty goofy standing on top of that box trying to be tall.

"We have become a nation of sheep!" he proclaimed. "Sheep, I tell you! Baa! Baa! Baa —"

"Excuse me, sir," I said, interrupting him in the middle of his third baa. He stopped short and stared at me, obviously startled that someone was actually paying attention to him. In fact, he was so startled that he stepped backward — and fell off his soapbox.

As he tumbled to the sidewalk, arms flailing, several passers-by chuckled. I held out my hand to help him up, but he just glared at me with a look of pure, white-hot fury. I was so thrown by it that I stepped backward myself — and tripped over his soapbox, and fell. Now there were two of us lying on the sidewalk, and even more passers-by began laughing.

Huggins jumped up and stood over me. I was afraid he'd stomp on me, all one hundred pounds of him. I was also afraid he'd pull a gun out of his jacket pocket and shoot me.

"Are you *mocking* me?" he hissed.

"Not at all, sir," I said, standing up quickly and brushing myself off. "I work for the *Daily Saratogian*, and I'd like to interview you."

Huggins's jaw dropped, and his angry eyes suddenly turned wide open and child-like. "Really?"

"You have a couple of minutes?"

His face turned all wary and suspicious again. "You sure this isn't some kind of joke?"

I hated to deceive the poor chump, but I said, "Of course it's not a joke." What the heck, maybe I *would* write up the interview. I'd try to convince Judy to stick it in the inside pages somewhere on a slow news day.

Of course, if Huggins turned out to be the murderer, then we'd be able to get him a spot on page one.

I took him to Bruegger's Bagels and offered to buy him lunch. I didn't have to offer twice. He proceeded to order three garlic bagels with honey-walnut cream cheese, two of which he gobbled down immediately. The third he stuffed in his pocket for later.

Large chunks of the first two bagels ended up in his thick beard, so he'd be able to eat them later, too. He was missing a couple of front teeth, which made it hard for him to chew efficiently. From a distance, he'd seemed about sixty; up close, I realized he was more like a sprightly eighty.

Between bites — and during bites — he treated me to a potpourri of his political wisdom. He was clearly an extremist, but after listening for several minutes I couldn't tell if he was way to the left of Jesse Jackson or way to the right of Newt the Grinch. Not only was he against big government, big business, and big unions, he was against a lot of little things, too. For instance, he was against little leagues, calling them "the ruination of our young boys." He was even against those little warning labels on cigarette packs — "medical fascism," he said.

I guess the key word here was "against." He was just plain against everything.

He finally took a break from listing the nation's evils to let out a long, loud, malodorous burp. I jumped in. "So, Mr. Huggins," I asked, "what did you mean about Jack Tamarack getting what he deserved?"

He eyed me cagily, and the air between us went through a subtle but definite change. "Wouldn't *you* like to know. Be quite a scoop for your newspaper, wouldn't it?"

My skin prickled, but I tried to play it casual, giving him a shrug. "Maybe, maybe not. Depends if you really have something."

"Yeah, I got something, all right. Oh, yeah." He was reveling in my attention and wasn't about to let it go. "You better believe I got something."

"Like what?" I said lightly, trying to sound jokey. "You gonna tell me you killed him yourself?"

Huggins hesitated, and for a moment I thought he was about to tell me just that.

Then he said, "No, but I know who *did* kill that sonufabitch."

My heart pounded. "Who?"

"Why should I tell *you?*" he sneered. "The *Saratogian* is just a rag. How many readers do you have — twelve?"

If I acted dismissive of this self-important little clown, maybe I could goad him into talking more. "You're just yanking my chain, Huggins. Here I buy you lunch, give you an interview, and then you feed me some stupid kind of line."

He pouted his lips. Bagel crumbs hung off of them. "It's not a line. I just can't tell you what I know."

"Yeah, sure."

"It's true. I promised his old man."

I threw Huggins a disbelieving look. "*Whose* old man?"

"Jack's old man, George Tamarack. Me and him grew up together in Stony Creek. We were both in the hospital last spring, George with his cancer and me with my heart problems, and he told me some things. Probably 'cause he thought I was dying. But

I *didn't* die, so he made me promise not to tell anyone."

Huggins pointed a bony forefinger at me. "And by God, I'm keeping my promise. I'm not like these peckerwood politicians that would screw a dead warthog if it would get them an extra vote . . ."

And off he went on another rant. I tried several more times to open him up, but he held tight.

I shut my ears to Huggins's raving and tried to figure out my next maneuver. Some way, somehow, I needed to convince Hack Sr. to talk to me.

But how?

I ended up taking the direct approach. First I got rid of Huggins, assuring him repeatedly as we said good-bye that I'd call him when the article came out. Then I hit a pay phone and called Hack Sr. at his home in South Glens Falls, twenty miles north of Saratoga. When he didn't answer, I guessed that he might be at the widow's house. So I drove over there and knocked with her big brass door knocker.

As I waited on the doorstep, I wondered what Hack Sr. could possibly have told Huggins last spring that might explain why Hack Jr. was killed this week. It seemed farfetched, and I was wondering if I was out of my depths with all this private eye stuff when the door opened.

Sure enough, it was Hack Sr. Judging by the grayish pallor of the old man's face, he'd slept even less last night than I did.

"Hello, Mr. Tamarack," I began.

His eyes narrowed. "You're the one, aren't you?"

"Pardon?"

"Susie told me all about you sticking your head under the door. What are you, a goddamn reporter?"

"No, sir. I'm trying to find out who killed your son."

A young boy appeared in the hallway — Hack Sr.'s seven-year-old grandson. He wore a bright Bugs Bunny T-shirt, but his eyes observed me somberly. Hack Sr. put a hand on the boy's shoulder. "Sean, go in the other room and turn on the TV."

Sean pointed at me. "Who's he? What is he talking about?"

"Go in the living room and watch TV."

"But, Grandpa —"

"*Go.*"

Sean took one last long look at me before tramping off unhappily. The old man watched him go, not speaking again until the kid had disappeared and we heard *Rugrats* come on.

Then he demanded, "Why are you bothering us? We already know who killed my son. It was that bastard Shmuckler."

"Shmuckler is my friend. He's not a killer."

"Horseshit."

"Just in case I'm right, Mr. Tamarack, do you want the wrong man thrown in jail for your son's murder?"

The old man winced with pain, whether emotional or physical I wasn't sure. "What the hell do you want from me?"

"Whatever you can give."

"I got nothing to give. *Nothing.*" The pain expanded, and contorted his whole face. "It's not right for a son to die before his father. It's not right!"

Then he went into another of his frightful coughing spasms and started to shut the door in my face.

But I stuck my foot in the way. Call me heartless, but what choice did I have? "Mr. Tamarack," I said grimly, "Yancy told me all about what you told him at the hospital."

Hack Sr.'s head snapped back in surprise, and he gasped. His spasm stopped so fast, I wondered if he'd faked it.

Meanwhile Sean ran into the room again. "Grandpa, you should sit down."

The old man forced a smile. "I'm okay,

bud. You can go back and watch TV."

Sean gave me an upset look, then reluctantly shuffled off. Hack Sr. turned back to me. "I got no clue what you're talking about. Yancy Huggins is a certified loony."

"Maybe so, but he was telling the truth on this."

The old man's shoulders sagged. "What did that half-wit tell you?"

*Not a heck of a lot,* I thought, but out loud I said, "Sir, I'd like to hear it straight from the horse's mouth. If you give me a clear understanding of exactly what you know, it'll be best for everyone."

"Why will that be best for everyone?"

"Because —" I began, but then, just like that, I *lost* it. My brain locked up tight. I coughed lightly into my hand, buying time. "You see, the thing is —" I continued, but not only was my brain locked, someone had thrown away the key.

I remembered this helpless feeling only too well. Back when I was an aspiring Hollywood screenwriter, this would sometimes happen to me in the middle of a big pitch meeting with some hot shot producer. One moment I'd be waxing eloquent about an exciting plot twist in a movie I was writing, then the next moment some mental doorway would slam shut — and I'd be sitting there with my tongue hanging out, like a dog who's been out in the sun too long. Highly embarrassing.

Hack Sr. eyed me curiously. Any second now he'd realize I was talking through my hat, and Huggins hadn't told me diddly-squat. Then Hack Sr. would clam up too. In desperation, I tried a line that I must have seen some variation of in a hundred different movies. "Mr. Tamarack," I said, "I don't want to tell the cops any more than I have to. But if you refuse to cooperate —"

"Look, this is just plain silly. What I told Yancy has nothing to do with my son's death."

"I'll be the judge of that. Either me or the police," I threatened, with as much severity as I could muster, hoping I sounded at least a little bit like Humphrey Bogart.

I guess watching *The Maltese Falcon* so many times in my twenties paid off, because my acting job worked. Hack Sr. waved his arm disgustedly, giving up. "All right, all right," he said. I was so excited, I felt like jumping up and down. "But I'm sure that sonufabitch Yancy already told you everything I know. It ain't much. All I know is, my son had dirt on Ducky Medwick."

*Ducky Medwick?* I tried not to let my astonishment show. "Uh-huh," I said noncommittally.

"So he leaned on Ducky, and Ducky leaned on the county chairmen, and that's how my son got endorsed for Congress."

"What dirt did your son have on Ducky?"

He lifted his shoulders. "Can't tell you. I asked, but he never said. Must have been awful big, though," Hack Sr. added, with a perverse sort of pride.

I nodded in agreement, thinking: how big *was* it?

Big enough that Ducky would kill the Hack to shut him up?

The other thing I was thinking: if the Hack's killer was State Senate Majority Leader Ducky Medwick, then I was definitely out of my depth.

*Way* out.

# 5

I decided to drive straight down to the State Capitol and confront Ducky immediately, on the theory that if you're standing at the edge of a deep murky pool and you're nervous about sticking your little toesies in, sometimes you have to just dive. It was Andrea's turn to pick the kids up from school, so I was free until six.

I got back in my rusty '85 Toyota Camry — even though I'm rich now, I somehow can't seem to let go of my old car — and headed south on the Northway to Albany. This was a rare trip for me. Albany may be only fifty minutes from Saratoga, but I hardly ever go there. Why bother? If you've ever been to Albany, then you know what I mean.

In all fairness, though, the State Capitol itself is pretty impressive. The building is one of those glorious French Renaissance extravaganzas they used to construct back when our country was young and full of hope. Everywhere you look, there are high domed ceilings, marble galore, and elegant gilt-framed paintings. The front staircase is so exquisitely carved, it's been nicknamed the "Million-Dollar Staircase." As my footsteps echoed along the hallowed hallways, the grandeur was so thick it felt like an effort walking through it.

Approaching Ducky's office on the third floor, I began feeling intimidated. Ducky had already beaten me once, when he caught me snooping under the bathroom door. What if he just threw me out of his office?

So I did a trick my father once taught me to do whenever I get scared before a meeting with some bigwig. I closed my eyes and pictured Ducky sitting on the toilet with his pants around his ankles, constipated, grunting loudly as he desperately tried to poop. It's hard to feel intimidated by a guy when you're imagining him in that position.

But my psyche job was wasted this time, because Ducky wasn't in. His efficient, gray-haired secretary informed me that he was out for the rest of the day. I asked if she knew where he was, or if he'd be in tomorrow, but she got all frosty on me.

"Who did you say you were with?" she asked, thin-lipped.

"I'm with the madmen and the dreamers," I said. She didn't crack a smile, but that was okay, I wasn't really expecting one.

I left her and was starting back downstairs

when I happened to notice, on the far wall, a listing of all the third-floor offices. The "Legal Counsel to the Senate Majority" — that must be the Hack's old office — was located in Room 313. On a whim, I turned around and walked back there.

The heavy wooden door to 313 was closed. I turned the knob, opened it . . . and suddenly found myself face-to-face with naked grief. A woman — the Hack's secretary? — was packing things in a large box and crying her eyes out. She looked over at me, not trying to cover up her tears.

It was kind of refreshing. Finally, a woman who wasn't obsessed with casseroles, or with using her dead husband's name to hustle a job she wasn't qualified for.

"I'm sending his personal stuff back home," the woman said. "It's so sad."

"I'm sorry." I took a closer look at her. It didn't hurt my eyes one bit. She was in her twenties or early thirties, with bleached blonde hair — not that that's really worth mentioning, since it seems like half the white women in America have bleached blonde hair these days. She did have a shape worth mentioning, though. It was the dead opposite of Susan Tamarack's waifishness. This lady had more curves than an Adirondack mountain road.

And she sure was distraught. Was she simply mourning her boss's death . . . or had he been more to her than just a boss?

The bleached blonde bombshell caught me staring. "Can I help you?" she asked irritably.

My face reddened. "No. Didn't mean to interrupt," I said, and withdrew, leaving her alone with her grief.

From Albany to Troy is only a hop, skip, and downwardly mobile jump away. I decided to drive right over to the Troy Police Department. On the streets of Troy, my rusty old car fit right in.

I told the cop at the front desk that I had information about Jack Tamarack's murder. He passed me straight through to the chief of police himself, Lou Coates, an overweight, middle-aged black man with a permanent scowl on his face. In his defense, if I had to spend all day in that windowless office of his, filled with the stench of stale cigarettes, I'd be scowling, too.

Sitting down in a cheap plastic chair with "Fuck the pigs" graffiti written in red marker on the seat, I gazed around at the chief's graying, grime-covered walls. When was the last time anyone had cleaned this joint? Evidently that job had been cut from the police budget.

"Whatchou got?" Chief Coates asked me belligerently, without preamble.

"I'm a friend of Will Shmuckler," I began, "and I'm doing some investigating on his behalf. I'm hoping we can work together."

The chief lit a cigarette. Pall Mall, filterless. "Whatchou got?" he repeated.

"Well, I'm following a couple of leads. Right now they're in the preliminary stages."

"In other words, you ain't got *bupkus*."

"I wouldn't put it that way, exactly —"

"If you ain't got *bupkus*, then why are you wasting my time?"

"Sir, I really think —"

"What's your name?"

"Jacob Burns. You've probably heard of me —"

"Bet your ass I have. John Walsh warned me you might come sniffing around."

John Walsh was this guy's counterpart at the Saratoga Springs Police Department. To put it mildly, Chief Walsh was not my biggest fan. But I beamed on Coates, trying to bluster my way through. "Good, I'm glad Walsh called. He must've told you how I solved two murders for him in Saratoga."

"No, he told me you were a royal pain in the *kishkes* who fucked up twice, big time, and got lucky. *That's* what he told me."

I kept right on beaming. "I love it when *goyim* use Yiddish. Where'd you learn the word *kishkes?*"

"Crown Heights. You want Yiddish, I'll give you Yiddish. If you don't watch your *tukhus,* you're gonna be *facocked.* You try to cover up for the *Shmuck,* I'll throw you in jail as an accessory to murder. You got that, *shlemazel?*"

I frowned. "I think the word you're looking for is *shlemiel.*"

The chief nodded. "Could be. Haven't been back to the Heights in years. Now get the fuck out of here and don't let me ever see your ugly *punimunim* again."

I got up and walked out, feeling good about multiculturalism but not so good otherwise. Being a private dick is a lonely job. No wonder so many of those guys hit the bottle.

Fortunately, unlike all the great private dicks of yore, I had a family to keep me relatively sane and sober. I went home and delayed answering all the anxious phone messages from Will so that I could hang out with the wife and kids for a while. I ate Andrea's delicious eggplant parmigiana and listened patiently as the boys regaled me with their computer stories. Or at least, I *pretended* to listen patiently.

Then, over dessert, I described my failed attempt to get hold of Senator Ducky at his office. "Why don't you just go to his house?" Bernie asked.

"Because I don't know where he lives, and it's not in the phone book."

"Then why don't you just look on the Internet?" demanded Derek.

"I don't think the Internet can give you addresses —"

"Sure it can! I read all about it in the *Dummy's Guide!*"

I stared at him. I knew my seven-year-old was precocious — he could already add and subtract better than most politicians — but was he reading *computer manuals* now?

Meanwhile the kid was saying, "All you have to do is access the People Tracker database."

"Access the what?"

"I'll show you," Derek said, jumping up from the table and racing to the computer room. His little brother put down his cup so quickly that milk sloshed onto the table, and then he ran to the computer room, too.

"You haven't been excused yet," Andrea called out, but Derek and Bernie either didn't hear her or didn't want to. She turned to me. "I don't think you should discuss your murder investigation in front of the kids."

"Why not? Even if we try to hide it, they'll just find out anyhow."

"But don't talk about it any more than you have to. I don't want them getting all upset and doing their weird nighttime stuff."

I knew what she meant. At our house, when the going gets tough, Derek walks in his sleep and Bernie pees in his bed. The last time our household got all caught up in a murder investigation, it took us months to get back to normal. So I promised Andrea to try to avoid talking about homicides from now on, at least at the dinner table.

After we got that settled, we trooped into the computer room. We watched with growing amazement as Derek's hands flashed here and there all over the keyboard, and the screen showed one incomprehensible (to me) message after another, until finally a message came up that I *did* understand. It was Ducky Medwick's home address in Clifton Park, New York.

"Incredible," I said, as Derek printed it out. "You're a genius."

"No, I'm not," he said, shrugging. "Any kid in my class could do this."

He may have been right. And that's the frightening part.

I tried to call Will to report in, but his phone was busy for half an hour. Probably off the hook again, so he could steal some sleep. I knew from experience, being wrongly accused of murder can kind of disrupt your sleep schedule.

Since I couldn't talk to Will, I spent some time playing Ms. PacMan with the kids — the one thing I really enjoy doing on the computer. Then after I put them to bed, I buzzed down to Ducky's house in Clifton Park. I guess I should take a moment to describe Clifton Park, though I really don't want to, because it's the dullest place in America. There's no downtown to speak of, no civic life, no volunteer fire department . . . just a lot of shopping malls.

On the positive side, Clifton Park does have some nicely built 70s-era ranch houses. Medwick, his wife, Linda, and their children, Barbara and Terry, ages thirteen and eleven — my kid had gotten all this info off the Internet somehow — lived in an especially sprawling ranch house on an especially large property at the end of an especially secluded cul-de-sac. The house probably cost an especially large sum of money. Personally, you couldn't have paid me to live there.

But hey, Ducky probably wouldn't have

wanted to live in *my* house, with its ninety-year-old quirks and occasionally obstreperous neighbors.

I walked up to the front door, setting off a motion detector that turned on the porch light. To calm my nerves, I conscientiously remembered to picture Ducky sitting on the toilet constipated.

But when the door opened, as far as its chain would allow, it wasn't Ducky standing there. It was his wife, Linda. I stared at her through the three-inch opening, my jaw hanging down in surprise.

Ducky's wife was the same hot babe I'd seen in the Hack's office, packing up his personal effects with tears in her eyes.

"Ms. Medwick?" I said hesitantly.

"Who *are* you?"

"My name's Jacob Burns. I'm looking for your husband."

"He's not here."

"Do you know when he'll be back?"

"What do you want?"

*I want to nail him for murder.* "I want to talk to him about an important matter. I'm with the *Daily Saratogian*. Here's my card." I handed her one of my two-year-old "Jacob Burns, Writer" cards from my wallet.

"I'll let him know," she said, and shut the door on me.

What was going on here? Was Ducky's wife really the Hack's secretary? But why? Obviously they didn't need the money.

Between Linda Medwick and Susan Tamarack, I was dealing with two very puzzling women. I walked back to my Toyota, annoyed at having no one around to answer my questions. One unfortunate reality of detective work is that in order to do an interrogation properly, it helps to have someone to interrogate. It's not like writing, where you can just go off by yourself and do your thing.

I resolved to wait in my car until Ducky came home. Of course, Linda might notice and call the cops on me, but I'd cross that bridge when I came to it.

I waited thirty minutes, until 9:45, when a car finally pulled up in Ducky's driveway. It still wasn't Ducky, though. He must be off at some late-night, cigar-filled political meeting. A gangly preteen boy hopped out of the backseat carrying a basketball, and said good night to the woman who was driving. Yet another bleached blonde, I noted. What's this world coming to? " 'Night, Terry. Good game," she told him, and zoomed off.

Terry aimed a jump shot at the basketball hoop in the driveway, getting a satisfying swish. Then he bounced the ball up the path toward the front door. I jumped out of my car and intercepted him.

"Excuse me, Terry," I called out.

He grabbed the basketball, pulling it tight to his body, and froze. I could practically hear his brain cells screaming, *"Don't talk to strangers!"*

"I didn't want to bother your mom this late," I said casually. "Do you know where I can find your dad?"

Terry had an open, honest face. In his confused eleven-year-old eyes, I could see *"Don't talk to strangers"* warring with *"Be polite."*

I felt like some kind of evil child molester, but I continued on. "It's just that your dad wanted me to give him something. For tomorrow's vote in the Senate."

Finally Terry spoke. "Dad's not home," he said. His voice broke a little on the last word, and a twinge of sadness crossed his face. What was that all about?

"Is he at a meeting? I could just go and give him this thing."

"No, he's at a hotel."

*Huh?* "Which hotel?"

"Holiday Inn. In Halfmoon. He's been there since Sunday."

Then, as if afraid he'd already said too

much, Terry hurried away and let himself in the front door.

The Holiday Inn in Halfmoon, fifteen miles north of Albany, was no doubt a hot spot for traveling salesmen on their way up I-87 to Plattsburgh or Montreal. But it wasn't exactly a place where you'd expect to find the majority leader of the New York State Senate fluffing his pillow.

Maybe that was the point, though. Maybe he didn't *want* anyone to find him.

Myself, I got lucky. I didn't have to bribe someone for a waiter's uniform and then sneak up to Ducky's room pretending to be room service in order to get hold of him. He was right downstairs in the hotel bar, sitting all by himself in the corner with a glass of amber liquid in his hand. Two other lone wolves sat in other corners with glasses in their hands, and behind the bar a chubby, dimwit-looking bartender yawned. B. J. Thomas's voice came over some tinny speakers, warbling about raindrops falling on your head. The television set was showing a commercial about how *you can reverse hair loss.*

But Ducky, bald though he was, ignored the commercial. He was ignoring everything except his glass. He sat there staring at it mindlessly as he swirled his drink around and around. I felt sorry for him. I was almost tempted to walk out and let the man suffer in peace.

Then Ducky looked up. His bleary eyes recognized me, and instantly his drunkenness seemed to fall away. He straightened his back, his eyes flashed, and he became once again the man I'd seen on the TV news so many times over the years, blasting away at governors, Democrats, criminals, and whoever else was unlucky enough to arouse his fury. He got the ironic nickname "Ducky" not because he resembled that friendly, waddling creature, but because he acted so positively mean and un-ducklike.

"What, are you *stalking* me?" he snapped as I walked up. "I'm calling the police."

"I doubt it," I replied. "I doubt you want anyone to know you're staying here."

That stopped him. "Who the hell are you?"

"Jacob Burns. I'm a friend of Will Shmuckler."

"Yeah, so what?"

I couldn't think of any nifty P.I. moves to pull on him, so I cut right to the chase. "Did you kill Jack Tamarack?"

He barked out a laugh. "What nonsense. Why would I do that?"

"Because he was blackmailing you."

His hand went involuntarily to his throat, but his voice stayed aggressive. "Where'd you hear *that?*"

"Never mind where I heard it. Where were you Monday night?"

"Jack Tamarack was not blackmailing me. Don't be preposterous."

"Give me one other reason why you'd endorse a lifelong hack, a guy who never even got elected to *dogcatcher,* to run for the United States Congress."

Before, I had believed that Ducky endorsed the Hack to reward him for twenty years of brownnosing; but upon reflection, that now seemed naive to me. You can't brownnose your way to the top, only to the middle.

"Jack Tamarack was a very capable man," Ducky said huffily.

"Yeah, right. The Hack never had an original idea in his life."

Ducky stared at me incredulously. "And you think that's a *negative?* What are you, an idiot? Listen, Burnside, or whatever your name is, the last thing I want is an independent-minded congressman. I want a guy who does exactly what I tell him, whether it's getting tax breaks for some local company or easing pollution regulations or *whatever.* I *wanted* a hack, Burnside, and that's why I got the county chairmen to pick Tamarack."

I almost believed him. But Hack Sr. had been so absolutely certain that his son was blackmailing this man.

"Now if you'll excuse me," Ducky continued sarcastically, "I was enjoying a little peace and quiet before you came along —"

"You still didn't answer me. Where were you Monday night?"

"None of your damn business."

"Are you separated from your wife?"

He glared at me but didn't answer. Instead he lifted his drink to his lips. It was time to aim a wild haymaker at him.

"Senator, was your wife having an affair with Jack Tamarack?"

Ducky stopped in mid-sip. Then he threw the glass at me. It slammed into my nose but luckily didn't break, just spilled scotch all over my face. Then Ducky stood up abruptly and left the bar.

I took that to mean yes.

# 6

When I got home, it was almost midnight —
but Derek Jeter wasn't in bed. For a crazed
moment, I was afraid some vicious murderer
had kidnapped him. But then I found him at
the computer, his tired, drawn face looking
ghastly in the screen's cold glow. The kid
would be a wreck tomorrow. Not good. The
first week of school was no time to relax bed-
time schedules.

"Derek, what are you doing up?" I began,
preparing to yell at him for sneaking out of
bed. But then he turned toward me and I
saw a familiar unfocused look in his eyes. He
was asleep.

"How you doing, kid?" I asked gently.

He nodded vaguely, then turned back to
the computer screen. I noticed he had a
bunch of newspaper articles about Jack
Tamarack listed on there.

"Honey, it's time to go to bed." I signed
off of AOL — I may be technologically challenged, but at least I know how to do *that* —
and lifted the kid up. He protested weakly,
then slumped against my body as I carried
him upstairs.

Once I lay him down in his own bed, he woke up. "Hi, Daddy," he said. "Was I sleep-walking?"

"Yup."

"What was I doing?"

"I don't know. You were at the computer."

"Oh, yeah. I was helping you solve the murder."

I sighed. "Sweetheart, it's okay, I really don't need help."

"But I don't want you to almost get killed, like last time."

I started to give some reassuring reply, but then I smelled something. Bernie Williams had peed in his bed.

Yes, it's hard to be hard-boiled when you've got two young sprats at home. I put some dry pants on the still-sleeping Bernie, and lay down with Derek until he was asleep, too. I was too tired to deal with Will, so I turned off the ringer on our phone in case he called me. Then I went to bed myself.

The next morning, Andrea and I talked it over and agreed it would be better for our family — and for Will, too — if I simply dumped the investigation in the cops' laps.

After all, they had infinitely more resources. I figured I now had enough grounds for suspicion against Senator Ducky that the cops would be forced to take my story seriously. So I called up Lou Coates, the African-American, Yiddish-speaking Troy police chief.

"Chief Coates," I said, when the receptionist finally put me through, "Ducky Medwick and his wife are separated. They split up on Sunday."

"*Nu?* What am I, a gossip columnist?"

"Jack Tamarack was killed on Monday."

"And the Mets won a doubleheader on Tuesday. So what?"

"So Jack Tamarack was having an affair with Ducky's wife."

There was a silence. Then the chief asked, "You have any evidence, or are you just ringing my *chatchkas?*"

Ringing my *chatchkas?* That was a new one on me. "No *direct* evidence, but —"

"But *shmut.* Don't be a *nudnick.* You got nothing. And I got no yen to go on a wild-goose chase against Ducky. 'Specially when we already got the dirty *mamzer* who did it: Will Shmuckler."

"If I can get you proof they were having an affair —"

"Do me a favor. Go shake your *shlong* at someone else."

He hung up. So did I. Chief Coates had

taken some liberties with his Yiddish, but that didn't really bother me. You're supposed to take liberties with Yiddish; that's what Yiddish is for.

What did bother me was that Chief Coates was clearly afraid to tangle with a powerful state senator. In upstate New York, it seems like everything in public life is about favors. If you want a government job, or a tax reassessment, or you just want your dried leaves removed from the curb for Pete's sake, you better know the right people.

And if you're like Lou Coates and you already have a government job, and you want to *keep* it, then you better keep the right people happy.

My musings were interrupted by an irate phone call from the one and only "dirty *mamzer*" himself. "Why the hell didn't you call me back yesterday?" he complained.

"Sorry, I did try —"

"I'm dying here. I got reporters hiding in my bushes now. I open my door to get the paper and they ambush me. I'm scared to go out for orange juice. My campaign events are getting canceled right and left. Give me some good news, I'm begging you."

I began to get worried about the guy. "Do you have people who can bring you food? I'll try to get down there today —"

"Screw that. Just give me some reason to hope."

I did my best. "Listen, Will, do you happen to know if Ducky Medwick's wife was the Hack's secretary?"

"Yeah, she was. Why?"

"You ever hear rumors she was having an affair with the Hack?"

Will figured out the implications immediately. All his frenzied angst disappeared. "Holy shit, that's fabulous! So you think Ducky killed him?"

"It's a possibility."

*"Oh man oh man oh man!"*

"Hey, don't come in your pants just yet."

"This would win me the election for sure! I'll be an innocent man, set up for a false murder rap by the corrupt Republican machine. Talk about getting the sympathy vote!"

Will's continuing obsession with his moribund campaign was getting on my nerves. "Susan Tamarack will get sympathy votes, too. Look what happened to Hillary's popularity when *her* husband had an affair."

"Yeah, but it didn't last. And Susan's gonna get hurt by Pierce."

"What do you mean?"

"You didn't hear? He announced his

candidacy last night."

I whistled through my teeth. "Amazing. He's actually bucking the bosses? Someone must've lent him a new set of balls."

"So now we got two Republican write-ins stealing each other's votes. Jake, we're gonna kick ass. All you gotta do is nail the killer before the election and get me off the hook!"

I sighed. "No sweat. And after that, I'll establish permanent world peace and pitch the Red Sox into the World Series."

"Just humor me, will you? I'm trying to keep my mind off the fact I may be going to jail for the next hundred and twenty years."

I didn't know how to respond to that.

"And Jake?"

"Yeah."

"Don't lose faith in yourself, you're the best. I love you, man."

*Yeah, yeah, I love you, too,* I thought as I hung up the phone. But my life sure would be a lot simpler if I'd just gotten a different college roommate. What was I supposed to do now —

Answer the doorbell, that's what. It was ringing. So I went to the door and opened it.

Standing there in front of me was the bleached blonde bombshell.

I'd never seen Linda Medwick in sunlight

before. With her soft skin and light smattering of freckles, she turned out to be one of those women who look even better in the daytime. Her low-cut, tight white T-shirt and short pink gym shorts didn't hurt her looks any, either.

"Come in," I said.

I held the door open for her, and she brushed against me as she walked past into the living room. For a second I wondered if it was intentional, then decided I was imagining things. She sat down on the sofa and crossed her legs.

"Can I get you something?" I asked.

She shook her head, her mane flying around as she did so. She'd done something extra to her hair this morning, and she looked like the second coming of Farrah Fawcett.

"My husband says you know about my affair with Jack," she said.

I perched on the chair across from the sofa. "Yes, I do," I answered.

"Why do you care about it?"

"You have to admit, it does give your husband a good motive."

She looked puzzled. "For what?"

"For murder."

She stared at me a moment, then threw out an unhappy laugh. "Ducky wouldn't kill anyone over me. He doesn't even *like* me. We're getting a divorce."

"When did he find out about you and the Ha— you and Jack?"

I didn't expect a straight answer, but she proceeded to actually give me one. Something smelled fishy here. On the other hand, if she was willing to spill the beans with so little effort on my part, who was I to complain?

Her answer was: "Ducky found out about us last week. It was *horrible*. I forgot to lock the door to Jack's office, and Ducky just walked in." She put her head in her hands. "Oh God, I'm so embarrassed."

Suddenly she burst into tears. I'd have suspected they were fake, except that she was crying for real when I caught her unawares in the Hack's office yesterday.

She gazed up at me with her moist hazel eyes. "I loved Jack, and now he's gone. I don't have anyone. I'm so lonely."

She sobbed some more, and I got up to give her a Kleenex. When I handed it to her, she gently took hold of my wrist. "Thank you," she said softly. "God, you don't know how much I need a little kindness right now. I'd give anything to just forget my troubles for a while."

She looked at me, her lips parted. I looked

back, and I couldn't help myself: I got that old familiar tightening in my jeans.

Hey, you probably think I'm a chump, falling for such a corny pickup line. But what can I say? Having a Farrah Fawcett lookalike in a skimpy white T-shirt suggestively stroking my arm just took my breath away. I never knew wrists could be so erogenous. And on top of that, it sure would be a kick to fool around with the wife of State Senate Majority Leader Ducky Medwick.

I guess men are just plain dogs.

But I guess I'll never know exactly *how* doggish we are. I like to think I would've resisted temptation, but I can't prove it, because just at that moment the phone rang. It broke the spell, and Farrah the Second let go of me.

"Excuse me," I said, blushing, and practically ran to the kitchen, where I grabbed the phone and said, "Hello?" Actually, that "Hello?" was more like a shout. I didn't quite have control of my voice yet.

"Is something wrong?" my wife said over the phone.

"No!" I shouted again, and then fought to rein in my volume and act normal. "Why would you think that?"

"Well, because you're shouting. And you sound out of breath."

"Oh, it's nothing. I just came in from outside. So what's up?"

"Bad news. I got a flat."

"What a drag."

"I made it to Matt's Garage, but it'll be a while before they get around to fixing it. Would you mind terribly giving me a lift to school? I have a class in forty minutes."

The trip would seriously eat into my day's sleuthing. On the other hand, it would give me an excuse to get away from the vixen in the other room. "Okay, honey," I said, "I'll be right there."

I hung up and headed back toward the living room. But Farrah the Second was already at my front door, on her way out. She turned back to me.

"I'm sorry," she said. "I didn't mean to come on to you like that."

*Yeah, I'll bet.* "Linda, why *did* you come here?"

She bit her lip and gave me a shy, scared-little-girl look, and in spite of everything, my jeans tightened again. *Dogs.*

"Jacob," she said tentatively, "could you keep my . . . you know . . . private? Would it be too much to ask?"

"I'm investigating a murder here."

"But my affair with Jack had nothing to do with his death, I'm *positive*. The night he

107

got killed, I was home. And Ducky was at the hotel."

"How do you know he was at the hotel?"

"Because he called me from there. We fought on the phone for an hour."

"Exactly what time was this call?"

Her eyes darted around nervously. I got the impression she was trying to remember when the Hack had been shot, so she could give an answer that would clear Ducky.

"I think around eight o'clock," she said.

Not exactly the world's most airtight alibi.

"If you won't do this for *me*," she went on plaintively, "what about my children? Do you want them to have to read in the newspaper all about their mom's sex life?"

I flashed on Linda's gangly eleven-year-old son. He'd seemed so vulnerable last night, cradling a basketball in his arms as he told me about his father staying at a hotel. The divorce would be tough enough on the poor kid, even without his mother's promiscuity becoming a major regional news story.

But now was no time to get all sensitive. I've always believed that Democrats need to learn to be just as cutthroat as Republicans. "Listen, you want something from me, then give me something. What dirt did Jack have on Ducky?"

She frowned. "I don't get you."

"Sure, you do. Your boyfriend was black-mailing your husband. That's how he got the big party endorsement." I had a sudden stroke of what felt like brilliance. "I'll bet you even helped him with the blackmail. You told Jack the dirt about your husband. So what was it?"

Farrah the Second shot me a venomous look. If looks could kill, I was maggot food for sure.

"Screw you," she hissed, and walked out.

For a two-year commuters' school, Northwoods Community College has a surprisingly beautiful campus. Okay, the buildings aren't much, just your basic institutional boxes, but they're located at the edge of a forest, with hiking trails out back and a clear view of the Adirondack foothills. It's almost enough to give you the illusion that you're at a classy place.

As I drove Andrea through the campus, it was teeming with students bustling to their 10:30 classes. Every last one of them was white, and I wouldn't be surprised if every last one was Christian, too. Beyond that, though, they came in all ages, shapes, and sizes.

A lot of these students were eighteen years old, not overly bright, with no clear idea why they were here. They chewed a lot of gum, drank a lot of beer, and bored me stiff when I used to teach at this joint.

Then there was another group of students, also fresh out of high school, but more focused and generally smarter. These were kids from small-town, working class families who already knew they wanted a B.A., but couldn't afford a four-year school for the whole four years. So they were planning to put in two years at Northwoods, then transfer to a "real college," as they would say. My heart went out to these kids.

But my favorite students of all were the older ones, the returning students in their twenties, thirties, forties, and even fifties. Most of these were men and women stuck in six-dollar-an-hour service jobs who were eager to better themselves and become nurses, physical therapists, or computer technicians. Sometimes you'd run into a homemaker hoping to return to the workforce after a decades-long hiatus.

As I pulled up in front of McCracken Hall, which houses the English Department, I wondered again: why did Susan Tamarack enroll in Rosalyn's Comp 102 course? With her husband about to become a United States congressman, and all the changes that would mean for both of them, surely she wasn't considering going back to work at this stage of her life.

And another question: did Susan know about her husband's affair? If only there were some way to —

Andrea broke into my thoughts. "I'm late, gotta run," she said, kissing me and hurrying out of the car. "Thanks for the ride!"

"No problem," I replied. I waited until she was safely out of sight. Then I parked the car and got out.

I had a plan.

Keeping my head down, I slinked inside McCracken. The main floor was full of people scurrying around like ants, but I didn't see anyone I knew. I slipped down the side stairs to the English Department.

Rosalyn's office, if I remembered correctly, was at the far left corner of the rear corridor. I tried to act nonchalant and slow my rapidly beating heart as I passed two students on my way back there.

*Don't be so uptight,* I told myself. After all, it wasn't like I was plotting to steal a computer or something truly valuable. All I wanted to do was borrow a stupid portfolio.

I located Rosalyn's office without incident. But it was locked. Now what?

Using my body to shield my larcenous activities from anyone who might be coming up the hall, I took out my keys and tried them all. No go. I guess that would be too easy.

Next I took out my Visa card, wiggled it under the lock, and tried to open the door that way. But it didn't work. No surprise there — I've never been able to pull off that trick. Somebody should hold a special course in lock picking for us sensitive *artiste* types who are trying to make it in the wild, woolly world of cops and robbers. Or maybe I could ask one of the prisoners in my Creative Writing class to give me some tips.

On the theory that my Visa card might be too stiff to wiggle properly, I took out my AAA card and tried that. I didn't have any real hope that it would work, I was just going through the motions.

But then I heard a small click. Miracle of miracles, something seemed to give — and when I turned the knob, the door actually opened!

My heart burst with pride. I felt like I had just completed an important rite of passage —

"Jacob," someone said.

*"Aauuh!"* I screamed.

"You okay?" Jeremy Wartheimer asked, as he stood there about two feet away from me. He was close enough that I could see the large pores in his unhealthy, acne-scarred skin. Jeremy was a colleague of Andrea's — her least favorite one.

"Sure, I'm fine," I said. "You just startled me a little, that's all."

Jeremy eyed me quizzically, then glanced over at Rosalyn's open door. Had he seen me unlock it with my AAA card? That would be a very bad scene. Andrea was up for tenure next year, and I doubted it would help her case any if her husband got caught breaking into her colleagues' offices. Palming the card, I stuffed my hand in my pocket as casually as I could.

"What's up?" Jeremy asked. "Is Roz in?"

"No."

"I'm surprised she left her door unlocked."

Desperate to distract him, I queried, "So how goes the struggle?"

"Well, you know how it is," he began, then launched into a lengthy detailed analysis of The Struggle.

You see, Jeremy Wartheimer was emphatically not a man who only stood for filberts. No, Jeremy was a Marxist in a big way, and a Trotskyite too, whatever that means. He would have made me nostalgic for the old days when I believed passionately that we could Change the World, except that he was such a jerk.

Jeremy and a couple of other teachers at the college — they called themselves a "communist cell" — had decided that the best way to bring about the long-awaited Revolution was to send frequent long memos to all the faculty members. Generally the memos were addressed like this: *"To our fellow worker citizens."* The memo itself would consist of ten or twenty pages of unbearably convoluted prose, which, if you cared enough to puzzle it out, usually boiled down to this basic message: In a capitalist society, true knowledge is impossible. Therefore, teachers know nothing. In fact, it is absurd for us to call ourselves *teachers.* We should all immediately inform our students that we're complete and total frauds.

Since this is not the sort of thing teachers usually like to say to their students, these Trotsky-inspired memos had no discernible effect besides making people cranky. However, that didn't seem to bother Jeremy and his fellow cell members in the slightest. They just kept plugging away.

I let Jeremy plug away at me for several minutes, long enough for him to forget about Rosalyn's unlocked door. Then I interrupted him in the middle of a harangue about "outmoded liberal humanist principles" and told him I had to be off.

But Jeremy stopped me. "Oh, Jacob," he said, "one more thing."

"Yes?"

His dead serious, dogma-infested face broke into an incongruously ingratiating smile. "Do you think you could read a screenplay I wrote?"

Good grief, was there any way out of this? I couldn't think of one. Since Jeremy was a colleague of Andrea's, I couldn't just go with my gut instinct and tell him to soak his nose with a rubber hose. "Sure, I'd love to," I said, feeling like a coward.

"Great, I'll go get it. I left it upstairs. I'll be right back." He dashed off toward the stairs, apparently eager to bring me his screenplay before I magically disappeared.

I followed Jeremy's example and did some dashing of my own, into Rosalyn's office. I was planning to throw open her desk drawers and do a quick search, but lo and behold, I got lucky. Right there in plain view on the edge of her desk was a pile of manila folders containing portfolios — and Susan Tamarack's was the third from the top. I grabbed it, stuffed it under my jacket, and made it back out to the hallway seconds before Jeremy reappeared.

"My screenplay is entitled *Contestation*," he said, handing it over gingerly, like a fragile treasure. "It's a comedy about the inadequate representation of working-class Americans in the electronic media."

"Sounds like a hit," I said. "I'll read it as soon as I get the chance." I waved Jeremy a quick good-bye, sped upstairs, and on an impulse tossed his screenplay into a garbage can in the front lobby. Then I walked quickly back to my car and got in. Before I even had the door closed, I was already eagerly examining my stolen loot.

My eagerness abated quickly, though, when I began to actually read. There were five essays in Susan Tamarack's manila folder. The first two, "My Mom's Death" and "What the Fourth of July Means to Me" were chock full of the kind of sentimental treacle that makes English teachers bald and sardonic before their time. Reading this stuff made me sympathetic to Jeremy, trying to add a little excitement to his life with Trotskyite intrigue.

Susan's third essay was about *Charlotte's Web*. It started off, *"This book is very good for kids. It teaches them that true friendship can save the life of a pig."*

And this person was running for *Congress*?

Ah, well. I guess there's no law that politicians have to be intelligent.

The fourth essay wasn't too promising either: "How to Make a Good Pancake." And when I saw the title to her fifth and last essay — "My Favorite Animal" — I was about ready to give up in despair.

But out of a sense of duty, I skimmed the thing. It sure was oddly written. Maybe Susan was in a hurry or stressed out when she wrote it, because it jumped around like a bad Hunter Thompson piece. She started out talking about her favorite animal — the turtle, in case you're wondering — and then somehow mysteriously segued into a discussion of her son's love for baseball. He would be playing in a Saratoga rec league this fall, the same one my own kids signed up for.

Then the essay did a sort of sideways shuffle into a long description of turtles' virtues. *They're very patient, and they never pass judgment on people,* she wrote. I couldn't really argue with that. I think I can say in all honesty that I've never had a turtle pass judgment on me. Though if one *did* pass judgment, I'm not sure how I would know.

After that she did a quick comparative analysis of turtles and people, in which people turned out to be decidedly inferior. In all fairness, this was not a badly written passage. But it was the next two paragraphs that grabbed my eyeballs and glued them to the page.

*"Like, for instance,"* Susan wrote, *"people get all sanctimonious when they hear about a woman who's getting beat up by her husband. They think, why doesn't she just leave him? But it's not that easy. It's really not. What if you've got no money of your own and not much education, and he's this really high-powered lawyer and everything? What do you do then?*

*"I think people should really put on the other person's shoes before they start criticizing his bunions."*

The essay stopped right there. Ordinarily I would have taken some time to contemplate that bunion metaphor. But I was too busy contemplating something else.

Was the Hack a wife beater?

And if he was . . . *what did Susan do about it?*

I got my car in gear and headed down the highway. It was high time to have a little chat with the widow.

# 7

Yes, it was high time indeed. But when I got to the widow's house, no one was there.

And when I hit the widow's campaign HQ, she wasn't there, either. Instead, there were five elderly ladies licking envelopes and four middle-aged guys working the phones. That was about nine more volunteers than we usually had working for Will even *before* he got busted. I stood at the front door and just watched for a few moments, feeling jealous.

Before I could step forward into the room, Oxymoron, the black Republican, appeared out of a side door and planted his large bulk in front of me. "Yeah?" he growled, folding his arms. "What do you want?"

"You probably remember me, I'm with the *Saratogian* —"

"I remember you," he said, not sounding all that nostalgic about it.

"Is the candidate here?" I asked. "I'd like to do an interview for the newspaper."

"She's not here."

"Could you tell me where she is?"

"No," Oxymoron said.

"What's with the attitude?" I blustered. "Don't you want some free press?"

"What did you say your name was?"

"Jacob Burns." I'm not above trying to use my fifteen minutes of fame to my advantage, so I continued, "You've probably heard of me. I wrote the movie *The Gas that Ate San Francisco.*"

Oxymoron stood there with his massive arms folded across his chest. "Yeah, I've heard of you, all right. Even saw your movie, thought it was a piece of crap. But I haven't seen your byline in the paper. So beat it."

He moved forward and I had to back up, almost banging my head into the door. I sidestepped. "You sure she's not in the back? I just have a couple quick questions," I said.

He put up his arms to grab me and shove me out of the room. But then a strange thing happened. My own skinny arms reflexively flew upward to ward him off . . . and the knuckles on my right hand somehow connected with his lower lip. It split open, and blood trickled out.

Oxymoron didn't take too kindly to that. In fact, he came at me with both fists. His first shot was a hard left aimed at my *shnoz*. I ducked under it just in time.

"Hey, I'm sorry!" I said. "I didn't mean to hit you!"

But Oxymoron wasn't listening. He came at me again. I was lucky to find a folding chair a couple of feet away. I grabbed it and flung it at him as hard as I could. That slowed him down enough so that I could make it out the door three seconds ahead of his next punch.

Ah well, I thought to myself as I hustled back to my car. Yet another setback for black-Jewish relations.

I went home and played phone tag with a pair of Shmuckler volunteers who'd left regretful messages that they were leaving the campaign. Then I called the Shmuck-man himself and gave him the latest investigation news, after first swearing him to secrecy. I didn't want him blurting anything to the press, because that might make Susan, Linda, Ducky *et al.* clam up.

Will was excited about my discoveries and would have kept me on the phone longer, but I had to take a break from the investigation to pick up Derek and Bernie at the bus stop. Then we spent the afternoon playing catch in the backyard. They were both having their first official league practices on Sunday, and they wanted to be ready. As Bernie explained, "Today is our *pre*-practice."

There's nothing in this world that gives me greater pleasure than playing baseball with Derek and Bernie. Or maybe *pleasure* isn't a profound enough word. Watching my sons dive for popups and race after ground balls brings back my own boyhood to me. When Mark McGwire and Sammy Sosa saved the game of baseball, they saved my childhood too.

After the boys and I were thoroughly pooped, we went inside for some apple juice, then headed upstairs to lie in bed and read together. It's quiet moments like this when we have our best talks, so after I read them a chapter of *Greatest World Series Thrillers*, I got the conversational ball rolling. "How was school today, guys?" I asked.

"Fine," they both replied. If I had my way, the word *fine* would be stricken from the English language. Then Derek asked, "Can I have computer time now?" and his little brother chimed in, "Me, too! Me, too!"

But I was too stubborn to give up just yet. "Come on, guys, tell me about school. What did you learn today?"

"Nothing," Derek said. "*Please* can I play on the computer?"

"Come on, you must've learned *something*."

"No, I didn't," he replied irritably. "Really, Dad, second grade is a *joke*. You know what we did in math today? It was, like, how much is ten plus eight? I'll bet even Bernie knows that, and he's just in kindergarten."

"Eighteen!" Bernie called out proudly.

"See, I'm right," Derek said triumphantly. "And reading is even worse, 'cause I have to sit there waiting for all the other kids to finish. And . . . they . . . read . . . about . . . this . . . slow. It's so boring! *Now* can I play on the computer?"

So this was how my child spent his days — getting bored silly? Three cheers for our ultra-homogenized, one-size-fits-all public school system. I felt like tearing my hair out.

Little Bernie, who is beginning to assume the peacemaker role in the family, realized I was feeling bad and decided to cheer me up. "Daddy, *I* learned something in school today."

"Well, that's certainly good to hear," I said. "What did you learn?"

"But I didn't really like learning it."

"What was it?"

"No, I don't want to talk about it."

"Oh, come on, Bernie."

"Yeah, tell us," his big brother said.

Finally Bernie gave in. "Well, this lady

came to class? Mrs. Demarco?"

"Uh-huh."

"And she talked to us about our private parts."

That threw me, all right. "Your what?"

Bernie giggled. "You know, our penises and stuff."

Derek spoke up. "Yeah, I remember her. Mrs. Demarco. She's *always* talking about private parts."

I wasn't sure whether to laugh or take this seriously. "What exactly does she tell you about private parts?"

"I don't know," Bernie said in a complaining voice. "It's, like, embarrassing. Why does this lady have to come in and talk to us about our penises?"

"Well," I said hesitantly, "I guess she wants to make sure the kids know their private parts are private, and no one else is allowed to mess with them."

"But it's *embarrassing*. How would you like to have some lady come in and start talking about *your* penis?"

"And your butt," Derek added.

"And vaginas," Bernie threw in.

"I always hated it when Mrs. Demarco came in," Derek said. "It was, like, weird."

"It's just really embarrassing," Bernie said. "Can we go down and play on the computer?"

I didn't answer right away. I was thinking, maybe this explains why our boys — especially the older one — were so into the computer. After a long day of wasting their brain cells at school, squirming in their seats and learning a little bit about their private parts but not much of anything else, they were probably desperate to exercise their noggins. Despite my fear and loathing of computers, I had to admit that the computer games we had, and the Internet stuff they were getting into lately, gave them a chance to mentally stimulate themselves. Unlike school.

On the other hand, maybe Derek was exaggerating the problem. And hopefully, after the first couple of weeks school would get more interesting —

"*Daddy,*" Derek said.

I shook myself. "Sure," I told them, "go play on the computer."

And that's what the three of us were doing two hours later, after dinner, when all hell broke loose.

Andrea was lying on the living room sofa reading a Georgette Heyer novel at the time. Meanwhile, the boys were showing me how to get information off the Internet about Susan Tamarack. I figured it wouldn't hurt to know what she was about.

I had planned to search out this info myself, without the kids' help, to keep them from getting more involved in the murder. But they came in the room and started giving me advice, and before I knew it, the computer search had turned into a group project.

Unfortunately, even with the kids' expert help I couldn't find out much. Susan Tamarack had not been a very public figure. I did learn that she originally met the Hack ten years ago, when she was a secretary in his office. Interesting — he seemed to have a thing for secretaries. With that as background, I was willing to bet that Susan guessed about his affair with his latest secretary. The widow's murder motives were piling up higher than a politician's promises.

After we exhausted the Internet's limited wisdom about Susan Tamarack, Bernie asked, "Daddy, can we play Triple Play now?"

"Just one more thing," I said. "Let's see what we can find out about Linda Medw—"

And then it happened: *KA-BOOM!* It came from right outside. Instantly the window behind us splintered open. A bullet thudded into the wall just above our heads.

*"Down!"* I yelled at the kids. *"Get down!"*

I shoved them off their chairs. We hurtled to the floor as another gunshot rang out, and another. It sounded like the shooter was in our driveway. Window shards rained down on us. Two more bullets hit the wall.

There was a brief silence, then Andrea screamed from the other room, *"Are you okay?!"*

"Yes! Stay where you are!"

The kids were whimpering. I crawled with them into the living room, where the shades were drawn and no one could see inside. I quickly reached up and shut off the lamp for good measure, as Andrea grabbed the portable phone and dialed 911. Then we all lay down on the rug and waited for the cops to come.

"Daddy?" Bernie said, his voice shaking with fear.

"Yes?"

"Is the computer okay?"

I couldn't stop myself. I started laughing hysterically.

"What's so funny?" Bernie asked, his feelings hurt.

I sobered up as much as I could. "Nothing, honey. Don't worry. The computer's fine."

The police came in waves. The first cop to

blare his siren our way was my friend and neighbor Dave, back from his little getaway with Madeline. Unfortunately he was out on patrol that evening, so he wasn't around when the shots were fired. By the time he got to our house, the gunman — or gun-woman — had already fled.

Dave's main job was to sit with us on the living room rug and keep us safe and relatively calm until reinforcements arrived. I was glad for his company, since he's much more *human* than the other local cops I've had run-ins with. Dave is the only black cop in town, and I think being an outsider has upped his sensitivity quotient.

After a couple of minutes of cowering, I went outside with Dave to do some quick surveillance by flashlight. We didn't find any muddy footprints or dropped guns. We did find a bunch of dried leaves on the driveway that I hadn't gotten around to raking up. They crackled loudly under our feet, and I wondered why I hadn't heard the crackling under the gunman's feet when I was at the computer. The window had been open about a foot.

We ended our surveillance when the other cops started coming. My opinion of Saratoga's finest was not improved by my encounters with them that night.

Not counting Dave, five other cops made the scene, including the grand poohbah himself, Chief Walsh. As I've mentioned, Chief Walsh was not exactly my biggest booster. He once tried to bust me for murder, and I tried to bust *him* for conspiracy to extort. Given how intensely we disliked each other, I guess he gets points for at least showing up at my house in the first place. But that's *all* he gets points for.

Andrea took the boys upstairs and went to bed with them while I told the chief and his square-jawed minions exactly what had happened. First I described the gunshots, then filled them in on my recent activities. "Because it's obvious," I declared, "that whoever shot at me was trying to stop my murder investigation — either by scaring me off or by killing me."

Chief Walsh eyed me dubiously. He was handsome and distingué, with classical features, clear blue eyes, and perfectly coifed silver hair, and I hated everything about him. I always thought he would have made a perfect Nazi colonel, casually sipping Rhine wine with his pinky extended as he sent victims off to the camps. "Have you learned anything in your 'investigation' that someone might actually be worried about?" Walsh asked with a tinge of sarcasm.

"Yeah, I might've learned a thing or two," I drawled, then hit them with both barrels blazing. "Jack Tamarack was blackmailing Senator Medwick, sleeping with Medwick's wife, and beating his own wife."

I expected to see all those square jaws dropping, but I was disappointed. Instead all their eyebrows began rising. "Do you have proof for any of this, or is it just gossip?" the chief asked.

"It's not gossip."

"So you have proof?"

"Well," I said defensively, "I'm still, you know . . ."

One of the two lieutenants in the room — a guy I knew and despised from before named Foxwell — cut in. "How do you know he was beating his wife?"

I couldn't very well say, "Because I stole her portfolio," so instead I hemmed and hawed for a moment. That gave Chief Walsh his opening.

"Listen, Burns," he said, "it's much more likely this whole thing was just a stupid prank."

"A *what?*"

Now he lifted his shoulders as well as his eyebrows. "Face it, you piss off a lot of people. I could name about ten guys in this town that would love to take a potshot at you. Hell, there's a few of them sitting right here in this room."

The lieutenants sitting on my living room sofa snickered. I was outraged. "Just a goddamn minute," I said. "Somebody took three 'potshots' at me and my sons. I fail to find that humorous!"

"Hey, we take it seriously and all," the chief said, "but I doubt they were actually trying to *kill* you."

"Thanks, that's so reassuring."

"Look, you were just three feet from the window. If they wanted to kill you, they could've walked right up to the window and put a bullet through your head."

I already knew the flaw in that theory. "But the shooter couldn't have walked up that close without me hearing him. His shoes would have crackled on the dried leaves, and I would've turned around and seen him. Maybe he realized that, so he decided to try and kill me from the sidewalk."

"I don't buy it," the chief said.

"Neither do I," said Foxwell. The other cops sprinkled around the room nodded in agreement.

I glared around at them all. "So what you're telling me is, you don't plan to even *look* for a connection between this shooting and the Hack's murder?"

Chief Walsh shrugged. "Well . . ." he began.

"In that case," I said, "why don't you take your lazy asses out of my house?"

As the chief and his bozos exited my front door, they were assaulted by a horde of reporters and cameramen. We don't get a lot of shootings here in bucolic Saratoga Springs, and I'm something of a local celeb, so the front curb of my house had already become home to three TV minivans. How did they get wind of this so quick? Media people must be descended from buzzards.

I wondered what Walsh would tell them. Probably some fancied up version of "no comment." Several media buzzards saw me watching through the window, and they waved and gestured for me to come outside and talk. But I was beat, so I just closed the shades again.

Meanwhile Dave came back in from outside, where he'd been doing more evidence-hunting on the driveway and sidewalk. Who knows — maybe the shooter left behind a business card by mistake.

"Find anything?" I asked.

He shook his head no. "I'll look again in the morning, but I kind of doubt we'll have much luck. Especially with the media stomping around all over the place."

"But they won't come on the driveway, right? I mean, you put up all that yellow police tape."

"Yeah, but that won't stop them. They'll just see it as an invitation to go under the tape and poke around."

Wonderful. Of course, having done the same thing myself at WTRO, I guess I couldn't complain. "Hey, thanks for trying. I appreciate it."

He checked his watch. "My shift is over now. You want me to stick around for a while? I know you've had a shock."

"No, that's okay," I said, but at the same time Andrea, coming down the stairs, exclaimed, "Yes, that would be great!"

So Dave stuck around for a couple of hours and watched the 11:00 news with us. It was quite a show. I had a starring role.

What had happened was, various buzzards kept ringing my doorbell and getting Derek and Bernie all riled up. Even Dave couldn't scare them off. So eventually, around 10:15, I'd decided to go outside and hold an impromptu news conference.

The first question came from an insipid-looking brunette with way too much makeup. "Mr. Burns, who do you think shot at your house? Chief Walsh says it was probably someone's sick idea of a joke."

I stood on the top step of my porch and looked out over the crowd. There were about fifteen buzzards and thirty neighbors. "Folks," I said, "I have a brief statement to make."

I waited until I was sure all the cameras were focused directly on me. Then I announced, "I am investigating the murder of Jack Tamarack. I have reason to believe that Will Shmuckler was falsely accused. Whoever shot those bullets through my window was trying to stop me from finding the real killer."

This time I got all the dropped jaws I could have asked for. Finally, when their amazement wore off, another overly made up lady buzzard asked me, "So who do you think *is* the real killer?"

"I don't know yet," I admitted, "but I'll find out." I gave the cameras my fiercest, most macho look. "And let me tell you this: nobody — but *nobody* — will scare me away. If they want to stop me, they'll have to kill me first."

*And they just might do that,* I thought, as I watched myself on TV. A chill went up my spine. I grabbed Andrea's hand.

Then Will Shmuckler came on our TV screen. He was standing on the front porch of his house by the Hudson. I was expecting this; Will had called twenty minutes ago to see if I was all right, and to let me know that his own personal set of media buzzards had banged on his front door, told him the whole story, and asked him for comments. "I gave them the works," he told me gleefully. "Best campaign speech I ever made."

Having seen him fumble and bumble his way through the Skidmore event just the other night, I was dubious. But when I saw him on TV, I had to agree. The Shmuck had done himself proud. I guess he was feeling more confident that my investigation was bearing fruit and he wouldn't go down for the murder. His confidence showed.

"I cannot begin to tell you how thankful I am," he pronounced, looking grave but forceful, "that my friend Jacob Burns and his family have not been hurt. I would hate to see Jacob's two young boys suffer because of their dad's heroic efforts to save me from this malicious, politically motivated accusation of murder.

"I hope that tonight's terrible near-tragedy will convince the police of what I've been saying all along: *I am an innocent man.* And I hope the voters of our 22nd District will understand exactly what's going on here. The powers that be want to wreck my

135

campaign. So they're destroying my reputation and threatening me with life in prison. I ask you: is this the kind of behavior you want to condone in this great democracy of ours? If you believe in our country, in truth, in *justice,* then please remember your cherished beliefs come Election Day."

Will looked good, better than I'd seen him since the campaign began. His hair was combed for once, and the camera angle made his proboscis a little less imposing than usual. He sounded good, too. It was a powerful speech.

Andrea and I looked at each other, and we were both thinking the same thing. *Was it possible?*

Was it possible that my old college buddy, liberal, Jewish, Democratic *Shmuckler* that he was, would actually get elected to the United States Congress?

# 8

I tossed and turned all night long, dreaming about faceless dark figures and large black guns. Every time I woke up and heard a car slink along in the early a.m. darkness, I wondered if it was the shooter coming back for another try.

On the other hand, the kids must have been really knocked out. Derek Jeter didn't walk in his sleep, or if he did, we didn't find out about it. And Bernie Williams didn't pee in his bed, either. We would definitely have found out about *that*.

The boys slept until seven-thirty, which is late for them. Then they came into our bed and cuddled. Happily it was Saturday, so no one had to rush off anywhere. Andrea read the boys two chapters of *Greatest World Series Thrillers*, and I was reading them yet another chapter — they're insatiable — when the phone rang. Probably some early-bird-gets-the-worm buzzard.

I grabbed the phone. "Yeah," I growled.
"This is Jeremy."
Huh? "Jeremy who?"
"Jeremy Wartheimer."

"Oh, right. How you doing?" *And why are you calling me before eight a.m. on a Saturday,* I wanted to ask, but didn't. No sense in alienating Andrea's colleagues. At least, not until she got tenure.

"I was calling to ask if you've read my screenplay yet."

Talk about pushy. "No, but I'm looking forward to it."

Actually, of course, I'd thrown his screenplay away, but there was no way I could tell him that. Maybe the next time he called, I'd simply pretend to have read it already. I could spew forth all the inanities that Hollywood producers spew when they're pretending to have read something, like: "Interesting work . . . A lot of good stuff in it . . . Reminds me of *The Godfather* . . ."

"So when do you think you'll read it?" Jeremy pressed.

I had to fight not to blow up at him. "Hey, cut me some slack. If you saw the TV news last night, then you know I've been kind of busy."

"I never watch TV. When you read my screenplay, you'll understand that I consider television an imperialist tool of the ruling classes."

What a turdball. My kids were wriggling around on the bed, impatient for me to get back to their book. "I have to get off the phone now. I'll read your screenplay as soon as I can —"

"Bullshit. You're not gonna read it."

"Sure, I will."

"No, you won't. I saw you throw it in the garbage in McCracken Hall."

Oh, God. "Listen, Jeremy, I'm — I'm sorry," I stuttered. "It's just I'm under a lot of pressure right now, and, um, look, why don't you give me another copy, I really do want to read it, okay?"

"Skip it. The truth is, I don't give a damn if you read my screenplay or not. I just want you to pass it along to your agent with a note saying how much you loved it."

"But I can't do that — unless I really *do* love it."

"Oh, yeah? Either you give me that note, or I tell Rosalyn all about you breaking into her office and stealing Susan Tamarack's portfolio."

Talk about stuttering. "How-how-how —"

His harsh laugh singed my ears. "How do I know? It wasn't rocket science. You were so *obvious*. First you stand outside Rosalyn's door palming a credit card, then you hide a manila folder under your jacket, and then when Rosalyn gives me the portfolios to look at, Susan Tamarack's is missing. So here's the deal, Burns. You're gonna fax me a letter addressed to your agent, signed by you, in which you inform him that my screenplay is the best thing since Fellini's *Satyricon*. That's spelled S-A-T-I-R-Y-C-O-N."

I was pretty sure he had the I and the Y mixed up, but now was no time to get technical. "Jeremy, this is preposterous —"

"I better get that fax by Monday morning, pal, or your wife's ass is grass. See, I won't just tell Rosalyn. I'll go to the department chairman, too."

"Look, please —"

But he hung up. I just sat there on the bed with the phone in my hands. *Jeez Louise*, people will stop at nothing to make it in Hollywood.

"Honey, what's wrong?" Andrea asked me worriedly.

"Uh, we better talk," I said. "Kids, why don't you go downstairs? Mommy and I need some private time."

"But I don't *want* to go downstairs," Bernie said, and his big brother added, "You're in the middle of the chapter!"

"You guys can go down and play on the computer."

"I don't *want* to play on the computer," Bernie said.

Now this was a first. "Sure, you do."

"No, I don't! What if someone shoots at us again?"

"Yeah!" Derek agreed. "They could kill us!"

"Sweethearts," Andrea said soothingly, "no one's going to shoot at the house again."

"How do you know?" Derek asked.

"And besides, they weren't really trying to kill us," I said, though I wasn't so sure that was true. "They were shooting above us, on purpose."

"How do you know?" Derek asked again.

Clearly this would not be easy.

Eventually we got the kids to go downstairs for some cereal. Then Andrea and I went back to bed, where I told her the whole sordid tale of my dastardly break-in at the English Department. As expected, Andrea was pissed. "First somebody shoots at us —"

"You mean above us —"

"— thanks to your investigation, and now you're endangering my job? What in God's name were you thinking?"

After several minutes of telling her I was sorry, I started getting pretty pissed myself. "Look, I screwed up. Now what the hell do you want me to do?"

"Why not just write that letter to your

agent? Then call him up and tell him to ignore it."

I gave that some thought. But as Bernie
would say, it was just too *embarrassing.* An-
drew, my agent, already thought I was a few
chromosomes short of a full mental deck. I
didn't want to give him any more ammuni-
tion to use against me.

I explained this to Andrea, but she wasn't
impressed. "Hey, I'd rather have you look
bad to your agent than have me get involved
in some scandal that might ruin my tenure
chances."

"Come on, do you really want to let
Jeremy blackmail us?"

"Of course not. He's the biggest ass in the
known universe. But what choice do we
have?"

"You know," I said, eyeing her thoughtfully, "I could always show you how to use
your AAA card."

She wrinkled her forehead, puzzled. But
when I told her my idea, she slowly started
grinning. Andrea may be the cautious type,
but luckily she's got a mischievous-kid
streak, too. And even luckier, she absolutely
couldn't stand Jeremy Wartheimer.

So we made our plan. Tomorrow was a
Sunday. Sometime in the morning Andrea
would drive to her campus and break into

Jeremy's office. Then she'd slip Susan Tamarack's folder back into his pile of portfolios without him even knowing. That would get me off the hook. I had never actually confessed to stealing anything, so I could just tell Jeremy that he'd misunderstood our phone conversation, and he must have misplaced the portfolio himself.

Only one catch: what if the AAA card snapped in half or whatever, and Andrea couldn't break in? What would we do then?

Well . . . we'd cross that Rubicon when we came to it.

The phone started ringing again shortly thereafter — buzzards on the prowl — so we took the phone off the hook. I've found that taking the phone off the hook takes care of a surprisingly large number of life's problems.

At five of nine, freshly showered and breakfasted, I lit out for the widow's house. I figured, this early on a Saturday morning I was bound to catch her. Even politicians — and Susan Tamarack was now, I supposed, a politician — have to sleep sometimes.

But no one was home at her place. Either that or they were avoiding me, because I rang the bell twice and banged the door knocker three times to no purpose.

Bummer. Leaning against one of the Corinthian columns, I was debating my next move when a post office van pulled up and the driver popped out. He reached in the passenger's seat for a large box, then came up the front walk toward me.

"Good morning," he said.

"Good morning," I replied. That box looked oddly familiar, and then it hit me: I'd seen Linda Medwick filling up this same box with the Hack's "personal stuff."

The mailman set the box down on the porch. "Could you sign for it, please?" he asked, holding out a clipboard and pen. Obviously he assumed I lived in the house.

I was tempted to sign the clipboard and abscond with the box. But I'd already gotten in enough trouble just for ripping off Jeremy Wartheimer. Imagine how much trouble I'd get into for ripping off the post office.

I mean, if there were two things I learned as a kid, they were: don't tear the tags off of mattresses, and don't mess with the U.S. mail. No way would I even consider fooling with the *federales* —

"Sir?" the mailman said impatiently, thrusting his clipboard and pen at me.

"Sorry, I . . . I . . ."

He eyed me questioningly.

"Never mind," I said, as I grabbed the clipboard and pen and signed, *"Michael Jones."*

"Thank you," the mailman said, and as soon as he drove out of sight, I grabbed the box, stuffed it in my car, and hauled ass to a secluded spot.

I know, I know, it was dumb. What can I say?

The secluded spot I chose was the far end of a Price Chopper parking lot, in the midst of a sea of abandoned shopping carts. I hopped in the backseat, tore the box open, and got down to work.

At the top of the box were loose odds and ends: key chains, wrapping paper, tea bags . . . all very innocuous, from what I could tell. It seemed funny that the Hack's mistress had been so conscientious about sending his stuff back to his wife.

Beneath these loose odds and ends, I found *more* loose odds and ends. And then more. I tossed them impatiently onto the seat. I found some long, official-looking documents — a sales tax analysis, an environmental study, and a report on HMOs — and leafed through them without finding anything of interest. Linda probably should have left them in the office for whoever took over the Hack's job, but I guess in her grief

145

she just threw in a bunch of stuff without thinking.

Then I came across two items that looked promising: the Hack's personal appointment calendar and his address book. I examined them hopefully, searching for some magic notation like: *"Sept. 6, 8:45 p.m.: go to WTRO to get whacked by Ducky Medwick."* But no such luck. If there was a clue hidden away inside all of these names, dates, and numbers, it eluded me.

I worked my way down through the box, burrowing past a yo-yo and three bags of M & M's, until I came to a couple of framed 5 X 7 photographs. The first photo featured little Sean in a T-ball uniform. The other photo was the same one I'd seen on the Hack's campaign brochure. It showed Susan gazing up adoringly at her husband while he gazed adoringly at the camera.

He looked smug, arrogant, and Republican. I stared into his eyes, trying to see if those were the eyes of a vicious wife beater.

Susan, for her part, looked waifish, obsequious, and a bit too much like a sweet little *wife,* if you know what I mean. But was she also an abused woman who lashed out at last and killed her abuser?

One thing was certain: no matter what this photograph seemed to show, Susan

Tamarack wasn't just a sweet little wife. Her seizing opportunity by the horns and running for Congress proved that.

I sat in my Toyota studying the photo and scratching my head, trying to reconcile all the contradictory aspects of this person. Then suddenly I noticed something. There was a second photo under the Plexiglas, hidden right behind this one. I could see one edge of the bottom photo barely sticking out.

I slid the Hack-Susan picture out of the way, and here's what greeted my puzzled eyes: a photo of some well-dressed man I didn't recognize handing a white envelope to Robert Pierce, of all people.

What the heck was *this* about?

Pierce was seated behind a desk. It looked like he was in his office, presumably at the State Assembly. The photo had been shot through the office window and looked grainy, like it had been enlarged. The two men seemed very serious and businesslike, but not antagonistic.

I couldn't see what was in that envelope. But I had a strong suspicion.

I mean, hey, a secret hidden photograph of a politician taking an envelope from someone . . . that thing had to have money inside. And not just cab money, either.

What was the Hack doing with this photograph? And where did he get it from?

I learned the answer to my second question easily enough, when I turned the picture over and saw the words "Zzypowski Investigations" stamped on the back. Then I took out the Hack's address book and found an address and phone number for somebody named "Zzyp." Maybe Chief Walsh was right, and I'm not the world's smartest sleuth, but at least I'm savvy enough to guess that Zzyp is short for Zzypowski.

I headed into Price Chopper for the pay phone. Would Zzyp be in his office on a Saturday morning? I dialed the number.

"Zzypowski Investigations," a sniffly voice answered.

"Is Mr. Zzypowski there?"

"That's me," he said, and then sneezed. "May I help you?"

"I hope so," I said, and hung up. Then I got in my car and made a beeline for his office.

I was excited about seeing what a real live P.I.'s office looked like. Ever since I fell into this sleuthing thing, I'd had fantasies about going professional and doing the whole Raymond Chandler number to the hilt. Renting a seedy old office somewhere, complete with battered Underwood typewriter, art deco ashtray, plus maybe a spittoon or two. With a fifth of bourbon and a gun in the bottom desk drawer. I'd sit by the window on cold, dreary January afternoons and play the saxophone.

So when I got to Zzypowski Investigations, it was a shock to my system. His office was located in a *mall*, for God's sake. A private dick in a mall? Further proof of the decline of civilization.

And Saratoga Mall was even more depressing than most malls. It was almost empty, since the majority of the mall's business had been preempted by another, newer mall right across the street. The wing of Saratoga Mall where Zzyp kept his office was especially dead, because Montgomery Ward, the main anchor store there, pulled out last spring and no one had come along to replace it.

I walked past the abandoned Montgomery Ward to the alcove in the far corner where Zzyp kept his office. There were no spittoons, ashtrays, or Underwoods, battered or otherwise. Just a Gateway computer bathed in bright fluorescent light. Forget the sax; mall Muzak wandered in through the door with me as I entered Zzyp's office.

Zzyp looked up from his computer

screen. "May I help you?" he said. His standard refrain, I guess. He had a red, stuffy nose, rheumy eyes, and thin forgettable hair. From what I could see of him behind the computer, his body wasn't too impressive, either. He could have been anywhere from thirty-five to fifty; he had the kind of dull, characterless face and physique that make it impossible to tell. Chandler must be turning over in his grave.

Not wanting to spend any more time in this place than I had to, I came straight to the point. "I'm wondering what you can tell me about this photograph," I said, and plopped it on the desk next to his computer.

Zzyp looked down at the photo, then up at me. Then he sneezed. "Where'd you get this?" he asked.

I was distracted by a strand of wet snot hanging from his nose, so I didn't answer right away.

"Where'd you get it?" he repeated.

I didn't want to explain about defrauding the post office, so I countered, "Why'd you give this photo to Jack Tamarack?"

He finally wiped his nose. Meanwhile he observed me craftily, and I realized that if it weren't for the head cold clouding his moist eyes, he might come across as a lot sharper than he did right now.

"How much is this little piece of knowledge worth to you?" he asked.

"Not much," I told him.

"Then I'm afraid I can't help you," he said, folding his arms and favoring me with a shiteating grin. Even his teeth looked rheumy.

I clicked into hard-ass mode. "Listen, bud, I know most of it already." I waved the photo at his face and unloaded all my best guesses on him. "You were helping Tamarack blackmail Pierce. This is a picture of Pierce taking a payoff from someone. All I'm asking you is, who's the other guy in the photo? You don't tell me, I'll find out somewhere else."

Zzyp hesitated, then said, "Go right ahead."

"Okay, suit yourself."

I started for the door, hoping I'd read his hesitation right and he'd call me back. Sure enough, he said, "Wait."

I turned. Zzyp sneezed twice, leaving a new, even wider rope of snot hanging down. I tried not to stare at it.

"Five hundred bucks," he said.

"I'll give you what's in my pocket. Hundred ten."

He gave an annoyed grunt, but said, "All right, all right, hand it over."

I handed it over.

"The guy in your photo is Dennis Sarafian." I blinked in confusion. "You know who he is?"

As a matter of fact, I did. I was surprised I hadn't recognized him in the first place. But then again, the photo was pretty fuzzy. And the one time I'd met Sarafian — or sort of met him — I'd only seen him in profile.

The sort-of meeting happened two years ago, just before I hit the Hollywood jackpot. I was so discouraged by my impecuniousness, I'd decided to bite the bullet and apply for a full-time job. One of the places I sent my resume was Sarafian Communications, a P.R. firm up in Queensbury, outside Glens Falls.

Sarafian's secretary called and asked me in for an interview, so I studied up on the company. Sarafian Communications handled a hodgepodge of corporate accounts, some as far away as Pennsylvania. But their *numero uno* client by far was Global Electronics, which is *the* biggest employer (after the government) in the Albany area. Global El, as it's nicknamed locally, manufactures everything from computer parts to microwave ovens to those tiny plastic outlet covers you put on when you're babyproofing your house.

Another thing Global El manufactures is pollution, big time. Four years ago, some government agency discovered that the sludge at the bottom of the Hudson River down below Albany is absolutely *loaded* with PCBs. It turned out most of the PCBs came from Global El.

So now the U.S. Environmental Protection Agency and the New York State Department of Environmental Conservation were trying to decide what to do about all of that evil gook. Should several highly contaminated miles of the river be dredged to get rid of the PCBs, as the region's environmentalists were demanding? Or should the PCBs be left alone in the sludge, as Global El was pushing for, on the theory that stirring them up could do even more damage to the river?

The issue was highly controversial and getting more so every year, with outraged newspaper editorials and TV sound bytes galore. Global El was making not-so-veiled threats that if they were forced to pay for dredging, they would move their operations — and their jobs — out of upstate New York. Given our tenuous local economy, these threats were not taken lightly.

Actually, it wasn't Global El making the threats; it was their spokesman, Dennis

Sarafian. The Global El honchos had farmed out their entire P.R. operation in upstate New York to Sarafian's company, putting him in charge of saving their collective corporate derrieres.

When I realized how married Sarafian was to Global El, I thought about skipping that job interview. Did I really want to be a corporate, pro-pollution lackey?

But Sarafian Communications had *good* clients too, like hospitals and colleges. So I bit the bullet and tried for the job after all. I put on my one suit, drove the half hour to Queensbury, and waited in the reception area for Sarafian to get off the phone and interview me.

I could see Sarafian's profile through the gauzy curtain that separated me from his office. I could hear his voice, too. He was explaining to some newspaper reporter that PCBs really aren't so bad, and a lot of them didn't even come from Global El in the first place, and they don't cause all that much cancer anyway, just a little. The *real* problem was that a bunch of radical environmental extremists are out to destroy our American way of life.

After listening to ten minutes of this, I couldn't take it anymore. Without even waiting for him to get off the phone, I left the building. I got back in my rusty old car and drove home, feeling more despairing about my career and my life and the world in general than I'd ever felt before. Then, that night, I got a phone call from my agent. Someone had just offered me a million dollars for my movie script.

And that was the last I'd thought about Dennis Sarafian until this very moment.

"So why was Sarafian giving Pierce a payoff?" I asked Zzyp.

"You want an awful lot of knowledge for a measly hundred ten bucks."

I took a stab at it. "Was Sarafian doing Global El's dirty work? Bribing Pierce to take a stand against dredging?"

"Like I say, you want a hell of a lot."

I came at him from another angle. "How'd you find out about this payoff, anyhow?"

He gave a self-deprecating wave of his hand. "In my business, you hear things."

"Uh huh. So you called the Hack and told him what you heard. You even offered to get him proof — for a price."

"Hey, it's called opposition research. Totally legal," Zzyp said. "All the politicians do it these days. I even put it on my business cards." He handed me one. "Big money in it."

I examined the card. In addition to "opposition research," Zzyp specialized in "bankruptcy investigations," "personal injuries," and "divorce work." Definitely not a Sam Spade type of guy — especially not with that snot still hanging from his nostril.

Nevertheless I said, "Very impressive," figuring the more I flattered him, the more information I'd get. "By the way," I added in a casual tone, "you ever do any *other* research for the Hack?"

He paused just long enough so I doubted he was telling the truth, then said, "No."

"Zzypowski, don't blow smoke up my ass. The Hack had dirt on Ducky Medwick, and a hundred to one he got it from you."

"I wish he did. Would've meant big bucks for sure. Look, I got a client coming in any minute, so if you don't mind . . ."

"I'll give you that five hundred bucks you wanted. If you tell me what the Hack had on Ducky."

"I told you already, I got no clue what you're talking about."

I took out my wallet. "Yeah, well, if you suddenly happen to *remember*, here's my card."

"Don't need it. You're Jacob Burns."

"How'd you know that?"

"Saw you on the tube last night. Actually,

I knew about you from before, when you solved those murders. Though the way I hear it, you solved them both *wrong* and just got lucky."

"Something like that."

"Word of advice." Zzyp leaned back in his chair. "You're not cut out for this game. Better get out before you get hurt."

"Thanks for the tip," I said. "But it's hard to take advice seriously from a guy with a three-inch booger hanging from his nose."

Childish, I know, but I was getting sick of every Tom, Dick and Harry reminding me of my shortcomings as a private dick. If I didn't watch it, I'd get a complex. I picked up the photograph and walked out.

I mean, hey, at least I wasn't doing divorce work.

# 9

"Opposition research."

I got the concept. But here's what I didn't get: what did the Hack actually *do* with his opposition research?

Maybe he showed Pierce the incriminating photograph and told him, *Don't you dare run against me for Congress, or I'll spread the word about your bribe.*

But wait a minute. This scenario couldn't be true, because Pierce *did* run against the Hack for Congress. He fought him for the party's endorsement. So what was going on here?

Another possibility: the Hack showed the bribery photo to Ducky and the county chairmen, and warned them that if they gave Pierce the nomination, the shit would hit the fan.

Puzzling. I drove back to Broadway, then went to my office to mull things over. By "office," I mean Madeline's Espresso Bar, which I've found is the best place on earth for deep ruminating. Also, they have free newspapers there.

Today's *Saratogian* featured a big front-page story by Judy Demarest about last night's shooting excitement. I'd given Judy the broad strokes of my investigation, leaving out such minor details as who was sleeping with whom, who was beating whom, and who was blackmailing whom. I wasn't ready to go public with all that yet — though if the cops kept sitting on their hands and my investigation got nowhere, I might be forced to.

The *Saratogian*, along with the *Albany Times Union*, *Schenectady Gazette*, and every other regional paper, printed lengthy excerpts of the Shmuck-man's stirring speech in favor of truth, justice, and his own campaign. They had photos of him too, looking tall, dark, and if not handsome, then at least impassioned. It was awesome publicity. Again I got that prickly feeling climbing up my spine, that maybe my old buddy actually had a shot to win.

From the *Times Union*, I learned that Pierce had two campaign rallies scheduled for midday down in Dutchess County, an hour and a quarter south of Saratoga. Much as I wanted to interrogate the guy, I decided to do it later when he was in a less public place, and easier to get to.

Also, there was another fellow I wanted to question first: Dennis Sarafian. If I got him to open up, I could pile more pressure on Pierce.

So I walked up Broadway toward my Camry, got in, and started off toward Sarafian's office. I made it about five feet before I stopped short. The car was making a loud *thumpa-thumpa* sound. And was it my imagination or was the car listing to the left?

I got out and looked at my front left tire. No, it wasn't my imagination. The thing was flatter than a Steve Forbes tax plan.

Both our cars getting flats in the same week — talk about bad luck.

Wait a minute — *luck?* I stooped down, ignoring a twinge of pain in my forty-one-year-old back, and examined the tire. It took a while, but I found it.

Someone had come up with a cute little way to slow down my investigation — with a jagged, three-inch-long tire slash.

I straightened back up and looked quickly around me. But I didn't see any bad guys running away. The sidewalks were full of pleasant-looking people going about their weekend shopping.

Yes, everything was perfectly normal, except that some creep had just slashed my tire in the middle of downtown on a beautiful September day.

Was it the same creep who had killed the

Hack? And almost killed me? How many creeps were running loose in this town, anyway? Even though it was seventy degrees out, I shivered.

I took a deep breath, leaned against the downward-sloping car hood, and tried to sort things out. Apparently someone had decided last night's warning wasn't enough, and I needed another one. Maybe Zzyp had followed me back to town from his office and done the dirty deed . . . but at whose behest?

I thought back to the murder weapon, with its filed-off serial numbers. It made the murder seem almost professional. Was the killer a hired gun? Could it even be Zzyp?

I looked up Broadway and my eyes locked on Susan Tamarack's campaign headquarters, less than a block away. Maybe Oxymoron had vandalized my car, out of general hatred for me and revenge for his split lip. With its half-rusted-out driver's side door, my Toyota was easily recognizable. If Oxymoron spotted it, he could have decided to have some spontaneous thrills. He seemed like the type that would enjoy that.

I considered going to the HQ to confront him, but since he'd almost rearranged my face the last time, I had trouble mustering up the enthusiasm. Instead I pulled out my AAA card and used it the way it was actually intended for a change, getting them to tow my car to a garage. To my eternal shame, I'm one of those guys who never learned how to fix a flat tire. In my defense, for most of my twenties and some of my thirties, I was too poor to afford a car.

Since I wasn't poor anymore, and I was in a hurry, I slipped the garage guys an extra twenty to take care of my car first. After they worked their magic, I got back in the Camry and chugged up the Northway to Sarafian's office in Queensbury, hoping to catch him before lunch. I kept looking behind me to see if someone was following, but I didn't spot anyone — although this is yet another private eye skill I haven't really mastered.

For a company with such an impressive client list, Sarafian Communications had a surprisingly humble headquarters. It was just a regular clapboard house in a middle-class neighborhood, with Sarafian and his people working on the bottom floor and Sarafian living upstairs.

I walked into his office and sat down in the reception area to wait. It hit me that I was sitting in the exact same spot where I'd sat when I applied for that job. And I was watching Sarafian's profile through the exact same gauzy curtains.

And I was overhearing the exact same kind of conversation. "My friend," Sarafian was saying into the phone, "we're putting out a press release in the next couple of weeks that'll blow the EPA, the DEC, and all the rest of these radical environmental types right out of the water. So if I were you, I'd just sit tight and not run any editorials for a while."

I felt like I'd entered a time warp. Two years ago, I just turned tail and slinked home. But today I said the heck with it. I got up, opened Sarafian's door, and strode inside. The receptionist, a willowy brunette with translucent skin, called out to me to stop, but I ignored her.

Sarafian, still in mid-harangue, gave me an irritated look. But then I took The Photograph out of my jacket pocket and held it up. Sarafian stared at it, then at me, and said into the phone, "Uh, listen, something just came up, I gotta run," and hung up.

"What do you want?" he snarled, skipping the small talk.

"Information," I replied.

"Then call the phone company."

I sized him up. He was in his late thirties and wore what looked like a thousand-dollar suit and a hundred-dollar haircut.

They did nothing to disguise his thin face, thin nose, thin hair, and sloping forehead, all of which combined to make him look like a ferret. On the positive side, he did have a strong jutting chin and aggressive eyes. If he had gone into show biz, he would have been an agent or producer, something slimy like that.

Interesting that Sarafian didn't ask who I was. Did he see me on TV last night, too?

"No, I'll skip the phone company," I said gruffly, shooting him my toughest Jesse Ventura glare. "I'll call the newspapers instead. Tell them I have a photo of you bribing a state assemblyman."

"Bullshit, that was a legitimate campaign contribution."

"Don't insult my intelligence."

He pointed at the photo. "You wanna know what's in that envelope? A thousand bucks. I reported it and everything."

"There's a lot more in there than just one grand."

"Oh, yeah?"

"Yeah. You were loading Pierce up with Global El cash. What was the payback — he was gonna fight against dredging?"

"Hey, it's *your* theory. You tell me."

I spread my palms and tried to put a conciliatory tone into my voice. "I got no desire to bust your chops. I'm investigating a murder, not a bribery. You make it easy for me, I'll do everything I can to make it easy for you."

"I know how to make it easy for both of us."

"How's that?"

"Just get the fuck out of my office — and stay out."

So much for sounding conciliatory. I went back to my Ventura routine, but that didn't work any better. Either the man really had nothing to fear or he was too afraid to open his mouth. I couldn't tell which.

Finally I stood up, growled, "I'll be back," and stalked out. Not a great exit line, I know, but it was the best I could think of. My morning coffee was wearing off, and I had the disheartening feeling that a *real* private eye would have brought this no-goodnik Sarafian to his knees begging for mercy in no time.

Luckily I had other fish to fry. One of my major fish, Susan Tamarack, had a 12:30 rally scheduled at the Knights of Columbus hall in Schuylerville, ten miles east of Saratoga. I grabbed a chocolate bar and coffee at Stewart's, upstate New York's version of 7-Eleven. Then I hit the road for beautiful downtown Schuylerville, driving past trailer parks, decrepit houses, and half-rotted pickups adorning front yards.

Schuylerville may be only ten miles away from Saratoga Springs geographically, but in other respects it's ten worlds away. For a small town, Saratoga has heaps of "cul-chah." We've got three classical music quartets, two ballet companies, and one folk music coffee shop. We even have Jews.

Schuylerville has none of these things. What it does have is an economy that's even worse than Troy's and a cultural insularity that's truly frightening.

When I entered the Knights of Columbus, which was filled with about a hundred of Susan Tamarack's supporters, my eyes were immediately struck by a huge surrealistic painting of the Crucifixion on the front wall. Warriors in red loincloths and evil-looking, yellow-faced guys in yarmulkes lurked all over the painting. Jesus was front and center, covered with blood.

The painting looked disturbingly familiar, and I quickly placed it: this was the same painting that was all over the local newspapers eight or nine years ago. At that time, the painting hung prominently in the auditorium of the Schuylerville public high school.

Now, when I said that Schuylerville has no Jews, I exaggerated. Actually, Schuylerville has about six Jews. Two of them, parents of high schoolers, went to the school board and complained that the painting violated the separation of church and state.

But the school board refused to take down the painting, so the New York Civil Liberties Union brought a lawsuit on the Jewish family's behalf. Then the fun really started. The family was ostracized, the kids were beaten up by their classmates, and the father's auction business was boycotted. On Yom Kippur, the Ku Klux Klan came to town to march on the Jewish family's house and burn some crosses.

We Saratoga Jews tried to reassure ourselves that Schuylerville was a whole different world, and It Couldn't Happen Here. But we were relieved when the courts finally ruled for the Jewish family, the painting was removed, and the furor died down.

But now here the painting was again, bringing back all those bad memories. It suddenly came to me that I was just deluding myself when I imagined that Will *Shmuckler* had any hope of getting elected. The 22nd District was full of backwater towns like Schuylerville that would never dream of supporting a Jewish candidate. Half the folks in this room probably believed in some kind of worldwide Jewish conspiracy. I wouldn't be shocked if a few of them even believed that Jews have horns.

I looked up at the painting. Sure enough, I saw a pair of dark red horns peeping out from underneath an evil guy's yarmulke.

I tried to erase all these thoughts from my mind and focus on the campaign rally. Phil Rogers, the whiny chairman of the Saratoga County GOP, was delivering his colorless opening remarks. I gazed around at the assembled throng — the men with their careworn faces and checked flannel shirts, the women with their faded sweatshirts. I sat next to a middle-aged couple that was quietly holding hands. The woman smiled hello.

It was disconcerting. These were good people — good parents, good workers, good husbands and wives. And yet, they just stood by silently when the KKK came to town.

Up at the podium Rogers stepped down and the widow stepped up, dressed all in black and looking sexy as hell. Something about her thin frame and big, fawnlike eyes made you want to hold her tight and take care of her. The crowd applauded, and she launched into her speech.

Or rather, *plodded*. The only half-decent part was where she talked about how much she loved her husband and wanted to carry on his work, fighting for the issues he believed in. But she never said what those issues actually were.

Not that the crowd seemed to mind. They clapped for her lustily. Who needs issues, anyway?

Even with Susan's sexy widow appeal, I was still surprised that so many people were attending her small-town rally. On a gorgeous day like today, why wasn't everyone out apple picking and leaf raking? But when she finished her speech and everyone immediately crowded around the three long tables at the far wall, I figured out what was going on. The tables were loaded with goodies, and not just the cheap salami and American cheese you find at an upstate Democratic rally. We were talking fried chicken, real mashed potatoes, and seven different kinds of soda. In impoverished Schuylerville, this was more than enough incentive to sit through an hour-long rally. Actually, it was just thirty minutes — I had to give Susan credit for that. Maybe she had nothing to say, but at least she said it quickly.

I was starved myself, so I filled up a plate with chicken and mashed potatoes while I waited for a chance to catch the widow in private. Since the food was paid for by the Republicans, I considered it my moral duty to consume as much of the stuff as I could.

Meanwhile Susan was constantly surrounded. When she got around to dating again, she'd have no trouble finding prospects. But it wasn't just the men who loved her. I kept hearing women congratulating her for her courage, saying things like "How do you ever find the strength?"

Courage? Strength? Personally, I saw Susan Tamarack as an opportunist trading on her dead husband's name to hustle a $140,000-a-year job she was hopelessly unsuited for.

Finally the woman of the hour broke free of her fans. She headed for a corner door and went through it to a hallway. I grabbed my plateful of grub and followed her.

I reached the hallway at the same moment she turned a corner into another hallway. I hurried onward, but before I hit that second hallway she was gone. It was dark here, far from the madding Schuylerville crowd, but after my eyes adjusted I was able to make out a WOMEN sign above a door. She must be inside there. I settled back against a wall and gnawed on a chicken leg, lying in wait.

I didn't hear anyone coming. I didn't see him, either. But suddenly I felt a cold hand on my shoulder.

I would have screamed, but my mouth

170

was full so I choked instead. Then I dropped my plastic plate, but it didn't go far. The mashed potatoes made it stick to my blue jeans.

Not that I was thinking about the state of my pants just then. I was staring into the eyes of Hack Sr. They gleamed angrily in the darkness.

"Come here," he hissed, and pulled me out of the hallway. I was so stunned, I let myself be pulled.

He led me into another hallway, in the opposite direction from where I'd come. Then he opened a door into a pitch black stairwell. I stopped dead. "Come here," he hissed again, louder this time now that we were far away from anyone who might hear us.

This was getting way too cloak and dagger for my tastes. Speaking of daggers, did he have any weapons of destruction hidden away in that bulky jacket of his? "What do you want?" I asked tremulously.

He shoved me into the stairwell, showing amazing strength for a sick old man. Thoroughly frightened by now, I was about to shove him back and haul ass out of there as fast as my running shoes could carry me. But then, without warning, he went into one of his patented coughing spasms. I'd have felt ridiculous shoving the guy. I felt ridiculous even being scared of him.

At last the hacking receded to the point where he could talk again, or at least croak out words.

"You're killing me," he gasped.

I didn't know how to respond. Even with the stairwell door open, I couldn't see his face, just a shadow.

After another few coughs, he was able to get out, "Why are you bothering her?"

"Look, how about we go back and get you some water?"

"*Why?*" he croaked again.

"Sir, I'm trying to solve a murder here," I said.

His voice was growing stronger. "Susan's got nothing to do with it!"

"I need to find that out for myself."

"The lady has been through hell. Her and the kid are all I got left." He poked my chest with his bony finger. "You fuck with her, you fuck with me."

"I'm not fucking with anybody. I just have a couple of questions."

"Like what?"

Somehow it didn't feel polite to ask the man if his son was a wife beater. I didn't feel like discussing his son's sexual peccadilloes, either. So I said, "I really do need to ask Susan."

He started coughing again. I finally re-membered the mashed potato plate sticking to my pants. I reached down to get it off of me, but Hack Sr. suddenly grabbed hold of my arm.

"I'm dying," he rasped.

"I'm sorry to hear that," I said.

"I got one month. Maybe two. You think I care about jail?"

He was still gripping my arm as tight as he could, and it started to hurt. But I didn't want to complain about minor arm pain to someone who'd just told me he was dying.

Hack Sr. himself wasn't burdened by any such concerns about social niceties, as his next words showed. "You bother Susan again," he wheezed, "so help me God, I'll shoot you. I'll blow your fucking brains out with my shotgun."

It seemed to me he was being a tad over-protective, but I didn't argue. Then the old man let go of my arm, coughed some more, and walked away.

After that cozy little *tête-à-tête* with Hack Sr., I somehow didn't feel up to tackling Susan just then. So I went back home to change my potatoed pants.

There was a note for me on the kitchen table. "J — We went to Mom's house. Feel safer there. Join us. — A." I crumpled up the note and threw it away, feeling guilty — not for the first time — about exposing my family to danger. Did I really have the right to do that?

But no way could I just leave Will swinging in the wind.

A ringing doorbell interrupted my ethical dilemma. Was it an annoying but harmless buzzard, or my favorite blonde bombshell dropping by for another go at seducing me, or a crazed killer? I grabbed one of the kids' baseball bats and went to the door.

It turned out to be the blonde bombshell's husband. He didn't look like a crazed killer. He looked haggard and worn, his shoulders hunched up against the autumn breezes.

How could I be feeling sorry for the all-powerful State Senate Majority Leader Ducky Medwick? Next to Alfonse D'Amato, Ducky was the New York politician I most loathed. But he was also a tired, wounded, cuckolded man. I opened the door and let him in.

He gave me a nod and entered wordlessly, sitting down on the same sofa his wife had lounged in yesterday when she put the moves on me. Despite myself, a tingle went through my nether regions at the memory. *Dogs.*

"Can I get you some coffee?" I asked.

"Thanks," Ducky answered.

"Be right back."

When I returned a couple of minutes later with a cup of hot java, he was leaning back in the sofa, eyes closed. He didn't seem to hear me come in. Was he asleep? "Here's your coffee," I said nervously, far too loud.

Without opening his eyes, or moving anything except his lips, Ducky asked, "Do you know how old I am?"

I sat down. "No."

"Sixty." The eyes slowly opened, but they had none of their usual vigor, just dull, aching pain. "I turned sixty last week."

"You don't look it." It's true, he didn't. Right then he looked about ninety.

"I'm dying," he said.

Shit, not another terminally ill old man. But he quickly dispelled that misunderstanding. "Not right away. I'm not sick. But I can't do what I used to, you know what I mean?"

He looked to me with mute appeal. But I didn't know what I was supposed to say, so I just nodded. He picked up his coffee, cradling the warm cup in his hands.

"I never should've married her," he said to his coffee. "She was nineteen. I was forty-five. It was stupid." He put the cup back down and looked me in the eye. "Now we have two kids.

I don't want them getting hurt."

Why was everyone hitting me with this "don't hurt the kids" thing? I must look like a softie. "I don't want that, either," I said.

He looked around the room as if noticing it for the first time. "Did someone really shoot at your house last night?"

I froze at the memory. "Yes." I wanted to ask, *Was it you?* but refrained. For the moment.

"And you honestly think they were trying to stop your investigation?"

"I do."

"But you're not stopping." It was a statement, not a question. "Phil Rogers called. The Saratoga chairman. He saw you at Susan Tamarack's rally today."

"News travels fast."

For the first time, a flash of Ducky's old fire leapt into his eyes. "Can't you get it through your thick skull that your friend Shmuckler killed Jack Tamarack? This shooting last night had nothing to do with Jack!"

"Look —"

"Because of your insane stubbornness, people will suffer. *Innocent* people!" Anger mixed with self-pity in his voice. "All I wanted was a simple divorce. 'Irreconcilable differences. The parties remain amicable.' Instead, the kids will have their mother's infidelities shouted out in every TV newscast! Everyone in the whole state will know about this! *Everyone!*"

True enough. And now at last I understood Ducky's deepest fears. They had nothing to do with his kids. Ducky was scared of being publicly branded as a cuckold. He was imagining his colleagues and the media buzzards tittering about him in the cloakroom of the State Senate.

I wasn't the only one who was worried about his shortcomings as a private dick. Power is perception, and if people began perceiving Ducky as half a man, his power was gone.

Now, I'd be the last guy to get upset if Senator Ducky Medwick lost power. But unfortunately, I do have these unpleasant things called scruples. I'm not Larry Flynt, or even worse, Kenneth Starr. "Senator," I said, "I see no reason to go public with what I know, as long as I can be convinced that you didn't kill the Hack yourself."

"Why in the world would I want to kill him?"

"Well, obviously, because he was sleeping with your wife."

Ducky snorted with disgust at my ignorance. "My wife never slept with Jack Tamarack."

"Sure, she did."

"Nonsense." His shoulders gave a shudder, then he said, "She was sleeping with Pierce."

My own shoulders snapped back in surprise. "Pierce?"

"Yeah, Pierce, the sonufabitch, my goddamn *protégé*." Now his words tumbled out fast and furious, like he'd been damming them in for a long time. "I go to his office last week to take him out for a beer. His secretary sees me coming, says don't go in there, he's busy. I laugh her off. Hey, I'm Ducky Medwick, I don't wait for anybody, I don't even wait for Pataki. So I go in Pierce's office. Linda is fucking him on the desk."

Ducky was so upset, his hands were shaking. Some of his coffee spilled onto the rug, but I didn't say anything. Ducky's story matched Linda's in every respect but one: the name of the guy she was *shtupping*. Kind of a key detail. So who was lying here . . . and why?

Luckily for my rug, Ducky finally got himself more or less under control. "So that night I packed up and left home," he continued. "What the hell else do you want to know, goddammit?"

"Look, I'm sorry."

"Sure, you are. You'll be telling Ducky

Medwick jokes just like all the rest of them."

The expression *"go fuck a duck"* came unbidden into my mind. I shook it off and tried to think of my next move. Should I tell Ducky what his wife had told me? Or should I play that close to the vest?

I decided to throw him a curveball while he was still off balance. "What was the Hack blackmailing you with?"

He looked rattled at my sudden change of topic, then rolled his eyes. "Don't be an idiot. I told you last time —"

"Look, you want me to protect your privacy? Then you better come clean on *everything*."

"But there's nothing to come clean on here!"

"If that's how you want to play it, fine. I'll just find out from Zzyp," I blustered.

"Zzyp?" he said, acting puzzled, like he'd never heard the name before.

And maybe he hadn't, I couldn't tell, but I kept hammering away. "You know exactly who I'm talking about. Zzypowski. I'll have to slip him a few grand for the info, which may kind of piss me off. I may get so pissed off, I'll decide to expose *all* your little scandals."

Ducky threw up his hands. "If I knew what you were talking about, I'd tell you, I swear."

"Cut the crap. Pierce was your protégé, you said so yourself. So why didn't you endorse him for Congress?"

"Because —"

"Because the Hack blackmailed you into endorsing *him* instead."

"You've got it all wrong —"

"Don't give me this baloney —"

"Will you just shut up and *listen?* Pierce refused to run!"

I stared at Ducky. "But I thought —"

"Yeah, everybody thought. See, at first he *was* running. But then when the Republican Committee met at the beginning of June, he told us behind closed doors at the last minute he was backing out. Asked us not to tell the media or anyone else. We tried to get him to run, or at least explain why he wasn't, but he said he had personal reasons."

*Personal reasons.* Yeah, they were personal, all right. Finally everything was coming together.

The Hack had used that photograph on Pierce, after all. That's how he forced Pierce to quit running.

But now that the Hack had been killed, Pierce was free to do whatever he wanted.

How convenient for him.

# 10

After Senator Ducky left, I called Will to give him the latest. He wasn't home, though. Instead I got a cheerful message: "You have reached the answering machine of Will Shmuckler on Saturday, September 11. I'm not home now, but you can find me at Crossgates Mall from four to five, the Latham Citizens Association monthly meeting from six-thirty to eight, and the Red Hook Town Council meeting after eight-thirty. Yes, folks, the Will Shmuckler for Congress Campaign is back on track. All on board!"

It was good to hear Will sounding upbeat again. Evidently his campaign events were no longer being canceled. I guess people weren't so sure anymore that he was a murderer.

Now if only I could convince the cops.

First, though, I better do the Daddy thing for a while, and try to avoid family chaos. I followed Andrea and the kids to Grandma's house in Lake Luzerne. The road to Lake Luzerne is a winding, two-lane divided highway, and I was pretty confident that if someone were tailing me, I would have

181

spotted him, even with my limited skills.

Grandma's house overlooks a large pond in the middle of a thick spruce forest that totally blocks out any signs of human life. You can sit on Grandma's back porch, gaze down at the pond, and pretend you're living in the sixteenth century. Except for one jarring note. The back porch is where Grandma keeps her computer.

The darn things are everywhere. Pretty soon they'll be attaching them to toilets, so you can log on to AOL while you're taking a Nixon.

Grandma — a.k.a. Hannah — had just returned from six months of tramping through Asia. She bought herself a Gateway to keep in touch with her new foreign friends via e-mail. Now she and her grandchildren like to sit at the computer, send messages all over the world, and laugh at me for being so ignorant about the Technology Revolution. It's disconcerting — *everyone* understands computers better than I do.

I can't help myself. I still miss Wite-Out. Remember that stuff? If you made a typo, you could just brush on Wite-Out, wait for it to dry, and then type right over it. I used to think Wite-Out was the coolest thing in the world. It had such a nice smell, too.

But who am I to complain? Grandma's

computer, and the expertise of my two boys and Grandma herself, enabled me to get Robert Pierce's phone number. I wish computers weren't so darn useful. It would be so much easier to truly hate them.

After two hours of getting no answer at Pierce's house, I finally reached him at 11:30. I hit him with vague threats about "damaging information" that had "come into my possession."

"What kind of 'damaging information'?" he asked, trying to sound sarcastic, but the tremor in his voice betrayed him.

"I'll tell you all about it. At your house. In thirty minutes."

"What? Tonight?"

"Right. Midnight. And just so you know, I'm telling my wife and mother-in-law I'm going over there." Actually, Andrea and Hannah were already sleeping, but Pierce didn't have to know that.

"Why are you telling *them?*" he asked.

"In case you get the urge to kill me," I said, and hung up.

So as you can see, the background for our late-night rendezvous wasn't all that congenial. The rendezvous itself was no better, though I must admit that listening to Pierce rant and rave at me was educational in a way. I had no idea there were so many synonyms for slimeball. My favorite was "scumsucking toad."

Finally I had enough. I got up from his kitchen chair and said, "Okay, Pierce, if all you're gonna do is call me names and stonewall me, I'll just take this charming little photograph to the cops."

"Go right ahead, you shit," he said. Evidently he'd run out of interesting epithets, and was going back to the tried and true. "That photo is meaningless."

"Then why was the Hack hiding it?"

"I got no idea. Look, you wanna know what's in that envelope Sarafian is giving me?"

"I already do. Money."

"One thousand bucks, that's all. It was a legitimate campaign contribution."

*Legitimate campaign contribution* — the identical words that Sarafian used. Had they been on the phone together, polishing their story? Or is "legitimate campaign contribution" a phrase that all scumsucking-toad politicians use?

"If it's so legit, why'd he pay you in cash?"

Pierce made a big show of shrugging. "You don't believe me, call my secretary in the morning. She'll give you a copy of my campaign finance disclosure form. Sarafian is on it, for one grand."

"What campaign was he giving you money for? You weren't running for anything then."

"Some people like to contribute in advance."

I took a couple of steps forward so I was standing over him. "Pierce, you're full of it. Sarafian was bribing you to oppose the Hudson River dredging."

Pierce looked up at me and smirked. "Really? Says who?"

"Okay, pal, answer me this. Why didn't you run for Congress until after the Hack was dead?"

"Personal reasons."

"Yeah, like the Hack was riding your ass about this bribe."

"Prove it."

"You don't get it, you dumb prick," I said. "I don't *have* to prove it. Right now, with my house getting shot at, the media is hanging on every word I say. All I gotta do is drop a couple of choice words about you and Sarafian, and you drop a couple of dozen points in the polls. 'Congresswoman Tamarack' — has a nice ring to it, don't you think?"

Suddenly Pierce slammed his fist on the kitchen table. "I wasn't bribed — and I wasn't blackmailed! My not running for

Congress wasn't about that!"

"Tell it to the newspapers."

"For Christ's sake, I was fucking Ducky's wife!" Pierce exploded, the veins in his forehead throbbing. Then he grabbed a heavy crystal salt shaker off the table, reared back his arm, and aimed at my head.

Oh God, I thought as I ducked, I hope he remembers about my wife and mother-in-law knowing where I am. But at the last moment he fired the salt shaker at the refrigerator instead. The salt shaker shattered, and the refrigerator got a huge dent.

Well, better the refrigerator than my head.

The sight of the ruined salt shaker seemed to calm Pierce down somewhat. "How could I look Ducky in the eye," he said through gritted teeth, "and ask him for an endorsement? The man had done everything in the world for me, and here I was screwing his wife!"

So Pierce and Ducky were both claiming that Linda slept with Pierce. But then why was Linda's story different?

"Pierce, don't try to play me," I said.

"I'm not —"

"Let's say you *were* sleeping with her. So what? You're still way too ambitious to let mere *morality* stand in the way of your career —"

"Shut up. You just hate me because I'm gonna win the election against your pathetic friend. You don't know jack shit about me."

"So educate me."

"Look, I'm not the ambitious asshole you think I am. I'm a small-town guy," he said earnestly. If he weren't a politician, I might have thought he was being sincere. "My three kids live a couple of miles from here. Sure, being a congressman sounded good. But there's a State Senate seat opening up next year, and I was planning to run for that instead. That way I can stay near my kids. And I don't need to go through Ducky to run for the State Senate, it's a different process."

"If you're so all-fired sensitive about Ducky," I said, "then how come this week you suddenly asked him to endorse you? After all, you're still having sex with his wife —"

"No, that's over. I ended it two months ago."

"Your nose is growing. Ducky walked in on you and Linda last week."

Pierce looked startled. "No way. Who told you that?"

"The quack man himself," I said triumphantly.

"But . . ."

"But what?"

Pierce blinked. "I don't get it. I really did break up with Linda. And as far as I know, Ducky never found out about us. So why would he make up this story?"

"*Someone's* making up a story, that's for damn sure."

Suddenly his eyes lost their baffled look and snapped into focus. "That would explain it, though."

"*What* would explain *what?*"

"Why Ducky is supporting Susan Tamarack instead of me. He must've found out somehow that me and Linda used to sleep together."

My head was spinning. If I believed Linda, she slept with the Hack last week. But Ducky said no, she slept with Pierce last week. Meanwhile Pierce said it wasn't last week, it was two months ago.

This was worse than Peyton Place. I never knew Republicans had so much fun. I stood up.

"I'll be in touch," I said.

Pierce eyed me worriedly. "Where are you going?"

"Home. Hanging around with Republicans is bad for my health."

"You're not going to spread malicious rumors about me, are you?"

"I might," I told him, "and I might not."

When I opened the door to Grandma's at one a.m., the phone was in mid-ring. I ran to it, hoping it hadn't already woken up my stressed-out family.

"Hello?"

"I can't believe it! Jacob Burns, the man himself! I finally found you!"

"Much to my chagrin. What's up, Shmuck? How'd the campaigning go today?"

"Great. I got some awful strange looks, but a lot of support, too. Hey, did you see the Channel 6 late-night news?"

"Can't say I did. Why?"

Like the ESPN sportscaster Chris Berman announcing a touchdown, Will shouted, *"He . . . could . . . go . . . all . . . the . . . way!"*

"Shmuck, don't shout at me, it's one in the morning. What have you been drinking?"

"Just coffee, baby, but in ten days it'll be champagne! Channel 6 took a poll. Pierce: twenty-four percent. The widow: twenty percent. William Shmuckler: *nineteen percent!* We're in striking distance, my man! We're on the move!"

"Wait a second. That doesn't add up to even *close* to a hundred."

"Because we've got undecideds coming

out the wazoo. Most of them are non-voters, so screw 'em. And the talking heads all said exactly what *I've* been saying: a lot of the birdbrains who say they're for Pierce or the widow won't actually go to the trouble of writing in their names. So the reality is, I'm probably winning!" There was a pause. "What do you say about that?"

"Nothing. I'm too stunned. I'm in total shock."

Will laughed. "So what exciting stuff have you found out today?"

Good question. I knew a lot more than I did before . . . but what did it all add up to?

"Come on, bro, what you got?" Will asked impatiently. "We need some good dirt on Pierce and the widow to put me over the top."

"Hey, one thing at a time. I'm trying to keep you out of jail, not get you elected."

"What's the difference? You do one, you do the other. Especially if you can prove Pierce or the widow killed him. It's gotta be one of those two."

"What? I thought you were all psyched to pin it on Ducky."

"Yeah, but I've been thinking. The motive is so obvious: either Pierce or Susan killed the Hack so that he — or she — could run for Congress."

"They have other possible motives, too."

"Like what?"

I considered informing Will about the photograph of Pierce. But I didn't trust him to keep that juicy tidbit out of the papers, and I wasn't ready to go public with it yet. "I'll tell you as soon as I can," I said.

"Tell me now," Will said. "Look, you don't know what I'm going through. Before I campaigned today, I had to spend two hours giving hair samples, tissue samples —"

"You're kidding me. They had a warrant for that?"

"No. They just asked me for it, and I said okay."

"You said *what?* Why'd you do that?"

"Why not? I'm innocent. Besides, it's better for my campaign if I can say I'm co-operating fully with the police."

"Look, you really should get a lawyer already. Like I said, I'll be glad to lend you the money —"

"I don't need your money, Jake, I just need a little good news after being treated like a goddamn criminal. Is that so much to ask?"

I sighed. "All right, lay off the Jewish guilt trip. You ready?"

"I'm way past ready."

So I broke down and told Will all about

the hidden photograph, and Pierce and Sarafian's explanation that the money was just a "legitimate campaign contribution."

"Legitimate, my ass," Will snorted.

"Hey, it's possible. With campaign finance laws the way they are, how can you tell a legit contribution from a bribe?"

"So what do you plan on doing about it?"

I'd figured that one out already. "I'll see Zzypowski first thing Monday morning, find out if a thousand bucks buys me a few more details on what really went down between Sarafian and Pierce."

A repeated thumping noise came over the phone, which puzzled me until Will explained it. "That sound you hear is me clapping with excitement. If you can prove Pierce took a bribe, and the Hack was busting his chops about it, then we've got a murder motive *and* a killer campaign issue! Now all we need is the goods on the widow."

"Wrong. All I need is to get off the phone and catch some sleep."

"Wait a minute, Jake —"

But I hung up, then pursued Plan A and took the phone off the hook. My adrenaline had run out and I was dog-tired. Acting like a hard-ass all day can wear a man out, especially if he's an *artiste* type like me. I almost stumbled and fell as I headed downstairs to the basement bedroom where Andrea and I sleep when we're at Grandma's house.

Before going to bed, though, I went to Derek Jeter and Bernie Williams's room to give them a kiss. As I opened the door, my nose was greeted by a most unwelcome smell. It didn't take any clever sleuthing to figure out that Bernie had peed in the bed again.

I guess I wouldn't be going to sleep just yet. I sighed and rummaged in the boys' suitcase for a fresh pair of underwear and pajama bottoms.

A private dick's work is never done.

The next morning, a Sunday, Andrea was planning to drive to her college so she could sneak into Jeremy Wartheimer's office. But she was stymied when she realized she didn't have the key to the front door of McCracken Hall, which is locked on weekends. The AAA card trick wouldn't work on the front door.

So she decided to put off her big burglary until Monday morning between nine and eleven, when Jeremy would be busy teaching his elective on "A Re-Deconstructive Analysis of Capitalist Literature." He only had two students in the class, but they always met for the full two hours. That would give Andrea plenty of time to do a re-deconstructive analysis of Jeremy's door lock.

With her criminal activities postponed, Andrea and I had time for a quiet breakfast in the kitchen. The boys were on the back porch with Grandma, showing her the Yankees' web site. Now that the kids were safely out of earshot — or so I thought — I brought Andrea up to date on all the black-mailing sex, and wife-beating.

But it turned out they *weren't* out of earshot. I discovered this later that day, much to my consternation, at Derek Jeter's first baseball practice.

The practice itself, at Saratoga's West Side Rec, was thoroughly entertaining. Charles Schulz, of *Peanuts* fame, once said that the reason little league is so funny is because kids love baseball so much — and yet they're so *bad* at it. I think he was right on the money. Watching these kids go through careful, elaborate windups before throwing the ball — only to miss their target by thirty feet — was funnier and more poignant than most Broadway plays.

Andrea, Bernie, and I sat in the bleachers eating Twizzlers and enjoying the action. Only one thing prevented me from fully relaxing: the fact that Hack Sr. was in the bleachers too, a couple of benches up. His grandson Sean was on Derek's team. The old man alternated between cheering on his grandson, coughing, and giving me the evil eye. I was almost glad when he had an especially horrible coughing spasm and headed off to the snack bar, presumably in search of something to drink.

At that point the team was playing a five-on-five scrimmage. Derek was at shortstop, and Sean was in the dugout waiting to bat. Bernie turned to me and asked, "Daddy, can I go sit in the dugout, too?"

Since it was just a practice, I didn't think the coaches would mind. The dugout was right next to us, so I could keep an eye on him. "Sure, go ahead," I said.

Bernie scampered down from the bleachers into the dugout. Then he walked straight up to Sean and asked, "Did your dad beat up your mom?"

Talk about mortifying. Andrea and I jumped up, intending to run over to the dugout and pull our son away from poor Sean. But something kept us rooted to the spot. I guess we really wanted to hear Sean's answer.

But Sean didn't speak right away. So my little five-year-old private eye continued his relentless interrogation. "Did your dad beat up your mom?" he repeated.

"I'm not supposed to talk about it," Sean finally answered.

"How come?" Bernie asked.

"Because people might vote against my dad."

"Oh." Bernie frowned in thought, then asked, "But isn't your dad dead?"

"Yeah, but now they might vote against my mom."

Bernie's forehead was so furrowed, it looked like you could plant rows of corn in it. Trying to figure out politics has the same effect on me. "You mean people might not like your mom because she got beat up?"

"I'm not supposed to talk about it," Sean said.

Then one of the coaches called out, "Sean, you're up next!"

He ran to get his bat. The interrogation was over just in time, because Hack Sr. was heading back toward us. He had a large soda in his hands. Meanwhile Bernie came running back up the bleachers. "Daddy, guess what?" he called out, obviously proud of himself. "I asked Sean about his dad beating up his mom!"

Several other parents in the bleachers turned startled eyes at me. "Be quiet, Bernie," I whispered urgently.

"Sean's not supposed to talk about it," Bernie went on, oblivious. "He said people might not vote for —"

"That's enough," Andrea said sharply. "We don't want to hear it." Especially because Hack Sr. was almost upon us, and he was listening.

Bernie looked hurt. "But I thought you wanted to know!" he complained loudly. "Don't you want to know if the Hack was beating her up and so then she killed him?!"

Hack Sr. was so busy staring at us, he tripped over a small tree root by the bleachers. As he fell forward and tried to steady himself, he hit the bleacher rail with his forearm. A bloody red gash opened on his wrist. He sank onto a bench.

"Mr. Tamarack!" I exclaimed. "Are you all right?"

For reply, he threw what was left of his soda at me.

I couldn't say I blamed him.

# 11

Bernie Williams's baseball practice, which began two hours later, was much less tense — thank God — but just as comical. A lot of these kids had never played baseball before, so they were running the bases backward, putting their gloves on the wrong hand, and in general acting unbearably cute.

I was disappointed that I had to go to prison before practice ended. As a teacher, not an inmate. Ordinarily, with so much going on in my life I might have canceled class. But today was the first day of the new semester, and I hated to disappoint the guys. When you're in jail, everyone you know — relatives, lawyers, social workers — is always promising you things and then not following through. So I do my best to be reliable.

I didn't *feel* too reliable, since I hadn't prepared at all for the class. Fortunately this was the fifth time I'd taught Creative Writing at the prison, so I more or less knew what I was doing.

But no amount of experience teaching in prisons can ever make you totally lose that seasick feeling you get in your stomach when the guards escort you down those hallways and the metal doors start clanging shut all around you.

These men weren't dogs, they were caged animals. Or at least that's how they were treated.

So I tried to treat them like men. When I came into the classroom and they were all hanging out by the front desk, I took care to shake their hands individually and look them in the eyes.

I'm a big believer in education and job training for prisoners. But still, my gut impression is there's nothing more important to these despised men than having someone simply shake their hands, look them in the eyes, and give them at least some modicum of respect.

Actually, another thing that means a lot to them is if you bring them homemade cookies. But the last time I tried that, I got so much grief from the guards — "How do we know those cookies don't contain contraband? What if those chocolate chips are really bullets?" — that I haven't tried it since.

As I went through my class list and took the roll for the first time, I came upon the name "Geronimo Owens." It belonged to a cheerful-looking, dark brown-skinned young man in the front row.

" 'Geronimo Owens.' Cool name," I said, just making conversation, trying to establish a little first-day-of-class rapport. "Were you named after the Apache chief?"

Geronimo's smiling face instantly turned blank. "Don't know," he mumbled, and looked away from me.

My mind must have been elsewhere, because I missed his obvious cues to shut up and lay off him. "So are you part Indian?" I asked.

Geronimo turned back to me, his face no longer blank. Instead it filled up with pure, unadulterated hatred. I seemed to be inspiring that emotion in a lot of people lately. If this were a dark alley, I'd be dead in five seconds, or at least missing a kneecap or two.

"Don't know," Geronimo answered me, in a voice colder than Pluto.

"Oh, sorry," I said quickly, then moved on as fast as I could to the next name on the list. I blushed hotly, feeling everyone in the class staring at me.

I understood, too late, what I had just done. I'd humiliated Geronimo in front of the other men by forcing him to admit that he knew little — if anything — about his parents.

200

I'd noticed this kind of dynamic before. Most of the inmates had virtually no contact with their fathers, and many of them had seriously messed up mothers, on crack and so on. But even though they shared similar family problems, they almost never talked about this stuff with one another. They were ashamed of their aloneness. They all tried to make it sound like they had much love waiting for them on the outside, be it from parents, girlfriends, big-time drug dealers, or whomever.

And here I'd busted through Geronimo's cheerful façade, without even meaning to. Phooey. What a way to start the new semester.

I managed to recover somewhat, giving the men a couple of writing exercises that they got into, and then doing theatre improvs. It helped that one of the men had been in my class last semester, and he acted like a *de facto* teaching assistant. He led one of the improvs himself, and when I asked for volunteers to read their writing aloud, he raised his hand immediately. Hopefully he wouldn't get grief from the other men for being a teacher's pet . . . though at six foot four and two hundred fifty pounds of hard jailhouse muscle, he could probably handle himself just fine.

When class was over, I chatted with him.

There were still a few minutes left before the guys had to be back in their cells for last count.

"What's up, Brooklyn?" I asked. "I thought you'd be out on parole by now."

"Yeah, fuck Pataki, what can I say?"

"That's too bad. You know, I wrote a letter for you to the board."

"I appreciate it, man. So what's up with you? I saw on TV about you getting shot at and everything. You gotta stay out of trouble, Mr. Burns. We need you in this fucking place."

"Hey, it's not my fault I got shot at."

"Yeah, that's what they all say," he joked. "So what happened?"

Several other guys from class were standing around listening, including Geronimo. I figured I might score a few points if I told them about my foray into the world of politics and murder, so I did. I laid out the entire story, because I knew if these men ever repeated the scandalous rumors I was telling them, it wouldn't matter. Since they were just prison inmates, no one would believe them.

When I finished, Brooklyn spoke up. "So the Hack got capped right before the big debate, huh? What was he gonna say in that debate?"

"I don't know."

"Well, I suggest you find out."

"Why?"

A couple of the men exchanged looks, like they were amused at my obtuseness. Then Geronimo stepped in. " 'Cause maybe someone popped the man to keep him from saying what he was gonna say. I'm surprised you ain't thought of that. What's the matter with you?"

Geronimo gave me a nasty sneer, and I realized he was paying me back for humiliating him. But I didn't mind. If Geronimo felt like we were even now, then he wouldn't spend the rest of the semester trying to *get* even.

Another reason I didn't mind his sneer was because I was too busy thinking about what he'd just said. "You got a point, Geronimo," I told him. And he did. Maybe the Hack *was* planning to say something in that debate, and someone found out.

But how would *I* find out?

Did the widow know?

A guard came by to say it was just three minutes until last count. The inmates went back to their cells and I went back to freedom. I ate dinner with my family and saw them off to their safe haven at Grandma's. I promised I'd be there in a little while. Then

I headed for the widow's house.

When I got there, it was already dark. It had started to rain too, a steady, miserable drizzle. The streets in Susan Tamarack's *chichi* neighborhood were deserted.

I got out of my car and shut the door. The sound was oddly muffled in the rain-soaked night. Pulling my baseball cap down low over my eyes, I walked toward the widow's front door.

Then I hesitated. What if Hack Sr. was spending the evening at the widow's house? I had no wish to confront him yet again. He might decide to shoot at me.

In fact, maybe he'd *already* tried to shoot at me, two nights ago. I kind of wished I had a gun myself — though I hadn't fired one since marksmanship practice at summer camp.

The front of the house was dark, but some thin light filtered in from the back. I walked up the driveway and around the side of the house, my feet squishing on the damp grass and fallen leaves, and found the source of the light. It came from Susan's empty kitchen. A half-eaten casserole sat on the counter, no doubt a remnant of all those casseroles I'd seen at the wake.

I stepped alongside the rear of the house toward the bedroom wing, where a couple of much fainter lights shone through partially opened curtains. In the first bedroom I came to, I looked through the narrow curtain opening and saw a night light on the wall. After a few moments, I was able to make out little Sean lying on his bed asleep, curled into a fetal position. I moved on.

The light in the next bedroom, judging by the way it flickered, came from a TV. I couldn't hear it, though; the sound was turned down or off. The curtains were shut almost all the way, so I had to press my face up close to the window to get a good view inside.

The TV, I now saw, was playing some old black-and-white Bette Davis movie. But the two people who were lying in the widow's bed together weren't watching it.

They had something much better to do.

The woman was on top and facing me, so I recognized her immediately. It was Susan. Her head thrown back, she was rocking gently back and forth.

The man was harder to see. His head was hidden by a pillow and some blankets. But then he reached up his hands and massaged the erect nipples on the widow's small breasts.

I recognized those hands — those gnarled, working man's hands.

They belonged to the dead man's father.

I stood there and stared.

Then the widow swirled her head to the side in a moment of passion, and her gaze hit the window. Her eyes widened and her mouth opened in a soundless scream.

I bolted and ran for the car.

Had she recognized me? Or had she just seen a shadowy face half-covered by an Adirondack Lumberjacks baseball cap?

I didn't know. I burned rubber out of there.

Maybe I shouldn't have run. Maybe I should have seized the moment to bang on the widow's door and give them both the third degree. After all, I'd caught them right at their most vulnerable. That's when they'd be most likely to open up and tell me the truth.

Either that or shoot me.

Was this a case of two lonely people coming together in their grief? Or were they sleeping together even before the Hack died?

Was his murder the result of an especially sordid love triangle?

"I'll tell you what *I* think. I think it's gross," Andrea said when I got back to Grandma's house and described what I'd seen. "Totally gross." She wrinkled her nose for emphasis.

"Why?"

"I'm picturing it. Sleeping with her father-in-law . . . I mean, she's younger than I am. Yecch."

"I think it's beautiful," I said, just to be ornery. "Love blossoming where you least expect it."

"Love I can see, but sex?"

"Speaking of sex . . ."

But she backed away from me. "Don't tell me seeing that turned you on."

"Not at all," I said, reaching for her. "It's all this talk about death that turns me on."

"You're weird."

"Your body is beautiful in the moonlight."

"Very weird."

"But handsome." I kissed her neck. "Incredibly handsome."

"No," she said, "just weird."

But I guess she was in the mood for weird, because before long we were tangled together in the double bed.

Afterward, as we lay with her head on my shoulder, she said, "Jake?"

"Yes, gorgeous?"

"How would you feel if, less than a week after you died, I was sleeping with your dad?"

"Come to think of it," I said, "it *is* kind of gross."

The next morning, Andrea and I got up early and went upstairs. She wanted to break out her AAA card and practice on Grandma's front door. Today was the day we were going to pull our scam on Jeremy Wartheimer.

The woman showed talent. She was able to break into the house three times in a row — the third time making it in less than twenty seconds, as Grandma and the boys watched.

The boys were thoroughly impressed, but Hannah just gave her daughter a puzzled frown. "Honey, why are you doing this?" she asked.

I answered for my wife, because even at age thirty-nine, she still feels uncomfortable lying to her mother. Myself, I got over any compulsion to tell the truth to my parents long ago. "We're just practicing, so in case we ever forget our keys, we can still get in the house this way," I explained.

"But I keep an extra key in the garage. You know that."

"But what if the extra key wasn't there for some reason?" Even as I said it, I realized how lame it sounded.

"What kind of foolishness are you up to now?" Hannah demanded crossly. "It's bad enough you run around like a chicken with your head cut off, putting my grandsons into who knows what kind of danger. Now you're getting my daughter mixed up in this, too?"

"Yay, Mommy's gonna be a private dick!" Bernie crowed.

"No, I'm not," Andrea said. "Really, Mom. It's just a little thing I'm doing."

"What is this 'little thing'?"

"Nothing important. Really."

But then Derek put in his two cents. "Mommy's gonna break into Jeremy Wartheimer's office and return the widow's portfolio that Daddy stole from Rosalyn."

Andrea and I stared at the little twerp. How did he know all this? We'd been careful never to talk about it when he was in the room. Jeez, both these kids had elephant ears. Andrea and I would have to start communicating in French.

Grandma was the first to find her tongue. "Could you say all that again, slower this time?"

So we had to fess up to the whole sordid business. In general, Hannah's a big supporter of mine, and vice versa. She never muttered an unkind word during all those

years when I was a struggling artist, con-
signing her beloved daughter to a life of gen-
teel poverty. But now Grandma had her
gloves off.

"You jeopardized *Andrea's tenure?*" she
yelled at me. "What were you thinking?"

Grandma waxed wroth for what felt like
forever. I was grateful that I had to drive the
kids to school, because it gave me an excuse
to escape. Hell hath no fury like a Grandma
pissed.

After dropping the kids off, I headed for
Madeline's to drink in the coffee and the
newspapers. I got lucky and found a parking
spot right outside, so I could keep an eye on
the car. The next time someone messed
with it, they might do something worse than
slash my tire.

As I got out of the car, I looked around
quickly to see if anyone was following. My
morning routine of going to Madeline's was
pretty well set, and if somebody knew that
they could lie in wait for me there. I didn't
see anyone, but somehow I didn't feel reassured. I managed not to run into the
espresso bar, despite a creepy feeling that
someone was aiming at my back. Once inside, I breathed heavily with relief.

My goal that morning was to take yet another stab at collaring the widow alone. But

once again I was thwarted. According to the papers, Susan had a morning appearance at some day care center down in Rensselaer County. No doubt she'd kiss a few babies and mouth a few platitudes, and no one would mention that the Republicans are always trying to cut funds for day care centers. Politics as usual.

I thought about heading south to harass Linda and Ducky, see if I could uncover the truth about Linda's whoopee-making. But I decided to work the bribery angle with Zzypowski instead. It was a tough choice: money or sex.

I sat at Madeline's and read the sports pages until it was late enough for the mall to be open and Zzyp to be in his office. Or rather, I *tried* to read the sports pages. Over the years I'd gotten to know a lot of Madeline's regulars, and now they kept coming up to me all morning to gossip about Will's case. Most of them had heard the latest poll results, and I got several offers to help out with the campaign.

Amazing what a good poll will do for you. Before, trying to get people to help Will's campaign was like trying to get my sons to go to the ballet.

But I wasn't ready yet to think about leafleting and canvassing. I left the coffee shop and drove to the mall.

At 10:15 on a mid-September Monday morning, Saratoga Mall was not exactly a bustling thoroughfare. In the entire wing of the mall where Zzyp kept his office, I only saw one other soul: a bored janitor pushing his broom along in a desultory way. I headed for Zzyp's office in the windowless alcove at the far corner. The door was unlocked, so I walked in.

He wasn't at his desk, where I'd seen him yesterday. Maybe he was in the back room. "Zzyp?" I called out tentatively.

The office seemed different somehow, like something was missing. Then I figured it out. Zzyp's computer was gone.

And another thing: there was an odor, not unpleasant really, kind of . . . earthy. Taking another few steps into the office, I noticed splashes of red paint on the floor behind Zzyp's desk. How odd, I thought —

But then I realized it wasn't paint.

I staggered backward, then turned around and almost ran out of there. To hell with this private eye impersonation. But I swallowed a couple of times and pushed myself forward, following the trail of blood.

Around the corner in the back room lay Zzypowski. There was a big hole in his chest and pools of dried blood all around him.

Enough already. It was time to get down to the serious business of puking my guts out. The bathroom door at the end of the back room was open, so I lurched over there, hoping I'd make it to the toilet before it was too late.

I made it, all right. But the toilet was otherwise occupied.

It was filled with electronic-looking *stuff* — busted motherboards and circuits and things. The bathroom floor all around it was littered with broken chunks of hard plastic. These were pieces of a computer, I realized. Someone had smashed Zzyp's computer, stomping the innards and bashing all the bytes to bits. Then they'd thrown into the toilet everything that would fit, no doubt flushing a few times.

I was so surprised I forgot to throw up. As I've mentioned, I'm not wild about computers myself. But still, this behavior seemed a bit extreme.

Obviously, there was something about Zzyp and his computer that someone had pretty strong feelings about.

Now what? I better get out of here before anyone found me. As Will's experience had shown, the police tend to get kind of suspicious when you're discovered next to a dead body. And the last thing I wanted was to give

Chief Walsh an excuse to act like an idiot at my expense.

But I didn't take off just yet. First I backed out of the bathroom and looked around. A wallet was lying next to Zzyp's left knee. I leaned down gingerly to pick it up, holding my breath so the smell of his blood wouldn't hit me too strongly. Now that I knew what that smell really was, it no longer struck me as pleasant.

I took the wallet to the front room and opened it, hoping for a slip of paper with someone's phone number, or a telltale receipt or something. But all I found were Zzyp's driver's license, P.I. license, credit cards, and cash. Of course, maybe whoever removed the wallet from Zzyp's pocket had also removed any clues that were in there.

But he'd left the cash. An honorable killer?

Fighting off another urge to do the sensitive *artiste* number and run away, I went back to Zzyp's corpse and felt his pockets. I had to shove his body around some in order to get to the pockets in back. But my efforts went for naught. His pockets were empty.

He had two file cabinets in the back room. I stepped over the body, carefully avoiding the blood, and went through the cabinets as quickly as I could. I skimmed through case files from about thirty insurance scams and forty messy divorces, but none of them seemed related to the Hack's murder.

Outside Zzyp's office the mall Muzak started up, reminding me that I was dangerously pushing my luck. I headed for the front room of the office and hurriedly opened the top two desk drawers. Pens, paper clips, staples . . . and, I was gratified to see, Wite-Out. But so far, nothing else.

I was about to open the bottom drawer when I noticed a movement out of the corner of my eye. Oh, shit. Through the front window, I could see the bored janitor heading straight for Zzyp's office door. I ducked down under the desk and shut my eyes tight, as if that could somehow keep him from seeing me.

Actually, maybe he'd seen me already. I waited for him to open the door. But nothing happened. Eventually I gathered enough courage to poke my head under the desk and check for the janitor's legs outside the door. His legs were gone.

I periscoped my head up over the desk and confirmed that his whole body was gone — at least temporarily. Then I tried the one place in the whole office that I hadn't tried yet: the bottom desk drawer. I opened it . . .

And found a bottle of Jack Daniel's whiskey.

*Finally.* Something in this godforsaken, Muzak-ridden nightmare of a place that Raymond Chandler would have approved of.

But nothing that would help me solve my murder case. Or maybe now I should say, *cases.*

Discouraged, I headed for the front door. But at the last moment I had a minor brainstorm and came back to the desk. I picked up the phone and pushed the "redial" button.

The phone rang twice, then someone answered.

"Hello?" she said.

Whose voice *was* that? It sounded familiar. "Hello?" I replied.

"Yes, *hello*," the woman said impatiently.

I slowly put down the phone. I'd heard all I needed to hear.

It was Susan Tamarack.

# 12

Unseen by the bored janitor or anyone else, I snuck out of Zzyp's office and fled the mall. I put the pedal to the metal of my old Toyota and zoomed off to the widow's house, car engine screaming. How had she gotten back so quickly from the day care center? She must have run out of babies to kiss.

There were four cars parked in her driveway. I strode resolutely to her front door and banged on the door knocker. By God, nothing would stop me from confronting this woman at last.

Except maybe Oxymoron. He opened the door. *"You!"* he cried out, clenching his fists. "You're fucking asking for it."

"I want to talk to her."

"Tough shit."

He started to shut the door in my face, so I said quickly, "Tell her I know who she slept with last night."

That stopped him. "What?"

"You heard me. Tell her."

Oxymoron stared at me uncertainly, then shut the door.

I stood there and waited. A minute passed. I was about to bang the knocker again, but then the door opened. This time Susan Tamarack herself was standing there. She was dressed in a black suit, sort of a combination campaigning/mourning suit. Very versatile. She was perfectly made up, her eyes flashed angrily, and she looked beautiful.

"That was you last night?" she hissed.

"That was me."

Without another word, she motioned me inside. We walked past several pairs of curious eyes in the living room. They all belonged to middle-aged men in suits with briefcases at their sides. It looked like the GOP had sent Susan some political consultants to help with her campaign. Did they hear my line about knowing who Susan slept with? I wondered what kind of spin they would put on their candidate's affair with her father-in-law.

I got the feeling Susan was wondering the same thing as we went down the hallway toward the bedrooms. She led me to the very last room, I guess so we'd be as far away as possible from her entourage. It was a guest room. She sat down on a chair and I sat on the edge of the bed.

We eyed each other. A wisp of soft black

hair came loose and fell over her cheek. "What do you want from me?" she said, her voice hard.

I hardly knew where to begin. "How long have you been sleeping with Jack's father?"

She threw me one of those hate-filled looks that I was so expert at inspiring. "You're gonna tell Shmuckler about this, huh? And your friend at the *Saratogian*. You're trying to destroy me."

I steeled myself against the sympathy I felt. "You don't like that question, here's another one. Did you kill your husband?"

She barked out an incredulous laugh. "Why would I do *that?*"

I ticked off the possible reasons on my fingers. "He was beating you. You were having an affair with his father. *He* was having an affair. Pick a reason. Any reason."

Actually, after all the conflicting stories I'd heard, I wasn't so sure the Hack *was* having an affair. But the widow didn't dispute anything I said, just sat there with her large eyes growing even larger. Finally the shock wore off long enough for her to ask, "How do you know all that?"

"Never mind how I know."

"I never told anyone about Jack hitting me."

"Why not?"

"He would've killed me."

I raised an eyebrow. Was she setting up a battered wife defense for herself, in case she got busted for her husband's murder?

"Well, he *might* have," she said stubbornly. "And besides, he was running for Congress. If I told people what he did, it would've ruined his campaign."

"So? Why should you care about his campaign?"

"Why should I care? I loved him."

"Oh, really. How long have you been having sex with his father?"

She grimaced. "Don't put it like that. You make it sound so disgusting."

"Why don't you explain it to me?"

She bit her lip — to keep from crying, it looked like. "The man is dying. I love him."

"Pretty liberated love life."

"Look, you have no idea what my life was like," Susan said bitterly, but at the same time something in her voice begged for understanding. "My husband could be very sweet sometimes, but he was a volcano, you know? Getting totally mad for no reason. And when he started running for Congress, he got worse. One night he wanted me to iron his pants and shine his shoes for the next day, and I told him I was too tired. And he hit me."

She bit her lip so hard I was afraid she'd draw blood. "He never hit me before. I knew he was under so much pressure from the campaign. Jack was from a poor family. This was all new and scary for him. So I tried to give him a break, you know?"

I nodded as if I did know. But really I didn't. I'm one of those people that, despite my best efforts to empathize, can never quite fully understand why abused women don't just *leave*.

"Jack promised he'd never hit me again. But he did. And then one night he didn't come home 'til after midnight, and I got suspicious, so I looked in his old e-mail. There was something from . . ."

She faltered, so I tried out a name. "From Linda Medwick."

Susan nodded. So now we had one more vote for a Linda-Hack liaison. Was Linda doing the horizontal hula with both Pierce *and* the Hack?

Meanwhile Susan was saying, "The next night, Jack called me from his cell phone. Said he was sleeping over at a supporter's house in Greene County. I got off the phone and started crying, and Jack's father — he was over our house that night, helping with Sean — anyway, he asked me what was wrong. So I told him. And he just held me, you know, and . . ."

Now the tears started falling down her cheeks in earnest, smudging her face with mascara. "George is such a great old man," she said. "Nothing like Jack. And I felt so terrible that George was, you know, *dying.* He's got nothing. Jack was his only child, and Jack was a jerk. So we were holding each other and, well, one thing led to another."

She looked at me defiantly through her tears. "And it wasn't disgusting. It was *love.*"

That word again. "Did he love you enough to kill Jack?"

"That's impossible," she answered sharply. "George was with me that night."

"Great alibi," I said sarcastically, trying to rile her into tripping up. "So the two of you have agreed to say that about each other?"

"It's the truth."

"You're saying the two of you were . . . *together?*"

She blushed and nodded.

"And your son was here at the time?"

She bared her teeth angrily. "No, he was sleeping at his friend's house. Whatever you may think about me, I'm a good mother. Sean doesn't know any of this."

Based on what I'd learned about kids' elephant ears, I doubted she was right. Besides, Sean had been home last night when Susan was with George. But I let it pass. "Okay, so maybe neither of you killed Jack. But what about Zzyp?"

I eyed her closely to see if the name got a rise out of her. But she didn't blink. "Who?"

I tried again. "You know who. Zzypowski."

Still no blinks. "Who's that?"

If she was faking it, she was doing a darn good job. Then again, if she'd managed to keep her affair with her husband's father a secret from her husband, she must have been good at faking things.

I thought back to the corpse I'd just had the pleasure of meeting. Now I'm no expert on morbidity, lividity, and all the other gross stuff that forensics experts use to figure out the time of death. But judging by the dryness of the blood, Zzyp had been killed before this morning. On the other hand, judging by the relative pleasantness of the blood smell and the unrottenness of the body, I figured Zzyp hadn't been dead for longer than a day. So that put the estimated — *very* estimated — time of death as yesterday. Which was a Sunday.

Why had Zzyp come into his office on a Sunday? Did he put in a call to Susan's house, and then wait in his office for someone to show up?

"Where were you yesterday?" I asked.

"Why?"

"Humor me."

She shrugged. "I'm doing all the stuff Jack scheduled for his own campaign. Yesterday I had breakfast at the Glens Falls Rotary Club, then lunch at the Silver Bay Elks, then something in Saranac Lake. I don't remember it all, it's just one thing after another." She checked her watch. "Right now I'm supposed to be in Ballston Spa at noon. My new campaign manager is already there, he's gonna kill me. I should've left ten minutes ago."

"So you were gone from home all day yesterday?"

She gave me a belligerent but bewildered look. "Yeah. So what?"

"Who was at your house?"

"George. He was taking care of Sean."

"You left them alone together all day? Even though George's health is so bad?"

"Oscar stopped by to help out."

"Oscar?"

"The guy who let you in just now."

"Oh." Oscar the Oxymoron. Had a nice ring to it.

"Look, I don't understand all these questions you're asking, and I really do have to go." She stood up and, with an airy toss of her head, said, "If you're so horrible and sleazy that you have to tell the whole world about my love life, go ahead. But in the meantime I have a campaign to run."

I didn't say anything. I was trying to square this feisty campaigner with the frightened waif who stayed silent while her husband beat her.

She tapped her foot impatiently. "You speak English? I'm saying *scram*."

I stood up, too. Then it hit me that with all the hot sex and other excitement going on, I'd forgotten to pursue the lead that Geronimo Owens had given me.

"One more thing," I said. "Before I go, I need a copy of the opening statement Jack was going to make at that debate, the night he got killed."

"Why?"

"Come on, the quicker you give it to me, the quicker you can get to your stupid Chamber of Commerce lunch or whatever."

"Yeah, but I don't know where a copy would be. Jack did his speechwriting at the office — along with everything else he did there," she added sourly, probably a reference to his shenanigans with Linda Medwick.

I couldn't resist one final question. "Why didn't you leave him?" I asked.

"Why don't you get out of my face," she answered, and stalked out.

I guess she knew I wouldn't really understand.

I got back in my Toyota, and drove far enough away from the house that I wouldn't have to worry about Oscar the Oxymoron jumping me. Then I parked the car, leaned my head against the seat, and collected my thoughts.

Zzyp called Susan's house yesterday. Then he got killed. Had that phone call set his murder in motion? And why did he call Susan's house in the first place?

Wait a minute. Maybe Zzyp was trying to sell Pierce's photo to *Susan,* the same way I figured he'd sold it to the Hack. Then Susan could use it to scare Pierce out of the race.

But why would Susan — or her faithful henchmen, Hack Sr. and Oxymoron — want to *kill* Zzyp, if he was just trying to sell them useful information?

I snapped my fingers. Was it possible that Pierce somehow got wind of Zzyp's plans? What if Zzyp called Pierce before calling Susan, and hit him up for hush money?

And then Pierce decided that instead of paying Zzyp to hush, he'd be better off killing him . . .

I was so excited by this new theory that I almost flooded the car when I started her up. I guess the old girl felt she had already done enough zooming in one day, thank you very much. It took some gentle sweet talking and careful gas pedal fluttering before she would consent to go anywhere.

After the car and I got our relationship straightened out, I realized I had a problem: I didn't know where I was going. According to the morning papers, Pierce was spending today campaigning in Lake Placid, two hours north. If you look at a map of the 22nd Congressional District, it resembles a giant lizard. The legislature gerrymandered it that way to keep out all those nasty urban voters from Albany and create a nice, safe Congressional seat for Republicans. It's highly convenient for them, but highly annoying for amateur sleuths who have to run all around the district trying to solve a murder.

I decided to call Pierce tonight and schedule another rendezvous at his house. For right now, maybe I should try to find out once and for all what that opening statement of the Hack's was going to be. Like Geronimo told me, that was an avenue I should have followed a long time ago. Ah, well. Did Philip Marlowe ever feel as incompetent as I often did?

Who knows, maybe that's why he drank.

Susan said the Hack did his writing at work, so maybe his old computer at the State House would still contain his statement. I pointed my Camry toward Albany, and fifty minutes later found myself inside the Capitol building.

As I climbed up the Million-Dollar Staircase to the third floor and walked down the corridor past all the marble sculptures and gilt-framed portraits of dead politicians, I wondered if the Hack's old office would be open. Would the blonde bombshell still be at her desk, even though her old boss was dead and her new boss was yet to be named?

The office, as it turned out, was locked. When I knocked on the door, no one answered.

Well, hell, that's what AAA cards were for. I took mine out of my wallet and waited for a break in the pedestrian hallway traffic, then set to work.

The time I'd put in training Andrea had been well spent. My card went through that fifty-year-old lock like a knife through butter. I opened the door, stepped inside —

And gasped. *Holy tamale.*

My gasp gave way to a grin. Linda Medwick was *in flagrante delicto* — I believe that's the expression — on the office desk with none other than Robert Pierce.

Wow. I'd now barged in on one dead body and two hot sex scenes in less than twenty-four hours. That must be some kind of record.

Watching these two paramours reminded me that having sex on top of a desk had long been a special fantasy of mine. My first college girlfriend once promised that for my twentieth birthday we'd make love on the front desk in the science lecture hall. But tragically, we broke up two weeks before my birthday. I should chat with Andrea about this unfulfilled fantasy —

Linda rather rudely broke into my thoughts. "Would you *mind?*" she asked, sounding annoyed but not the least bit embarrassed. I had to admire her coolness. I guess those generous endowments of hers, now strutting their stuff in full view, had also endowed her with generous self-esteem — at least as regards her impact on men.

For his part, though, Pierce looked like he wanted to do the bug thing and crawl under a rug. His "private parts," as Bernie would call them, were shrinking right before my very eyes.

"No, I don't mind," I said to Linda, feigning casualness. "I'll look the other way while you get yourselves together."

I turned around and folded my arms as, behind me, Linda screeched, "Kindly have the *decency* to *leave!*"

"Sorry, I'm not going anywhere," I said. "So forget about cooking up a cover story together. I'll talk to *you* alone, then I'll talk to *him* alone."

Naked and shrunken though he was, Pierce had regained some of his dignity. "I refuse to discuss anything with you."

The door to the hallway was still open. Three guys in navy blue sport jackets were wandering by. "Excuse me, sirs," I called out. "There's something I'd like to show you in Mr. Tamarack's office."

The men hesitated, then one of them gave an amused half-grin and said, "Sure." They headed my way. Little did they know the thrill they were in for.

But Linda yelled out, "All right! We'll talk!"

So I barred the doorway to the three men. "Sorry, fellas. Change of plans," I said, as I shut the door on them.

Linda and Pierce put their clothes back on. I told Pierce to leave the office for fifteen minutes, then come back.

"You can't order me around," Pierce said hotly, some of his natural arrogance returning along with his clothes.

"Sure, I can order you around all I want," I said. "Knowledge is power, and I'm a Robert Pierce expert. See you in fifteen."

Pierce glowered at me, looking like he wanted to wring my neck. But he didn't say anything, just stalked out. As he headed off, I couldn't resist a parting shot. "And you better not let me catch you in the hallway eavesdropping," I warned him. "Go take a cold shower."

Then I turned to Linda. The low-cut neckline of her slinky yellow dress was askew, and one of her assets was popping out. I figured she did that on purpose to distract me, so I determinedly ignored it, forcing my eyes to focus on her face instead.

"Okay, bombshell," I said cheerfully. "Spill it."

# 13

"You pathetic private eye wannabe," Linda spit out, but I stopped her.

"So what's up with you and Pierce and the Hack?" I asked. "You guys do threesomes?"

She smashed the desktop, hard, with her fist. Then she did a strange thing. She leaned against the desk, threw back her head, and laughed so hard her breasts jiggled. There wasn't much joy in that laughter, though, just irony and disgust.

Finally I asked, "You almost through?"

"Yeah, I'm *through*, all right," she said acidly. "Just my luck, I come along after Bill and Monica. Now every pissant politician in America is scared the voters'll find out he's not a model of Christian purity."

"So Pierce is scared?"

"You kidding? You're all scared shitless, *all* of you. *Men*." Her lips curled. "If I could do it over again, I'd can the bombshell routine, go to law school instead. Worst thing ever happened to me was these stupid boobs." With that she stuffed her wayward left breast back into her skimpy dress.

"Why don't we get back to the facts."

"Yeah, sure, *facts*. What the hell is a fact?"

This lady would be perfect as a Jerry Springer guest. "How long have you been sleeping with Pierce?" I asked.

"Hey, I don't need to talk to you. I don't have a political career for you to ruin."

"But you do have a family that could be ruined," I reminded her, and instantly felt like a real asshole.

I expected her to scream at me, but I guess she decided it wouldn't do any good. Instead she said, "How the hell should I know when I started fucking him? When did that old Congressman die — Mo Wilson?"

That seemed like a non sequitur, but I humored her. "Last May."

"Then the answer's May. I took Robert to bed a week later."

Something clicked. "Was there a connection between Congressman Wilson dying and your taking Pierce to bed?"

"Hell, yes. My sonufabitch husband, *Ducky,* was too much of a wimp to run for Congress. He likes being a big duck in a small pond. Said he's too old to go to Washington and start over."

"But you wanted to go."

Linda's face twisted with outrage. "*I'm* not too old to start over! What does Ducky expect me to do, spend the rest of my life in that lousy house in the most boring suburb in the universe? I want to have fun! I'm not ready to die just yet, thank you very much!"

"And you figured Pierce was gonna run for Congress," I prodded.

She eyed me challengingly, like she was trying to shock me, and said harshly, "Right. So I made up an excuse to go in his office. Talk about a pushover. Took me five minutes tops before I was fucking his brains out. I will say one thing for him, though, at least he can get it up. Unlike Ducky, who refuses to take Viagra because he's afraid he'll get a heart attack."

This was way more detail than I needed. Although it did occur to me that after a decade plus of being married to a predatory shark like Linda, I might have trouble getting it up myself.

"So you and Pierce became lovers. And you were hoping, what, he gets elected, and then you divorce Ducky, marry Pierce, and go to Washington?"

Linda nodded. "Why not? This Congressional seat is so safe, I figured Robert could survive a tiny little sexual scandal and still get reelected. We'd just have to be discreet, that's all. I'd wait a few months after divorcing Ducky before I married Robert. Then it's good-bye Clifton Park, hello

Washington. Party with the big boys while I still have my looks."

"Did Robert know you were planning to marry him?"

"Are you kidding? He was talking marriage the first day."

I eyed her skeptically. She shrugged. "I'm very good in bed," she said matter-of-factly.

I was tempted to ask her, if she was so good in bed, then why was Ducky having trouble getting it up? Instead I said, "But Robert didn't run for Congress after all."

She frowned bitterly. "No. He said he would, but then the bastard double-crossed me."

"Why?"

For the first time her hazel eyes showed uncertainty. "I don't know."

"Come on, why'd he change his mind about running? You must have some idea."

"He wouldn't tell me. Believe me, I tried everything. I screamed, I sweet-talked, I gave blow jobs, I threatened to leave him, but nothing worked."

"Was he being blackmailed?"

"About our affair? No, nobody knew. We were so careful it was ridiculous."

"What if he was being blackmailed about something else?"

She cocked her head at me. "Maybe. But

he would have told me. Why, is there something you know about?"

I sidestepped her question and tried out Pierce's own explanation on her. "Maybe he felt guilty asking Ducky to push him for Congress, when here he was doing the boogie woogie with Ducky's wife."

She shook her head in exasperation, her Farrah Fawcett do flying around her shoulders. "Why don't you ask *him?* I really don't know. I was so pissed off I split up with him."

"He said it was the other way around."

"In his dreams." She gave a sardonic grin. "I told him I loved him, but I couldn't deal with cheating on my husband anymore."

Her story sounded more real than Pierce's. I was beginning to get a feel for this lady's *modus operandi.* "But then, after the Hack died, and Pierce decided to run for Congress after all . . ."

". . . I called him up and said I'd been missing him unbearably all these lonely months, and I was desperate to see him again and caress his gorgeous body."

"I take it he didn't need much convincing."

"No."

"Even though this could destroy his campaign."

"Hey, men aren't the smartest creatures in the world."

"When did you call him up to get back together?"

"Last night. You just broke up our big oh-God-I-missed-you-so-much fuck."

"Wait a minute. You're lying. You were already sleeping with Pierce last week."

"What gives you that idea?"

"Your husband told me."

"You talked to Ducky?" I didn't answer. Linda looked puzzled. "Look, I don't know why Ducky would lie about this. But it's Jack I was sleeping with last week, not Pierce. I ought to remember who I sleep with. I'm not *that* big of a slut."

I felt hopelessly befuddled. Was there some magic P.I. technique I was missing? I shifted gears. "Okay, back up a few months. When Pierce refused to run, and Jack got the nomination instead . . ."

She knew where I was going, and nodded. "Right, that's when I started sleeping with Jack. The guy had been hitting on me for two years, ever since I went to work for him."

Linda was sitting in her chair now, talking in a conversational tone. She seemed to actually enjoy answering my questions. Maybe it had been a long time since she'd been honest with anyone.

I tried to keep the tone light, hoping something useful would spill out of her. "Why'd you take this job, anyway? I'm surprised you'd want to be a secretary."

"It beats being stuck all day in the suburb from hell. Ducky and Jack worked out a deal where I got paid for nine to five, but I didn't have to do much work. And if I wanted to get my hair done or whatever, I could just take off."

"Nice. But I assume the Hack hitting on you wasn't part of the deal."

"No, he thought that up on his own. I didn't go for it."

"Why not?"

"Why waste my time? I figured he was going nowhere, just a lifetime ass kisser. I was shocked when he asked Ducky and the rest to endorse him, and they actually said yes. You know what? I think he ran for Congress to impress me."

"And it worked."

"Well enough that I gave him what he wanted."

"But he was married."

"So?"

"You really thought he'd divorce his wife and marry you?"

"What can I tell you? Every man I ever

slept with has asked me to marry him."

The woman had about as much sexual self-doubt as Madonna. Talk about narcissistic.

But what if something happened to shake up her exalted opinion of herself?

"So according to you, everything was going great between you and the Hack until . . ."

"Until he got blasted. Just my luck."

I took a breath. "Was it really luck?"

She cocked her head. "What do you mean?"

"Maybe the truth is, he said he *wouldn't* marry you. And you were so mad at him for resisting your feminine charms, and refusing to spirit you away to Washington, that you shot him."

She shoved her chair back and stood up, no longer enjoying our little chat. "Give it a rest. I'd never care enough about any man to *shoot* him. And besides, Jack had already filed for divorce — though he was keeping it secret till after the election." She opened the door to go out. "Hey, it's been real, sweetheart, but your fifteen minutes are up."

I had one more question. "Do you know what Jack was planning to talk about at that radio debate, the night he got killed?"

"Yeah. Cutting taxes, and family values.

Why is it the family values guys are always so easy to seduce?"

I didn't have an answer to that, but I realized I did have yet another question. "How can you hate men so much, but be so into sex?"

"Because I like seeing how stupid you get," Linda said, and walked out.

Pierce wasn't back yet, so I turned on the Hack's computer. Fortunately there was no password, and despite my computer illiteracy, I found his campaign documents quickly enough — they were all stashed in a file called "Congress." But reading through the stuff was like swimming through mud. I mean, how many times can you read "capital gains tax cuts" and "preserving the moral fiber of our society" without going bug-eyed?

There were three different speeches in his computer, labeled "20 minutes," "10 minutes," and "2 minutes." I was almost finished with the task of reading them when I discovered an interesting notation at the bottom of the two-minute speech: "for debate intro, cut 30 seconds — 100 words." So this must be the speech he planned to use at the radio debate. It would have worked just as well as a lullaby.

"I don't have all day," someone snarled at

240

me from across the room.

It was Pierce. The Hack's speeches must have done some of their lullaby work on me, because I hadn't even heard Pierce come in. I woke up fast and attacked. "You lied to me last night," I said.

"What are you talking about?" he asked aggressively.

"You said you weren't seeing Linda anymore."

"I wasn't. Not until today."

I laughed abruptly. "You expect me to believe that?"

"It's true. She called me last night, right after you left."

So his story matched Linda's. Miracle of miracles, maybe people were actually being straight with me for a change. "What did Linda say last night that got you running down here all of a sudden?"

Pierce shifted in his seat and his face unexpectedly reddened. He looked shy, like a teenage girl talking about a first date. "She said she missed me and wanted to get back together."

"How sweet. And what did *you* say?"

His old belligerence returned. "Well, it's pretty obvious what I said, isn't it?"

"Yes, it is. You were willing to risk your whole campaign for her?" He sat there glowering. "What happened to your campaign appearances in Lake Placid?"

"I blew them off. I said I was sick."

"There's something fishy here, Pierce. No politician I ever heard of would just *blow off* a campaign appearance. Not with one week left before a very close election."

"Look, I love Linda. She's the best thing that ever happened to me."

I stared at the poor lovestruck clown and he looked away, embarrassed. *Good God,* I was thinking, *if Linda Medwick is the best thing that ever happened to you, then you've had a pretty sorry life.*

I hated to burst his bubble, but . . . "Did you know she was sleeping with the Hack?"

Pierce's eyes jumped. His jaw went slack. "Bullshit."

I was tempted to believe he really didn't know. But then that old joke came to me: How can you tell when a politician is lying? When his lips move.

I stood over Pierce and put my face three inches from his, just like in the TV cop shows. "Bullshit yourself. You knew about the Hack, all right. Is that why you killed him?"

"What?!"

"You pulled an O. J. Simpson."

"Hey —"

"Her fucking the Hack kind of *bothered* you, didn't it?"

"Look here," he said, starting to get up.

But I pushed him back in the chair. "Sit down," I told him. He looked like he was about to either burst out crying or kill me. If only I could get him mad enough to say something he shouldn't . . . "Linda says the only reason she's having sex with you is she's trying to find out if you killed the Hack."

Pierce's eyes jumped again, then he finally found his tongue. "That's a lie!" he shouted.

He tried to get up again, but I slapped him. He was too stunned to fight back. I was pretty stunned myself. I don't think I ever slapped anyone before in my life.

"Listen, you fool," I said. "What did Zzyp have on you? And you better tell me the fucking truth this time!"

"I told you the truth *last* time! I never heard of any guy named Zzyp!"

"Did he know about you and Linda?"

Pierce screamed in frustration, "Will you please *believe* me —"

"Fat chance. When's the last time you talked to Zzyp?"

*"Never."*

"Tell it to the judge. I saw Zzyp's cell phone records," I lied.

Actually, I was starting to believe Pierce

really *didn't* know Zzyp, and I was about ready to give up on this line of questioning. But my last-ditch fib about cell phones worked, and Pierce finally crumpled.

"I swear to God," he said plaintively, "the first time I ever heard of this guy Zzyp was when you mentioned him two nights ago. And the first time I talked to him was yesterday. He called me totally out of the blue."

Aha! "What did he say to you?"

"He said he had information that would help me win the election. He offered to sell it for twenty thousand bucks."

"What information?"

"I don't know. I told him I didn't want it."

"You really expect me to buy that? *Puh!*" I spit out. In honor of Yancy Huggins, the only honest politician (besides Will) that I'd met lately, I borrowed one of his lines. "You'd screw a dead warthog if you thought it would help you win."

"Hey, I didn't say no because I'm a nice guy. You'd told me Zzyp was mixed up in your murder investigation. I didn't want any part of it. That's why I hung up on him."

"You're lying through your gums, pal," I sneered. "Zzyp called you because he had dirt on you. He offered to sell it to you for twenty grand . . . or else he'd sell it to Susan Tamarack and your campaign would be as finished as yesterday's fish."

He threw up his hands. "Hey, if you want to find out why Zzyp was calling me, just ask him yourself."

"I can't."

"Why not?"

"You know why. Because he's dead."

Pierce's eyes did their patented jumping-out-of-the-head maneuver. Impressive. But was he truly astonished by Zzyp's death, or just faking it? Maybe his eye thing was the equivalent of Clinton's lip thing — a habitual gesture you make when you're being deceitful.

I didn't get a chance to explore that further, because just then Linda walked in. Pierce turned to her, and his whole face hardened. As for Linda, her jaw was so tight you could have used it for a hammer.

This was one lovers' quarrel I did not want to be in the middle of. Especially since I had started it.

"See you lovebirds later," I said, and stepped out.

# 14

After spending half an hour with the likes of Linda Medwick and Robert Pierce, I felt like going home and taking a long shower. But that wasn't meant to be. As I walked down the hall, I passed Ducky Medwick's office — and who should come barreling out of there but the quacker himself. Two suits in their late twenties hurried to keep up with him.

I was feeling sorry for Ducky, being married to a ballbuster like Linda, until he opened his mouth. "You *cretins*," he shouted at his two aides, "why didn't you *tell* me that bill was coming up today?!"

"I'm sorry, sir," one aide stammered, and the other one whimpered, "We didn't know."

"You didn't know?! What the hell do I pay you for, you worthless sacks of —"

"Senator Medwick," I interrupted.

He whirled, and was about to yell at me too until he saw who I was. Then his eyes filled with impotent rage. At least that's how they looked to me, but after talking to Linda maybe I had impotence on my mind. *"What?"* he snapped.

"We need to talk."

"Talk to my secretary. Make an appointment. I've got a crisis here, thanks to these morons." Throwing them a glare that made them cringe, he walked away from me.

I raised my voice. "Senator, we need to talk *immediately*."

"No can do," he called over his shoulder.

With his morons beside him, he was at the top of the steps now, heading down. I stopped him the only way I knew how. "Ducky," I called out, "why did you lie about who your wife was sleeping with!"

That stopped him, all right. Stopped him cold.

But meanwhile, the morons were so stunned they forgot to watch where they were going. Like amateur vaudevillians, they simultaneously slipped on the steps, clutched at each other for support, and tumbled head over heels in tandem down to the landing below. I could hear them yelping in pain.

Ducky paid no attention to their squeals. He made a sudden turnaround and came toward me, seething with that impotent rage I mentioned before. Then he wheeled away from me and strode back into his office.

I followed him. We walked through his reception area, complete with efficient gray-haired secretary, and into his inner office. Then he closed the door.

I looked around. There were photos of Ducky's two kids lining the bookcase, but none of his wife.

He started right in. "So what do you *imagine* that you know about Linda?"

"You said you caught her with Pierce. But really, it was the Hack."

"So what? It wasn't *me* she was fucking, that's all I care about."

"Why did you lie?"

He stomped his foot. "Goddamn it, I've got a gun control bill to kill. You know what the NRA is gonna say if I'm not out there on the Senate floor in less than ten minutes?"

"You can still make it if you cut the shit."

He gave a low growl. "This is humiliating, you know."

"I can't help that."

"You're enjoying every minute of this, you lousy —"

"Hey, if it means anything, I think you deserve better than her." I tried a joke. "Not that I think all that highly of you, either."

That broke the tension — somewhat. Ducky snorted. "Alright, the truth? Yeah, she was fucking Jack. Why'd I lie? So you and the cops won't go around thinking she killed him, in some kind of crazy lover's thing."

"Do *you* think she killed him?"

He lifted his shoulders. "Hell if I know. Frankly, I'm wondering how much I really understand that woman."

I nodded. "Now what about you?"

"What *about* me?"

"Did *you* kill him in some crazy lover's thing?"

"I have an alibi."

"Yeah, I heard it. Not exactly airtight."

He frowned. "I don't remember telling you my alibi."

"Linda did. She said you were on the phone with her."

He waved his arms dismissively. "That may be *her* alibi, but it's not mine. I was in the hotel bar all night, when Jack was killed. You can ask the bartender."

"So Linda lied to me about that phone call?"

"What, that surprises you? She called me up and asked me to lie, too. Screw that. I'll protect the bitch to a degree, but no way am I gonna mess up my *own* alibi."

I sat silently, thinking. Ducky seemed awfully proud of this alibi of his, but maybe I should check it out anyway.

"You got any more degrading questions

for me?" Ducky said. "I have to get the hell downstairs."

"Tell me, why'd you support the widow for Congress instead of Pierce?"

"*Why?* Because when I got home that night after catching Linda with Jack, she treated me to a detailed list of every man she ever slept with. Including Pierce. So I'll be damned if I'm gonna support *him*. For all I know he's fucking my wife even as we speak!"

Actually, there was a pretty good chance he was right.

But I didn't mention it.


Dying for a shower though I was, I made one more stop on my way north. I pulled in at the Holiday Inn in Halfmoon and bellied up to the bar.

It was a quarter to four, generally a depressing time to be in a bar, and today was no exception. I was happy about one thing, though: the night bartender was already on duty. It was the same guy I'd seen last time. I took a close look at him. His fat face and puffy eyes made him look like ESPN's Chris Berman, but without the spark. This guy seemed like someone who spent a lot of his life lying around, scarfing down potato chips and Bud, and *watching* Chris Berman.

"Good afternoon," I greeted him cheerily.

"Afternoon," he answered morosely.

"Samuel Adams, please."

"Yeah," he replied, lumbering over to the refrigerator and getting me one.

I put a fiver on the bar and told him to keep the change. That brightened him up a little. "Thanks," he said.

"Pretty slow today, huh?"

"About like usual."

"Must be kind of romantic, being a bartender at a hotel."

He squinted at me dubiously. "Romantic?"

"Sure. Ships passing in the night and so on. You get any famous people here?"

"Nah. Just salesmen."

"Really? I thought I saw Senator Medwick in here the other night."

For the first time, the bartender's face turned animated. "Ducky's a good guy."

"He's always been one of my favorite politicians. He's hell on Democrats."

"Yeah, he's the best."

I threw a ten on the bar, trying to brighten up the bartender even more, get him loose. "Hey, hit me with a shot of Jack. Get yourself one too, if you want. I sold seventeen computers today."

"Congratulations," he said, and brought

out two shot glasses. He hadn't needed much encouragement.

"So you get a chance to talk to Ducky? He's always struck me as a real straight shooter."

And that's all it took. The bartender waved the Jack Daniel's bottle toward me and said confidentially, "Between you, me, and Mr. Daniels, Ducky's gonna hook me up with a state job. Get me out of this hellhole."

"You're kidding."

"Nope."

"That's fabulous. Why's he doing that for you?"

All of a sudden the bartender's face turned dull again. He picked up a dirty napkin from the bar and threw it away before finally answering me. "I don't know, he just is. Guess he liked me."

"Why?"

His eyes narrowed, looking like small black mancala stones inside of his flabby face. "Who are you, anyway?"

I threw caution to the winds. "Is he giving you a job because you're giving him a fake alibi?"

He gulped, and his voice came out in a squeak. "I don't know what you're talking about."

I put my beer glass down on the bar. "You realize you're committing a crime. Obstructing justice, it's called."

"Hey —"

"Ducky'll hook you up with a state job, all right. Pressing license plates."

He opened his mouth, then shut it, then reopened it, and then re-shut it.

And this time it stayed shut.

I held up my palms. "Your secret is safe with me," I said. "Play it straight and I won't tell the cops. Hell, I won't even tell Ducky. But *you* better tell *me:* what really went down between you two?"

The bartender turned his back to me and began washing glasses. I harangued him for five minutes straight, about angry cops and crowded jails and the interesting sexual habits of inmates, but he just stood there stoically and kept on washing. Ducky had picked the right guy to back up his alibi, no question.

And there was also no question, at least to me, that his alibi was about as reliable as an astrological forecast.

I would have wandered around the hotel chatting up clerks and maids and so forth, but by now it was already past four o'clock. That shower was calling me. If I cranked up the old Toyota as fast as she could go, I'd make it back by 4:45. That would give me just enough time to grab a few minutes' worth of watery bathroom heaven before the kids came home from their friends' house and I had to take on Daddy duty. Hopefully those precious minutes would help me mellow out from my long day of interrogations. Then I wouldn't find myself yelling at the kids for no reason except my own tension.

The Toyota was in a good mood and I managed to get home by 4:44. Nevertheless, that shower was not meant to be. There were two cops standing outside my front door. One of them was my old nemesis, Chief Walsh. Uh oh. As I pulled into the driveway, Walsh and the other cop, Lieutenant Foxwell, eyed me grimly.

I walked up to them with fake jauntiness and said, "Hi, what's up? You get a lead on who shot at me?"

"May we come in?" Walsh asked, with exaggerated pleasantness.

"Look, I was about to take a shower, and my kids are coming home any minute. What is it you want to talk about?"

Walsh gave me an incongruous wink. "We think you know."

The smug bastard. I was pretty sure I *did* know.

The cops must have found Zzyp's body. And they must have found out somehow that I was there at the scene of the crime.

I kept my cool as best I could. "If you want to come in, be my guests," I said, unlocking the door. "But I better call my friend and ask her not to bring my kids home until you're already gone. For some reason, my kids don't like being around cops. And they seem to have a special loathing for *you*," I added, turning to Chief Walsh. "I wonder why."

He stroked his chin, as if giving the matter thought. "Who knows?" he said. "Kids are funny."

"True. I mean, just because somebody once tried to pin a false murder rap on your daddy, that's no reason to hold a grudge. Won't you sit down?"

Walsh and Foxwell gave each other a look and sat down. I went into the computer room to get the portable phone. The window that had been shot through was still boarded up; I made a mental note to get the thing fixed as soon as I had time. The way things were going, that might not be until October. Then the phone rang, before I got a chance to make my call. I picked up. "Hello?"

"Burns, where's my goddamn fax?"

*What?* I needed some serious aspirin. Who was calling me, and why? "Fax?"

"Don't play games with me. Your deadline was this morning," said the man whose voice I was now able to place. Jeremy Wartheimer. "You don't get me my fax by five p.m. — that's fifteen minutes, scuzzbag — and I walk right across the hall to the head of the English Department. Bet Andrea will be real pleased with you when she finds out, won't she?"

I looked over at the answering machine. There were too many blinks to count, meaning I had a lot of messages. What were they? Was one of them from my wife, announcing that she'd succeeded in her top-secret assignment and returned Susan Tamarack's portfolio? Or would her message say that her AAA card had let us down and the mission was aborted?

I'd give anything to be able to hit the "play" button on that machine. But how could I listen to Andrea's message about attempted breaking and entering when my two least favorite cops were sitting in the next room? Their lucky day: they had just placed me at the scene of a murder. No doubt they'd enjoy harassing me about breaking and entering, too.

"You hear me, you dickweed?" Wartheimer said.

Hell, you only live once. I decided to have faith in Andrea and AAA and take a chance. "Listen, Jeremy, there's been a misunderstanding —"

"Yeah? Then misunderstand *this* —"

"I never took anyone's portfolio." I was careful not to say "Susan Tamarack's portfolio" in case the cops were eavesdropping.

"What, you're gonna try to *deny* it?" Wartheimer said incredulously. "You admitted Saturday on the phone that you took it!"

"I admitted nothing of the sort. You were talking so fast I couldn't get a word in edgewise."

"You are so full of —"

"You must have misplaced it."

"I didn't misplace anything and you know it —"

"Have you checked? Where *are* the portfolios, anyway?"

"Right here on my desk, and Susan Tamarack's portfolio is not one of them —"

There was a sudden silence on the phone. Then I heard Wartheimer saying two words that pleased me no end: "Shit! Fuck!"

*Yes!* "What happened? Did you find it?"

"You put it back on my desk, you —"

"Don't be silly. How could *I* put it back? I haven't been to the campus today."

"Then Andrea did it."

"Yeah, right. You think if I stole some-one's portfolio, I'd tell Andrea? Forget it. Look, seriously, don't feel bad, Jeremy. I'm always misplacing stuff and thinking some-one must have taken it."

Wartheimer sputtered, "You — you —"

"Hey, I gotta go. Good luck with your screenplay. Sorry I couldn't help."

Then I hung up the phone, feeling exul-tant. But when I looked up, I got an un-pleasant surprise: Chief Walsh's blue Nazi eyes were gleaming at me. He'd slipped into the computer room without my noticing. "What's this about stealing someone's port-folio?" he asked.

"It's nothing. The guy's delusional," I said airily. "Now if you'll excuse me, I have to call my friend."

Luckily I reached Janet before she left her house, and she agreed to keep Derek and Bernie until six. "They're no trouble at all," she reassured me. "They've been playing with my kids on the computer ever since they got here."

Great. Whatever happened to playing in the backyard?

But now was no time to get caught up in computer phobia. Taking a deep breath, I went back into the living room and faced the dreaded cop duo. "Okay, I'm all yours. What did you want to see me about?"

"Where were you yesterday?" the chief began.

"This is excellent," I said, beaming and rubbing my hands. "Now I get to see how the real pros do an interrogation."

"I'll do it any way I damn please," said the chief. "You don't like it, I'll book you on suspicion of murder."

I feigned puzzlement. "What, now you think *I* killed the Hack?"

Turning to Foxwell, the chief pointed a disdainful finger at me. "Isn't he pathetic?"

"No question," Foxwell agreed.

"You boys mind clueing me in on *why* I'm pathetic?"

"Not at all," Chief Walsh said pleasantly. "You're pathetic because you're trying to act like you weren't at Zzypowski's office this morning, messing around with his corpse. Whereas we have the janitor's description of a guy with black curly hair and a big nose, which fits you to a tee —"

"Hey, there's lots of us big-nosed, curly-haired guys running around," I said flippantly. "It's an epidemic."

"But they don't all have your fingerprints." I gave a quick start — how could I have been so dumb? The chief gave a nasty grin. "That's right. We did a computer match of prints that were all over the scene — the cabinets, the drawers, even *Zzyp's wallet* — to some prints of yours that we just happen to have on file. And guess what? Perfect match. What do you think of that?"

"What can I say? I'm delighted to hear that a small-time, birdbrain cop like yourself could figure out how to use computers. By God, if you can do it, *anyone* can. You give hope to the rest of us."

"Hope is not what I'm giving you."

"Okay, I'll bite. What *are* you giving me? What's your theory?"

"Nothing complex. You went in his office yesterday, pulled a gun, and shot him. Then you trashed his computer. But after you got home, you realized you left something behind. So today you came back looking for it."

"And why, pray tell, did I kill this man?"

"Maybe as a favor for your pal Will."

"For Will? *Why?*"

"Because Zzypowski specialized in opposition research. He knew things. Maybe he knew things about Will." The chief stretched his legs out comfortably and crossed his ankles. "Or maybe you just killed him because you've had writer's block for God knows how long, and you were looking for a new thrill."

"I've got a wife, two kids, and a minivan. I doubt I fit the personality profile for thrill killers."

"You'd be surprised."

"You never cease to amaze me, Chief. Whose butt did you kiss to get this job, anyway? Or did you pay some politician a 'finder's fee'?"

"This is all very enjoyable, Burns, and personally I'd love nothing better than to sit all day with you and chew the fat. But I do have this pesky murder investigation to run. So listen up. It's like this." He leaned forward and, in the same mock-friendly voice, continued, "Either you give me everything — *now* — or I bust you as a material witness and drop you off in City Jail. Judge Klausner takes Tuesdays off ever since his operation, so you'll be down there till at least Wednesday. Sound like fun?"

Actually, no. I once had the privilege of spending a night in that jail, and it was an Unforgettable Experience. The putrid smells, the abusive guards, the crazed drunk chanting "Hare Krishna" all night long . . .

So I decided to spill my guts out to Chief Walsh. After all, we *were* on the same side, right? Much as I despised the man, we both

261

wanted to nail whoever was running around shooting people.

I didn't spill *everything*, though. I kept mum about Susan's unusual sex life. I told myself it probably wasn't relevant to Zzyp's death, so why mention it? And staying quiet — for now — about Susan's affair with Hack Sr. gave me more leverage to use on both of them.

Also, I must confess there was some kind of . . . call it prudishness, maybe, or that hard-to-kill sensitive *artiste* in me . . . which made me want to keep their affair hidden.

But I did inform the chief about plenty of other entertaining stuff, like Linda Medwick's hijinks, and Zzyp's final phone call to the widow's house, and my suspicion that Zzyp had dirt on both Pierce and Ducky. "Incidentally, if Ducky hits you with an alibi, I'd advise you to check it thoroughly," I said, and described my encounter with the bartender.

I was pretty proud of myself for finding the hole in Ducky's alibi. But I got the disturbing impression that whenever I talked about Ducky, the chief's eyes glazed over. Finally I called him on it. "Look," I said, annoyed, "you have to admit, Ducky had strong motives to kill both men. The Hack, because he was fucking his wife. And Zzyp, because —"

The chief yawned loudly at me. "Face it, Burns, your friend Shmuckler is the fool who killed the Hack. And when the smoke clears on this new murder, we're gonna find out he popped Zzypowski too — assuming you didn't do it for him."

"How intriguing. What incredible insights," I said, clapping my hands together. "And according to your brilliant theory, who was it that took those pot shots at me and the kids? Was that Will, also?"

The chief didn't deign to answer. He stood up, and so did his lieutenant. "Thanks for your time," he said. "Don't leave the jurisdiction. We'll be back."

"Chief Walsh, may I remind you of something," I said politely, then lowered my voice as deep as it would go. I'm not saying I hit bass, but I came close. "Last time you messed with me, I almost got your ass fired. This time, there might not be any 'almost' about it."

All of the chief's pretenses at civility disappeared. "You shithead," he exploded, and before I could react he was shoving me up against the living room wall. "One more word out of you, and I will throw your sorry ass in jail and I will enjoy it. You got that?"

Behind the chief, his lieutenant watched silently. I didn't say anything myself, just stood there burning up. Then the two of them walked out.

# 15

I cussed and screamed in my empty house until I calmed down enough to be fit for human contact. Then I called Judy Demarest at the *Daily Saratogian.*

"Hey, Jude," I said when she came on the line, "you better print up an extra ten thousand copies of your paper tomorrow."

"Why on earth should I do that?"

"Because I'm about to feed you a major scoop," I said, and proceeded to tell her everything I'd just told Chief Walsh. Judy practically salivated over the phone as she promised to set aside the whole top half of tomorrow's page one.

The 22nd District Congressional race was about to take yet another bizarre twist. The scandal about Pierce taking an envelope of cash would seriously damage — if not cripple — his campaign. Meanwhile Zzyp's phone call to Susan Tamarack's house would muddy her up, too.

Yes, things were definitely looking up for Will Shmuckler.

Furthermore, all this publicity would turn up the heat on Chief Walsh. I smiled at that.

If he thought he could scare me off by throwing his weight around a little, he had another think coming.

I took two aspirins and my long-awaited hot shower, and began to feel like an approximation of my old self. As the $H_2O$ poured over my body, it occurred to me that in the seven hours since stumbling over Zzyp's corpse, I had harangued Susan Tamarack, Robert Pierce, both Medwicks . . . in other words, all of my major suspects but one. The father-in-law.

Except he wasn't just a father-in-law — he was also a father. Would the man go so far as to kill his own son?

I was toweling off when the doorbell rang, so I jumped into my jeans and headed downstairs. I started to open the door, then got a sudden fear that whoever was standing on my front porch might be about to shoot me in the head.

But I got lucky. It was Derek and Bernie, jumping up and down with excitement at seeing me. "Daddy! Daddy!" they shouted in unison, as I gathered them into my arms. I called out thanks and a good-bye to Janet, who was still in the car — "I'm on my way to Boy Scouts," she explained as she drove off — and brought the kids inside.

Bernie looked searchingly into my eyes.

"Daddy, did anyone shoot at you today?"

Good grief. "No, honey," I said.

" 'Cause they said on TV, somebody got killed at the mall."

While I was trying to figure out a kid-friendly way to respond, Derek interrupted. "Hey, Daddy!" he chortled. "I made up a joke! The guy who shot at our window was a real *pain!* Get it?"

I must have been distracted or something, because the pun slipped right by me. "Get what?"

Derek's little brother jumped in. "It could be 'pain,' like if you're hurting —"

"No!" Derek shrieked. "*I* want to tell it!"

But Bernie kept right on going. "Or 'pane,' like window pane!"

"No fair!" Derek howled. "I wanted to tell it myself!"

"So did I!"

"Listen, guys," I said.

Derek burst into tears. "It was *my* joke!"

Bernie was wailing too. "No, it wasn't!"

My headache came back full force. "Please —"

"Yes, it was!"

"No, it wasn't!"

"Please be quiet!" I said loudly.

"But, Daddy —"

*"Be quiet!"* I yelled, loud enough for them

to hear it in Albany.

This is not a technique they recommend in the parenting magazines, I know. But sometimes you have to go with your gut, and sometimes your gut says, *scream.*

In this case, it worked. The boys were stunned into silence, and I was stunned into thinking about why they were acting like pains. No doubt they were tense as hell and scared of getting shot at again, just like me.

"Listen, kids, let's start over. I haven't cooked dinner yet. Would you like frozen waffles?"

"Yay! Waffles!" they shouted, and everything was okay again.

Well, *almost* everything. "Daddy?" Bernie asked anxiously. "Can we go sleep at Grandma's again tonight?"

"Sure, that's the plan. Mommy's driving there straight from work. After we eat our waffles, we'll drive up there, too."

"Good," Derek said, "because I don't think the murderer knows where Grandma's house is."

"No, he probably doesn't," I said. Then, when both boys goggled at me with frightened eyes, I amended that to, "I'm *sure* he doesn't."

Derek, always the literalist, asked, "Why are you sure?"

"Well," I stuttered, and then came up with, "Because Grandma has a different last name from us."

Thank God, that seemed to satisfy them. Derek went off on a different tangent. "Hey, Daddy, guess what? We were on the computer at our friends' house —"

"*I* wanna tell it!" Bernie shouted. "*I* want to tell this one!"

I girded myself for another sibling battle. But amazingly, Derek just said, "Okay." I guess he didn't want to hear me scream again.

"We looked for stuff about Jack Tamarack in all these different search engines," Bernie said, and then stopped. "*Search engine,* that means —"

"It's okay, kiddo, I do know what a search engine is."

"I wasn't sure. 'Cause with computers, you're kind of, like . . ."

"Yeah, I know what I'm like. So what did you find out about the Hack?"

"Nothing, but we found some cool stuff about his dad." He took a folded up printout from his jacket pocket. "Here."

I opened the printout and began reading. It was an article from the *Schenectady Gazette,* back in June. Some enterprising reporter had tracked down George Tamarack and asked him if he planned to vote for his son in the upcoming election. The reporter had caught wind of the fact that Hack Sr. used to run the Plumbers and Pipefitters Union local, and was still an active Democrat in South Glens Falls.

"I'll vote for the Democrat, of course," Hack Sr. was quoted as saying. "I don't know what the heck happened to Jack. I try to bring the kid up right, but he goes off to law school and turns Republican on me. Fights against the working man and hangs out with a bunch of downstaters wearing fancy suits. I hope he gets killed in the election."

*I hope he gets killed in the election.* Pretty eerie.

It sounded like Hack Sr. was trying to be funny. But knowing him like I did, I could feel the anger behind the humor. And telling a reporter — on the record — that you're voting against your own son . . . that's heavy stuff.

Not that Hack Sr. would kill Hack Jr. just for the crime of being Republican. But if he'd been wrought up about his son for years, and then found out his son was beating the woman he loved . . .

Yes, *loved.* No matter how kinky I may have found it, the truth was undeniable:

Hack Sr. was madly in love with his daughter-in-law.

I was eager to interrogate the man in person, but I couldn't go off and leave my kids. "Boys," I said, "I need to make a quick phone call for a minute."

"A kid minute or a grownup minute?" Derek asked. My sons have discovered that when a kid says "a minute," it usually means a real minute; but when a grownup says "a minute," it can mean anywhere from a real minute to half an hour.

"I guess I mean a grownup minute," I admitted. "Why don't you go play on the computer?"

"I'm tired of the computer," Bernie said.

"Look, if you're scared of getting shot at again, we can move it into the dining room."

"No, I'm *tired* of it."

"Me, too!" Derek chimed in.

Would wonders never cease.

A few minutes later, after I set the kids up with magic markers so they could draw pictures of their favorite Yankee players, I went upstairs to call Hack Sr. There was no answer at his house in South Glens Falls, so I tried the widow's place. Sure enough, he picked up the phone with a cough and a hello.

"Mr. Tamarack, this is Jake Burns."

Another couple of coughs, then: "So fucking what?"

Okay, so that's how we were playing it. I
steeled myself. "Look, I want you to know, I
haven't told the newspapers or the cops
about you having sex with your son's wife."

He didn't say anything or even cough, but
I could hear his labored breathing.

"And I'm hoping I don't *have* to tell them
about it."

"You son of a —"

"Calm down. And don't go into one of
your fits, either. Just tell me: what did you
and Zzyp talk about yesterday?"

Of course, I wasn't sure Hack Sr. really
did talk to Zzyp yesterday — or ever. But if I
*sounded* sure, maybe I'd confuse the old man
into admitting it.

As it turned out, though, I didn't need any
tricky subterfuges to get him to open up. "If
that's all you want, why didn't you just say
so in the first place? Hell, I'll be glad to tell
you that. I already told the cops ten minutes
ago, when they came by here."

It was good to know that despite Chief
Walsh's attitude problem, he was following
up on the lead I gave him. "Okay, so tell
me."

"Sure. This fellow Zzypowski called up
yesterday. First he asks for Susan. I say she's

272

not home, but I'm her father-in-law and campaign manager, and can I help him with something? I'm not really her manager, but sometimes I tell people that just to keep 'em off her back."

"Uh huh."

"So the guy says yeah, you can help me with something, and I can help *you*. Says, I got information *vis-à-vis* your campaign opponent that'll shoot him dead out of the water. Says, you give me twenty grand and I'll lay it on you. Even claims the deal is legal. 'Opposition research,' he calls it."

"So what'd you tell him?" I asked impatiently.

"I say, hey, if this is for real, I'll go for it, sure. Pay the twenty myself out of my pension. God knows *I* won't ever be needing that money. Not in this lifetime, anyway."

"Did he explain what you'd be getting for your money?"

"No, he wanted to show me in person. I was stuck babysitting all day yesterday, so we were gonna meet at his office today at noon. Only by the time I got there, the cops were crawling all around and he was dead."

I thought about what the old man was telling me. It made sense. It was logical.

It might even be true.

273

"So who do you think killed him?" I ventured. "Pierce?"

"Why Pierce?"

I frowned into the mouthpiece of the phone. "Isn't it obvious? Pierce must have found out that Zzyp was going to sell you information about him —"

"Whoa, hold on. Zzyp wasn't gonna sell me any information about Pierce."

Huh? "But you just said —"

"No, I didn't. Zzyp was gonna sell me stuff about Will Shmuckler."

*Oh, Lord.* I just sat there with the phone in my hand. Then Hack Sr. started cackling, and it hit me that he was pulling my leg.

"Got you there, didn't I?" he said.

"You're just bullshitting me, right?"

"Makes you think that?" he asked, still laughing.

"Give me a break. Zzyp had the goods on Pierce, I have the photograph to prove it. If he wanted to sell you something, *that's* what he would sell."

"Hey, I don't give a flying fuck in a rolling doughnut if you believe me or not. I'll tell you, though," he added teasingly, "them cops seemed to believe me pretty good."

Aspirin or no aspirin, some little imp was banging bongos in my brain. "I don't get it. Why would you lie about this?"

"Hey, if I *was* lying, it would be darn good campaign strategy, don't you think?"

"What do you mean?"

"Use your noodle. You're telling the cops Zzyp had dirt on Pierce. Meanwhile *I* tell the cops Zzyp had dirt on *Shmuckler.* When the media gets hold of it, they'll put it all together and figure out *both* of those guys had motive to kill Zzyp. The only one who comes out of this smelling like a rose is Susan. She'll win with sixty percent, easy."

Downstairs, my kids were begging loudly, "Daddy, has it been a grownup minute yet? We're *hungry!*" Trying to shut out their voices, I said into the phone, "I can't believe you'd pull this."

He gave a half-chuckle, half-cough. "Hey, never underestimate an old union man."

"But whoever shot Zzyp probably shot Jack, too! Don't you want your son's killer to get thrown in jail?"

Hack Sr.'s voice turned harsh. "My son is dead. Susan's not. You don't get it, do you? I'd do anything for Susan. *Anything.*"

It sounded like he was about to hang up, so I spoke quickly. "Listen, you crazy old man, you better go back to the cops."

"Why should I?"

"You tell them the truth about Zzyp. If

you don't, I'll tell them the truth about you and Susan."

But Hack Sr. didn't answer, just slammed down the phone. I wanted to call him right back but the kids were climbing up the stairs, whining for their waffles. Then the doorbell rang and the kids whined even louder. Bernie started crying. He assumed, quite rightly, that the ringing doorbell meant his dinner would be delayed even longer.

Once again my gut urged me to scream. This time I held it in. I clamped my mouth shut, afraid that if I opened it I'd explode, and headed for the door. It was Will. He stood there in an old gray windbreaker, looking distressed — not at all like a guy who might be elected to Congress in less than two weeks.

"Care for some waffles?" I asked.

"Did the cops talk to you yet?" he asked in return.

Both kids were crying now. "Shmuck-man, if I don't toast a few waffles this very kid minute, somebody in this house is gonna die. Either the kids will kill me or I'll kill them."

Seven minutes later, with the waffles toasted, cut, and drowned in syrup, Will and I made our way to the living room. "So what were you doing in this guy Zzypowski's office?" he said.

"How'd you know I was there?"

He shot me a puzzled look. "Didn't you get my phone messages?"

Jeez, I'd forgotten all about those messages. "I've been kind of busy."

"The cops brought me in and questioned me all over again, after they found out you were in Zzypowski's office. They wanted to know if I sent you."

"Well, you didn't, so I assume you just told them the truth."

"Of course. But why *were* you there?"

"To get to the bottom of Zzyp's nefarious activities. I think he was holding out on me about something."

"Like what?"

"He got killed before I could find out."

Will frowned. "This is so infuriating."

"No kidding."

"Did you hear the latest poll?"

"Yeah, you told me a couple of days ago —"

"No, there was a new one today, on 'Live at Five.' Pierce: twenty-three; the widow: twenty-three; and good old Shmuck: twenty-four."

"*What?!*"

"That's right, I'm actually ahead."

There was a sadness in his voice, but I ignored it. "Wow. Congratulations, Congressman Shmuck!" I put out my hand and slapped him five, but his hand barely slapped back. "Come on, jump up and down!"

"I know. I should be happy, but I'm not." Slumped down low in the sofa, he looked gloomy and forlorn, nothing like the Type A guy I knew and more or less loved. "This whole murder business has wiped me out."

"I know what you mean," I said. Having been a murder suspect myself once, I knew it was no barrel of monkeys.

He gazed up at me. "Did you ever feel like you were in someone else's body?"

I sat on the sofa beside him. "You're afraid of going to prison," I said.

"It's not just that," he replied. "Everywhere I go, people talk to me about all this surreal weirdness I know nothing about. Like the Hack's murder, and you getting shot at, and now this whole new murder. And I'm realizing, I never — *never* — get to talk to anyone about any of the things that made me want to run for office in the first place. Things like the environment, or health care, or *foreign policy* for God's sake. Once — just once — I'd like for someone to ask me about East Timor."

"But that's politics, Will. Even without

these murders, it would still be like that."

He got up and paced up and down the living room. "But my campaign was supposed to be *different*. I had such big plans." The sparkle returned to his eyes as he went on. "I was gonna fly in twenty ex–death row inmates who turned out to be innocent, and hold a big press conference so the voters could really *see* these men. And I was gonna do another press conference with parents whose kids died because they didn't have health insurance. And I was gonna buy a bunch of guns on the Internet or at gun shows or somewhere and hold them up at my speeches to show how we need tougher gun control."

"You can still do all that, Will."

"No, I can't. I don't have the money to organize it, and anyway I'm too numb from all the bullshit. I'm, like, where's the next shock coming from?"

"Actually," I said hesitantly, "I can pretty much tell you where it's coming from."

He eyed me sharply. I didn't relish giving him the news, but I figured he should be prepared. "Hack Sr. told the cops he got a call from Zzyp right before he died, and Zzyp offered to sell him some dirt on you."

"That's preposterous!"

"Of course. The old man's lying through his teeth."

"But why?"

"To make it look like you had a motive to kill Zzyp."

"He's trying to *frame* me?"

"Yeah. So people won't vote for you."

Finally Will understood. His eyes widened in dismay, then he sank back down onto the sofa.

I gave him a light, joking punch on the shoulder. "Hey, be flattered, Shmuck-man. For him to frame you is a compliment. He thinks you're a legitimate threat to win the election."

Will put a pillow over his head, and when his voice came out, it was muffled. "Yeah, there goes my big one-percent lead, all right." He removed the pillow and gave me an earnest look. "Jake, the hell with politics. Maybe I should just quit the race."

"You're not serious, are you?"

He threw up his hands. "Look, what's the point? So far my campaign is connected somehow to two people getting killed. And you and your sons almost got killed, too. It's not worth it."

I stared at Will with concern, thinking again how out of character he was acting. I wasn't used to seeing him in this Hamletesque "to be or not to be" mode. For a moment I wondered if there might be some hidden reason why Zzyp's murder had hit Will so hard. But that didn't make sense — I mean, Will had never even met Zzyp.

The silence between us grew uncomfortably long, until Will broke it with an unhappy laugh. "Nah, screw it," he said, "I'm not really serious about quitting, hell no. I'll go ahead and play their game. I'll futz with the truth and make personal attacks and ignore the issues and do anything else I have to do to get elected, just like every other goddamn politician." He pointed an emphatic finger at me. "But once I'm in office, by God, that's when I'll get to do what *I* want to do. I'll fight for what I believe in."

As I stared into his brown eyes, which were now shining with righteous passion, I thought to myself: Is this how all politicians start out? Was Richard Milhous once an innocent, well-meaning man?

You know, he probably was.

After Will left, I grabbed a waffle for myself and finally listened to all those phone messages. There were calls from Andrea, the media, and prospective campaign volunteers. Trying to act like a responsible husband after all the stress I'd been causing the family lately, I called Andrea back at Grandma's house. But I ignored everyone else. I didn't have time.

The kids and I piled into the car and headed out to the *Daily Saratogian*. I gave Judy the photo of Pierce, Sarafian, and that fateful envelope. The photo would be prominently displayed alongside tomorrow's big exposé.

That job accomplished, we headed north to Grandma's. We had a pretty peaceful evening, all things considered. Then again, peaceful evenings are a lot easier to have when you're surrounded by trees and crickets and stars.

Andrea entertained us with the tale of her successful B and E into Jeremy Wartheimer's office. The kids were thrilled to have a Mommy who was a real live burglar — although, as our five year old solemnly pointed out, "Mommy's a *good* burglar, not a bad burglar." As for Hannah, she stopped being quite so ticked off at me, now that her daughter's tenure was no longer in danger.

To keep the mood calm, I downplayed my involvement in Zzyp's death. No need to get Grandma all riled up again. Also, I was hoping to avoid getting Bernie upset to the point where he would pee in Grandma's sheets again tonight.

So after we watched a few innings of the Yankees crushing the Tampa Bay Devil Rays by about 200 to 0, Grandma headed for her room while the rest of us went downstairs to bed. I had no trouble falling asleep, but then I had the strangest dream.

I dreamed someone had a hand over my mouth and was whispering softly in my ear, "Say one word and I blow your wife's head off."

I tried to wake up, but I couldn't. Then I tried to scream, but I couldn't do that, either. It was like there was something covering my mouth —

Oh, shit. Something *was* covering my mouth.

This wasn't a dream.

# 16

Again the whisper came: "Now stand up. Real slow, and real quiet."

The hand finally came away from my mouth. I stood up — real slow, and real quiet. Andrea, with her usual fall allergies, kept right on snoring behind me.

I still couldn't make out who I was dealing with. Out here in the woods, far from the city lights, all I could see was a shadow. I didn't even see any gun, but from that rude remark about blowing Andrea's head off, I assumed he had one. I say "he"; it was hard to tell from the whispering, but I thought the person was a man.

I felt something in my back — a gun barrel. Good thing I hadn't tried to call his bluff about the gun. The barrel prodded me forward, and no words were required for me to figure out what he wanted: I was supposed to walk forward and out the door.

Only one problem. It was so dark, I walked straight into a wall. I stubbed my toes, but more important, made a loud bumping noise that sounded to my terrified ears like a thunderclap. Andrea had always had an amazing talent for snoring her way through any noise short of a hydrogen bomb. She better show that talent tonight — or she'd get killed, too.

Wait a minute. *She'd get killed, too* — what was I thinking? Was I expecting to get shot?

Yes, I realized, that's *exactly* what I was expecting. I panicked, and walked into the wall again. Another — and louder — bumping noise. The gunman gave a low, angry hiss. "Sorry," I whispered, inanely apologetic, like I was somehow at fault.

On my third try I made it out the door into the downstairs hallway, with the gunman close behind. "Outside," he whispered hoarsely.

"Let me get my shoes," I whispered back, trying to gain time.

He answered with his gun barrel. So outside we went, after I stumbled into two more walls looking for the outside door. By the time I made it out there, my big toes were smarting. Of course, that was the least of my worries.

The gunman followed me out, and as soon as he shut the door behind him he started breathing loudly, in uneven rasps. I still couldn't see him, but now I knew who he was. He must have been fighting to keep his breath quiet the whole time we were inside the house.

"Mr. Tamarack!" I said. I wouldn't be thinking of him as "Hack Sr." anymore; any man with a gun in his hand automatically becomes a "mister." "What are *you* doing here?"

Even as I said it, I knew it sounded dumb. It was perfectly obvious what he was doing here: holding a gun to my head and threatening to shoot me with it.

Another thing he was doing was going into a coughing fit. I didn't offer to get him a glass of water, though. That's one disadvantage to holding guns on people — they may call you mister, but they're less eager to do you favors.

There must have been clouds covering the moon and stars, because I couldn't even discern the outline of Mr. T.'s body. I tried to tell from the sounds he made whether the coughing was making him double over. If so, then maybe I should make a run for it. Since I could barely see him, he could probably barely see me.

But as my two sons had noticed earlier, "probably" can be the scariest word in the English language. What if Mr. T.'s night vision was better than mine? There was always the danger that he was a big carrot eater, and right now he was watching every move I made with owl-like eyes.

Before I could make up my mind about fleeing, the coughing fit subsided. Then Mr. T. rasped, "To the pond!"

"Why?" I asked, for lack of anything better to say.

I felt that familiar gun barrel at my ribs. *"Go!"*

So I went.

From Grandma's house to the pond, there's a narrow gravel road about seventy-five yards long. With giant spruce trees looming on either side of me, I was more or less able to steer myself down the middle of the road.

A cold wind was blowing against my chest, through my thin cotton pajamas. The small, jagged gravel bit into my bruised toes, but I barely noticed. My eyes were desperately searching the darkness for some kind of weapon, like a long stick. Judging by the sound of crunching gravel, Mr. T. was staying a steady couple of yards behind me. I needed to distract him somehow.

"I don't get it, Mr. Tamarack," I said. "Did you kill Zzyp?"

When he didn't answer, I stopped and turned toward him. He stopped too, and snarled, "Keep moving."

I kept moving. "And what about your son? You killed him too, didn't you? But why?"

Mr. T. still didn't answer. It wasn't fair. I thought murderers were supposed to be eager to talk about their evil deeds to whomever they were about to kill. Some perverse instinct to brag, or confess. That's what happens in all the movies and TV shows. So why wasn't it happening now?

I talked faster and shriller, still trying to get Mr. T. flustered. "You killed your son because he was beating Susan, right? And because you wanted her all to yourself. You only had a couple of months left to live, and you couldn't wait."

Finally he spoke — or rather growled. "I know what you're trying to do, Burns. Forget it. Won't work."

"I gotta tell you, Mr. Tamarack, that's pretty sick, having sex with your son's wife."

"You wouldn't understand."

"Sure, I do. You took advantage of her when she was too battered and upset to say no."

Mr. T. gave a low growl. "Listen, you piece of garbage, you say one more word about me and Susan and I'll shoot you on the spot."

I took him at his word and shut up. But

after a few moments of silently death-marching toward the pond, I began again. "Here's what I still don't get. Why'd you kill Zzyp?" Then suddenly it hit me. "I know — because he found out somehow about you and Susan. And he threatened to tell Pierce all about it, unless you paid him. So you paid him with your gun."

"Nice theory."

"But it's true, isn't it? And that's why you're killing *me*. You're scared I'll tell Shmuckler about your affair."

"Damn right, I'm scared you'll tell him."

"I won't do that, I swear."

"Horseshit. You're just like everyone else these days, the politicians, the media, you don't care whose life you ruin."

"I'm not like that, Mr. Tamarack," I pleaded. "I haven't told Will yet, and I don't plan to."

"Is that so?" he said sarcastically. "You sure threatened me plenty about telling the cops."

"Look, all I was trying to do was find your son's killer!"

"Well, bully for you. I'll give you some news, pal: You'll never threaten me and Susan again — ever. Now turn left."

If we had kept going straight, we'd have gone another hundred yards and wound up at a neighbor's house. But turning left pointed us toward a grassy clearing on the edge of the pond.

The wind must have blown the clouds away from the moon, because I could see a fat crescent reflecting off the water. I made out a big shape in front of us in the middle of the clearing. It was a pickup truck — Mr. T.'s, I realized.

And now I realized, too, what the old man's plan was. He was going to pop me here by the pond, so he could jump in his pickup right afterward and take off. Also, maybe he was hoping that at this distance the gunshot wouldn't awaken my family, and he'd have extra time for his getaway.

Even the moonlight reflecting off the pond was playing into Mr. T.'s hands. He'd be able to see me well enough to kill me with one shot. I wondered, would he shoot me with some ceremony, maybe give me a little warning? Or would he, experienced killer that he now was, just pull the trigger with no fanfare at all?

Judging by the pronounced lack of ceremony he'd shown so far, I was pretty sure he'd go for the latter scenario. The only warning I'd get would be the nanosecond between the crack of the gun and the bullet smacking my chest.

I had to hand it to Mr. T., he'd come up with a darn good plan. I couldn't see any flaws whatsoever —

Until he started coughing.

Without even thinking, I leapt around the back of the pickup and crouched down low behind the driver's door.

Through his coughs, Mr. T. sputtered out, "Fuck!" Then somehow he managed to stifle the coughing and hush up. I strained my ears to hear him. But I couldn't hear a thing. Maybe it was just my imagination, but the nighttime forest noises suddenly seemed to get twice as loud.

I thought about running into the forest. But it would take me a good fifteen strides to make it out of the clearing. That was about twelve or thirteen strides too many —

*CRACK!* Oh, shit. I felt the bullet hit my leg through my pajamas. I started to yelp with pain. Then I realized it hadn't hit my leg after all, just the pajamas themselves.

But with the next shot I might not get so lucky. I couldn't see Mr. T.; he must be aiming at me from underneath the truck. Damn. I looked down at my legs, wondering if there was some way I could hide them. My pajamas were bright orange, and seemed to attract every wayward bit of moonlight in the entire clearing.

Mr. T. shot again. This time he missed, but I could swear I felt the air from the passing bullet flutter my PJs at the knees. I quickly stepped out of my pajama bottoms and threw them away from me. I had a decent tan left over from summer weekends at the beach. Hopefully my legs would be dark enough that he couldn't make them out from his vantage point under the truck. I needed every edge I could get.

There weren't any gunshots or other human noises for a while. I took advantage of the temporary lull to rip off my orange pajama top, too. I felt a little weird, standing naked in the moonlight battling an old man to the death. But what the heck.

Suddenly I heard a soft rasping to my left — Mr. T.'s breathing. He was coming around the front of the pickup. Quickly and silently, I slipped around to the rear of the truck and kept on going up the other side until I was next to the passenger seat. Then I stopped and listened. Was Mr. T. still chasing me, or had he stopped also?

At first I couldn't hear anything but those darn animals and bugs. But my ears were gradually becoming accustomed to the forest, and I was able to make out that soft rasping again. To my right this time — he was coming at me from the other direction now. *All around the mulberry bush, the monkey chased the weasel.* . . . Stepping as lightly as I could, I retraced my steps around the pickup and wound up right back where I'd started, alongside the driver's seat.

I wasn't enjoying this game much. The gun was taking all the fun out of it. But I did have one advantage — I could hear the old man breathing, but I doubted he could hear me.

The long minutes of stress were making his lungs work harder and his breathing grow louder. Now I could hear him clearly as he switched directions again, working his way up the right side of the pickup and then around the front.

Time for me to stop acting like a weasel. I crouched down beside the pickup's front left fender, getting ready to jump him as soon as he came close enough. I listened to that rasping approach. It was taking forever.

But then, all at once, his head and gun arm appeared around the front of the pickup.

I sprang upward, flailing at him. My left arm hit his right arm, and the gun went off. I stumbled against the front bumper and fell down. Luckily, he was falling, too. Had the bullet hit him? No — he scrambled up, and so did I. We faced each other. Any moment now he'd shoot me dead.

Then I noticed a key fact: he didn't have the gun anymore. I must have knocked it loose when I attacked him.

His eyes darted around looking for the gun. Mine did too. We both spotted it at the same time. It was gray and shiny and glinting in the moonlight about three yards away, down a small hill.

He was closer to the gun, so he had a two-step head start. But at last old age and illness took their toll. I caught up to him and shoved him hard on his left hip, knocking him sideways. While he was regaining his footing, I beat him to the gun. I picked it up and waved it in his face.

"Hands up!" I yelled. Any cliché in a storm.

He just stood there and stared at me. Or at least, I thought he was staring at me. With the pond and the moon behind him, I couldn't see his eyes. I couldn't tell if he was about to make one last all-or-nothing leap at my throat, or if he was going to put his hands up. Maybe he couldn't tell, either.

"Don't make me shoot you!" I shouted frantically. *"Put your hands up!"*

Still his hands didn't rise. His breathing was growing louder and louder, which probably heralded a horrible coughing fit. Meanwhile I thought I saw his legs bending at the knees. I definitely saw his arms come out from his sides. I sensed he was about to lunge at me.

Great. I'd have to kill an old man while he was in the middle of coughing his poor lungs out.

"Mr. Tamarack," I said desperately, "Susan doesn't want you dead. She wants you alive. She needs you."

Now my clichés were really starting to bother me. I was sure I sounded too corny for Mr. T. to pay me any attention.

But luckily the clichés seemed to hit the spot. Mr. T. slowly put his arms back down to his sides and straightened his legs. Then he burst out into the worst coughing spasm I'd ever seen him have, and that was saying something. He gasped and doubled over in pain for what must have been a full minute or two. I was afraid he would die on me anyway, whether I shot him or not. Actually, him dying of natural causes here and now might be the best thing that could possibly happen.

But he didn't die. Slowly his coughs subsided and he straightened up.

"Let's go back up to the house and get warm," I said.

He nodded and silently began trudging

up the path to Grandma's house. I stayed right behind him, the gun held high. I didn't think he'd try anything, but why take chances?

As we went up the front steps, a light came on in Grandma's living room. The gunshots must have woken somebody up. When Mr. T. opened the front door, with me on his heels, we were immediately greeted by the sight of Andrea, Bernie, Derek, and Grandma all standing in the living room staring at us. That's when I remembered I was still stark naked.

Grandma found her tongue first. "What in God's name?"

"It's a long story. Mr. Tamarack," I said, keeping the gun trained on him, "why don't you go sit on the sofa. Hannah, do me a favor and call 911. And Andrea, how about getting me a robe?"

"What about me?" Bernie asked.

"Yeah," Derek chimed in. "What should *we* do?"

"Just thank God it's over," I told them.

# 17

But it *wasn't* over.

Hack Sr. — now that he didn't have a gun anymore, I was thinking of him as Hack Sr. again — sat on Grandma's living room sofa not saying a word. He did plenty of coughing, though. I felt silly getting a glass of water for a man who had just almost killed me, and who I was now holding a gun on. But I didn't want to be stuck listening to him hacking until the police came, so I brought him a drink.

When the local Lake Luzerne cops arrived fifteen long minutes later and took him away, he was still mute. I guess he was thinking up what story to tell. Because later that night, when Saratoga's finest showed up at the Warren County Jail to interrogate him, he was ready for them.

He confessed to Chief Walsh and Lieutenant Foxwell that he was trying to kill me, but he refused to explain why. Furthermore, he categorically denied killing either Zzyp or his son.

Chief Walsh came to Grandma's house early the next morning and told me about

Hack Sr.'s denial. "But that's ridiculous," I said, outraged that Walsh actually seemed to believe him. "I'm telling you, he basically *confessed*. When he was marching me off to the pond."

Walsh gave an irritating shrug. "Not according to him."

"But —"

"He says you kept telling him he killed these people, and he didn't say no because he didn't feel like getting into it with you. So you took that to mean yes, but it didn't."

I tried to remember last night's mostly one-sided conversation. Technically, Hack Sr. might be right — he didn't explicitly state that he killed anyone. "But still," I said, noticing a whine in my voice and adjusting to get rid of it, "just from the way he spoke, it was obvious he agreed with what I was saying."

Walsh shifted gears. "By the way, why *was* the old man trying to kill you? Not that I blame him, of course."

"I haven't the foggiest," I replied, still giving Susan Tamarack and her family a wee bit of privacy after everything they'd been through.

The chief poked away at me with more questions, but I stoutly professed ignorance. "Look, Burns," he declared finally, exasperated, "you may think you're cute. But you're obstructing two murder investigations."

He had a point, and eventually I'm sure I would have given in, but it turned out I didn't have to. Later that day, the police were able to match Hack Sr.'s gun to the bullet they recovered from Zzyp's body. That was all the evidence they needed to book him for Zzyp's murder.

Interestingly, Hack Sr.'s gun had filed-off serial numbers — just like the other gun that had killed Hack Jr. That convinced the cops that Hack Sr. had done both killings.

Hack Sr. held fast, though. He continued to deny the allegations and defy the allegators. He did amend his story, now claiming that he went to see Zzyp early Sunday evening about a campaign matter and found him dead on the floor with the gun beside him.

Zzyp's wing of the mall was deserted at that hour, Hack Sr. said, and he was frightened the killer might still be lurking nearby. So he picked up the gun and took it with him for protection when he left Zzyp's office.

Then he never gave it to the cops because, in his words, "I didn't want anybody knowing I was at this fellow Zzyp's office in the first place. Wasn't nobody's business." He claimed he was planning to ditch the gun that night, but then decided to shoot me with it instead.

The way I learned about Hack Sr.'s revised statement was from Dave, my cop friend. It was Dave, too, who rang my doorbell two days later and gave me the word: Hack Sr. had finally broken down and confessed to both murders.

The old guy was still acting cagey about his motives, though. All he told the cops was: "I killed 'em because I wanted to. Ain't that good enough for you?"

And it *was* good enough. The cops had their man. So I figured there was no need to inform them about the wife beating and illicit sex that had motivated Hack Sr. to kill his own son.

I still wasn't exactly sure why he killed Zzyp, and maybe I never would be. But I let it go and allowed my life to return to normal. My family moved back home to Saratoga, we got the busted window repaired, and my kids lost their fear of sitting in the computer room. With the bad guy captured and in jail, Bernie Williams had three dry nights in a row and Derek Jeter didn't walk in his sleep — at least, so far as we knew.

As for the Shmuck-man, his "to be or not to be" moment was long forgotten and he campaigned with renewed zest. He still wasn't talking about real issues much, or if he was, the media buzzards didn't report it. But they did report, repeatedly, his impassioned declarations about having been an innocent man unjustly accused. He came across great on TV, like the hero of a real-life courtroom drama.

His two opponents rocked back on their heels. Inspired by Judy's scoop in the *Saratogian*, the buzzards were all over Pierce for details about his dealings with Sarafian; and even though both of them steadfastly protested that they were 110-percent pure, Pierce's campaign was on the skids. I wondered if Linda Medwick was still sleeping with him. Probably not.

Meanwhile, Susan Tamarack had cut way back on her campaign appearances after her father-in-law was arrested. On the positive side, the media gave her a lot of sympathy for having a husband who got killed and a father-in-law who went postal. But there were also whisperings that she herself might have been involved somehow in one or both of the murders. No one had anything concrete, and none of the buzzards wanted to take on the poor grieving widow until they did. There was enough of an unsavory aura surrounding her, though, that her campaign suffered.

On Friday morning, I sat in the back room of Madeline's and read the latest poll results in the newspaper. They showed: Robert Pierce, eighteen percent; Susan Tamarack, twenty-eight percent; and William Isaac Shmuckler, *thirty-six percent.*

I was thrilled for Will — and for myself, too. For the past few days I'd been indulging in a nifty new fantasy, and now, as I sipped my café au lait and reread the poll results, my fantasy felt more and more real. It went like this: Andrea would take a year's leave of absence from her job, we'd move down to Washington, and I'd be the Shmuck's legislative aide.

Andrea and I had stayed up half of last night talking about this, and we both agreed it could be a very cool adventure. I was enjoying my sabbatical from writing, but sometimes I felt like I was drifting. It would be great to have some exciting work that really gave me a sense of purpose.

As for Andrea, she was more than ready to take some time off from teaching. She thought the department chairman would give her a leave of absence without prejudice to her tenure application, and she could use her free time to write the children's book she'd been meaning to write for years.

So I had called the Shmuck first thing this morning. We'd made arrangements to meet at Madeline's in the afternoon, about five hours from now, and I was planning to ask him for a job then. God knows after everything I'd done for him, I deserved a job. How much do legislative aides make, I wondered, and what does it cost to live in Washington . . .

My morning daydreaming was interrupted when Susan Tamarack walked into the espresso bar. She headed straight toward me.

I stood up. She was dressed in black, as always, but she looked even more waiflike than before. Despite all those casseroles, she must have lost five or ten pounds — and she didn't have five or ten pounds to lose. Her face was pale and drawn.

"Ms. Tamarack, I can't tell you how sorry I am," I said, quite sincerely.

She studied me for a moment, then said, "I appreciate your not telling anyone about . . . you know."

I nodded, embarrassed. "No problem."

She sat down and I did too, feeling uncomfortable as hell. "Here's what I don't get," she began. "If you *did* tell people about me and my father-in-law, it would kill my campaign. Your buddy would win for sure. So why don't you do it?"

I squirmed in my seat. I had pondered the exact same question. Thirty years of recent political history, from Watergate to Willie Horton to Monica, told me that I was a sap for not revealing everything I knew. I should fight the Republicans any way I could. Dirty tricks and slimy tactics are the name of this politics game.

But I couldn't help myself. Some foolish remnant of idealism prevented me from using irrelevant personal attacks to get votes.

The widow studied me some more. She seemed to decide something. "You're a good man," she said quietly.

"Yeah, well, I try not to be *too* good. No future in it."

She put her hand on mine. The sudden contact made me uneasy — was she flirting? — but I couldn't think of a polite way to remove my hand.

"Mr. Burns, I need your help," she said.

"With what?"

"I want you to find out who killed my husband."

*Come again?* Now I did remove my hand. "Susan —"

She stopped me. "It wasn't George."

"But he confessed."

"He lied."

"Why would he confess to a murder he didn't commit?"

"To protect me."

"I don't get it."

"He thinks I killed Jack. And Zzypowski, too."

I stared at her. "Why would he think that?"

"Hey, I had plenty of reason to kill Jack," she said harshly. "He was abusive. He was a sadist. He cheated on me."

A jolt of electricity shot through me. Whoa, maybe she really *did* kill her husband. "What about Zzyp? Why would you kill *him*?"

She shook her head impatiently. "I don't know what George is thinking. He won't explain it to me. He won't even *talk* to me. I go to see him in jail and he just . . ." Her voice caught in her throat. "It's horrible. He's so depressed, he's losing his mind."

She looked on the verge of crying, but I tried not to let that distract me. "Wait a minute. If he won't even talk to you, then how do you know he thinks you're the murderer?"

"Because why else would he say *he's* the murderer?"

"Maybe it's true. He did try to kill *me*."

"Look, I know George. He didn't do it!"

"There's another thing. You told me that you and George were together the night Jack was killed. So George must know you didn't do it."

She looked abashed. "George and I weren't really together that night. I was seeing a lawyer about filing for divorce."

"Wait a minute. Linda Medwick said your husband was filing, not you."

Her lips parted. "He was? The bastard. But anyway, I couldn't very well use the lawyer as an alibi. If word got out I was divorcing Jack, it would ruin my campaign. I'm supposed to be the grieving widow and all that."

I rolled my eyes. It hadn't taken this woman long to turn into a typical conniving politician.

The widow caught my disapproval. "Look, why *shouldn't* I get some benefits out of my husband dying?" she declared defiantly. "After everything I put up with from that bastard, it's only fair I should get *something*."

"Like a Congressional seat?"

She gripped the edge of the table. "You don't have to like me. But George doesn't deserve to die in prison. They won't even give him bail, because they say he's dangerous. That's insane!"

"Not to me."

"Mr. Burns, I'm sorry about what he did to you. I'm sure he's sorry, too. He's a loving man, a good man, like you."

"Cut the flattery, huh?"

"Will you help me?"

"Why don't you just go to the cops?"

"I did. They wouldn't even *listen* to me." Her lips trembled and the waterworks started. "George Tamarack deserves to die a decent death, in his bed, surrounded by people he loves. I'm begging you, *please*. If you won't do it for George, or me, then do it for my son. You're our only hope."

She was leaning forward, and one of her tears fell into my café au lait. I sighed. "So what's your theory on who done it?"

"Oh, Mr. Burns," she breathed, "thank you."

"Don't thank me yet. I haven't said yes to anything. So let me guess: You're figuring Pierce for the killer, aren't you?"

She pushed a wayward lock of wavy black hair back from her forehead. "Do you remember, you asked me once what Jack was planning to say in that radio debate?"

I eyed her quizzically. "Yeah, you claimed you didn't know. What, is this *another* lie you told me?"

"I didn't trust you then. And anyway, I *don't* know, not really." She leaned forward. "But the night before the debate, I over-heard Jack talking to someone on the phone. He said something like, 'Be sure to listen to WTRO tomorrow. I've got something that'll knock their socks off.' "

"Knock *whose* socks off?"

"I'm not sure. And then he said, 'They won't be calling me the Hack anymore after tomorrow night. Everyone'll know, I'm my own man.' "

I sipped my café au lait *cum* tear drop thoughtfully. "*I'm my own man.* Does that mean, instead of being Ducky Medwick's man?"

She bobbed her head vigorously up and down. "See, Jack was paranoid everyone was laughing at him behind his back. He knew people thought of him as a nobody, a yes-man to Ducky who just happened to be in the right place at the right time. Jack didn't discuss it with me — he never dis-cussed *anything* with me — but I'd hear him on the phone with people. He was scared Will Shmuckler would keep calling him a 'puppet of the party bosses' and stuff like that, and eventually it would stick in people's minds, and he'd lose the election."

"Get real. There's no way he was gonna lose."

"Everyone knew that but him. Jack was always insecure. He knew his Dad didn't approve of him, and deep down he felt like he didn't really *deserve* to be a congressman. So he wanted to do something to prove himself."

I circled the rim of the coffee cup with my finger. "And you think he was planning to prove himself how — by saying something in the debate that would be damaging to Ducky? That doesn't seem logical."

She threw me a frustrated look. "I'm telling you, he *wasn't* logical. He was so scared of losing that election, he went off the deep end! He beat me for looking at him the wrong way. He screamed constantly at our son. And he was fucking Ducky Medwick's wife! So don't tell me about *logical*. What that man did has nothing to do with *logical!*"

The veins stuck out in the widow's forehead and the pulse in her neck was throbbing. It struck me that she might not be acting too incredibly logical herself. Again I wondered if her father-in-law/lover was right, and she really did kill her husband and Zzyp.

But if that was the case, then why would she come to me? Maybe she felt guilty about

George taking the rap for her, and she was hoping against hope that I could find some plausible alternative suspect to toss to the police.

"Mr. Burns, if you want money, I can pay you —"

I put up my hand. "Enough already, I'll take the case."

As soon as the words escaped my mouth, I regretted them. I mean, the man who had confessed to both murders and almost certainly committed them was behind bars; my wife and kids were calm again, and so was my mother-in-law; and my man Shmuckler was about to become the first-ever Jewish liberal Democratic congressman from the 22nd District. Why couldn't I just leave well enough alone? All I had to do was say no to this woman, and I'd get to spend a quiet morning sipping yuppie beverages and doing the *New York Times* crossword puzzle.

But I guess just like everyone else, I was a sucker for a grieving widow. I picked up my café au lait and drank some more of her tears. Then I got down to work.

Susan and I went out to her car, a Volvo that used to be her husband's. We searched the glove compartment and map tray for any slips of paper or other stuff that might possibly tell us what he was planning to say in the debate that never was. But we came up empty.

I decided to confess to Susan about stealing her mail. She glared at me for a moment, then shrugged it off. We went to my Toyota, pulled the box of the Hack's personal effects out of my trunk, and scavenged it anew for evidence. But we found nothing striking, just the same random personal miscellany and boring official documents. I thought Susan would break down when she found a photograph of the Hack with their son, but she bit her lip and kept on going.

Then we went to her house and scoured for clues there. She hadn't gotten around to going through his clothes and things yet, so they were pretty much the way he'd left them when he died. We tried the pockets of his suit jackets, the drawers of his bedside table, and the desk where he paid his bills. But we didn't hit on anything that seemed useful. We did find a long computer printout in his desk, entitled "Campaign Finance Disclosure Form," which recorded all of his campaign income and expenses; but I saw nothing in there that looked suspicious.

No, let me rephrase that. I saw *a lot* of suspicious things in there, since big contributions from big corporations *always* make me suspicious. However, I saw nothing that looked positively illegal.

Apparently this operation was a bust. I sat back in the Hack's chair and closed my eyes for a moment.

"How about calling Linda Medwick?" the widow suggested. "Maybe he told *her* what he was planning to say."

Just what I needed — another skirmish with the blonde bombshell. That *New York Times* crossword felt mighty inviting right about now. "Did your husband have a safety deposit box?"

"Not that I know of."

"There must be some special place where he kept his private stuff. All men have one." Maybe not *all* men, but I certainly do. Excess cash, condoms, etc., always go in the back of my sock and underwear drawer. Come to think of it . . . "What about his sock and underwear drawer? Have we checked that yet?"

"No, but there's nothing there. I should know, I washed the man's dirty underpants for ten years."

I stood up. "Let's check anyway."

About twenty-five seconds later, I was sitting on the Hack's bed feeling like Sherlock Holmes. No, I hadn't found a copy of that final undelivered radio speech. But in the very back of that drawer, stuffed inside a pair of long underwear that Susan said the Hack never wore, I'd found something equally fascinating: a second computerized printout of the Campaign Finance Disclosure Form.

This disclosure form was different, though. It was unexpurgated. There were several "contributions" that hadn't been listed on the other printout, and some expenditures, too. The expenditure that grabbed my eyeballs and held them was one dated May 31 that read: "$20,000 — Zzypowski Research."

I felt goose bumps rising. May 31 — that was right before Robert Pierce dropped out of the race. I'd bet my entire nest egg the timing was no coincidence: The Hack had paid Zzyp for info, then immediately used it to blackmail Pierce into dropping out.

My goose bumps rose even higher when I realized the $20,000 figure rang a bell. It was the identical sum Hack Sr. had mentioned to me.

I stared down at the printout, which shook in my excited hands. Everyone and his brother had been blowing smoke at me for a week and a half, but now at last the fog was clearing. When you came right down to it, the solution to these murders was really simple.

One man had the exact same motive for both killings. Jack Tamarack spent $20,000 to blackmail Robert Pierce — and Pierce whacked him. Then George Tamarack was about to spend $20,000 so *he* could blackmail Pierce — but Pierce stopped that by whacking Zzyp.

And finally, I had the kind of evidence that even cops would have to pay attention to.

"Find anything good?" Susan asked, looking over my shoulder.

"You bet your ass," I replied.

# 18

Unlike Chief Coates's office in Troy, Chief Walsh's office in Saratoga had *mucho* class. But as Walsh leaned back in his antique leather chair and frowned at me from behind his oak desk, it occurred to me that despite his distinguished silver hair and perfect unwrinkled suit, the man himself had about as much class as Joey Buttafuoco.

"For Christ's sake already," he said, irritated, "your boy Shmuck is off the hook. The other guy confessed. Quit bothering me."

I angrily slapped the two campaign finance forms onto Walsh's desk. My gesture would have been more impressive if the forms hadn't slipped right off the desk and onto the floor. "Look, this is major new evidence."

"Yeah, major new evidence you got a bug up your ass. I'm not going off half-cocked on some half-baked vendetta against Robert Pierce."

"It's not a vendetta —"

"What's the problem, you got the hots for the widow?"

What a jerk. "At least let me look through

Zzyp's files, see if I can find proof for this blackmail scenario."

"You already went through his files, remember? When you found his body."

"I was in a hurry. Maybe I missed something."

"You didn't. We went through them ourselves. Nothing there but seedy sex and insurance scams."

"Come on, Chief," I wheedled, "just go in your back room, get me the files, and then I'll leave you alone."

"Can't do it. We examined Zzyp's files onsite. They're still there."

I gave him a look. This sounded like yet another example of his sloppiness — or unwillingness to get involved in any political controversies. Sensing my exasperation, the chief defended himself. "You can't just confiscate a P.I.'s client files. They're confidential, like a lawyer's."

"You don't expect me to believe a mere technicality like that would stop you."

"Believe what you want. I don't like having my evidence thrown out in court. We did take a *quick* peek at his files right after the murder. And we were gonna ask the judge to let us examine them in detail. But now that the killer's confessed, we don't need to."

"Yes, you do. You need to reopen the whole —"

"Wrong. *You* need to get the hell out of my office."

I grabbed the campaign forms off the floor and stood up. Clearly it was useless asking the local police chief to investigate crooked local politicians. "You'll look pretty damn stupid when I crack this case."

"Crack your head is more like it. Don't blame me if you piss someone off and get yourself killed."

"How sweet. You're actually worried about me."

"That'll be the day."

I would have stayed and bantered some more, but since Walsh refused to help me out, there was a mission I wanted to accomplish pronto: sneak into Zzyp's office somehow and search through his files again. This time I'd do it right. Maybe the chief was bothered by legal impediments, but I wasn't.

How would I get in there, though? I wasn't in the mood for another AAA B and E. I'd had more than enough of that lately, thank you very much. Also, I had a better idea. I'd go see the mall manager and tell him I was interested in renting out Zzyp's old office.

The mall was in such dire economic straits that I guessed this approach would get quick results, and I was right. The mall manager was a guy in his twenties who looked eager and freshly scrubbed, like this was his first Big Responsible Job. When I entered his brightly lit, faux-cheerful office and told him what I wanted, he almost began drooling right before my eyes.

"Sure, I'll be glad to show you the office. We can go right now," Freshly Scrubbed said, jumping out of his chair. "It's a wonderful space. Mr. Zzypowski was very happy there, and please rest assured, we've never had *any* crime problems before. We have complete twenty-four-hour security with at least two well-trained security guards on the premises at all times . . ."

He babbled on for the entire walk to Zzyp's office. It was almost as irritating as the Muzak version of "Eleanor Rigby" playing over the loudspeakers. People who turn beautiful songs into Muzak should be strung up, shot, and sent to outer space.

Freshly Scrubbed's oral motor kept right on running as he unlocked the door and we walked in. Then he took a break from his monologue at last and asked, "So what will you be using this office for?"

I didn't want to mention my name or my

million-dollar movie, in case he recognized them and realized I was connected with Zzyp's death. "I'm a writer," I said.

"A writer? How interesting," he said doubtfully. I could hear the alarm bells going off in his brain: *This guy's a writer? That means he won't be able to pay the rent.* "What do you write?"

"All kinds of things," I blustered. "National magazines, internet marketing, and so forth."

He frowned. "Internet marketing — is that well paying?"

I threw him a wink. "*Very.* Listen, this office feels very promising, but I need to see if it's a good writing environment."

"I'm sure it would be —"

"There's only one way I can really find out for sure."

"What's that?"

"I have to actually, you know, do some writing here. Do you think I could hang out here for thirty minutes while I test the place out?"

He eyed me warily. "I don't know, that's kind of an unusual request."

I gave a self-deprecating smile. "It's an artistic temperament thing. You know how writers are."

He smiled back condescendingly, as if to

say he knew *exactly* how writers are. "Okay," he said, "no problem. I'll be back in half an hour."

"Good. I have a real positive feeling about this space. It has writer vibes."

"Writer vibes. Glad to hear it," Freshly Scrubbed said as he walked away. No doubt he'd go back to his office and tell his colleagues about the eccentric writer who was testing out the "writer vibes" in Zzyp's office. I'd better get those files examined fast, before people wandered by to gawk at me.

First I went through Zzyp's desk and found the same paper clips and Wite-Out I'd found last time. In fact, everything was just like it had been before, with one exception: The quart of Jack Daniel's in the bottom drawer had gone from almost full to almost empty. Hmm. Maybe this was how those well-trained security guards entertained themselves on dull weekday afternoons.

Then I headed for the back room to search through Zzyp's cabinets. Since I didn't really know what I was looking for, I looked through everything. I began with the insurance files and their seedy tales of arsons, fake thefts, and accident victims who were supposedly crippled for life but actually played handball daily at the Y. All very enlightening, but there was nothing even remotely related to my murders.

The divorce files looked even less useful. No variety here: every single case was about infidelity. I must admit, though, I enjoyed the photographs of all those adulterous couples kissing, petting, and, well, coupling. You know those reality-based TV shows like *Cops* and *Rescue 911*? Somebody could make a lot of money off of a show like that called *Adultery*.

But after thirty or so files, even the most pornographic of the photos began to lose their charm. As I flipped rapidly through the nude bodies in the "Wilson, Kate" file, I wasn't paying too much attention. Then suddenly something hit my eye. Startled, I took a closer look at the happy-go-lucky adulterers in the photograph.

I didn't recognize the woman. But I recognized the man, all right. Kate Wilson's philandering hubbie — or by now, I suppose, *ex*-hubbie — was none other than Dennis Sarafian.

Kate must have gotten a hefty divorce settlement, because there were a lot of other hot photos in this file, too. They featured Denny baby with no less than five different women. I couldn't help getting jealous. The guy was ferret-faced and balding, but here

he was with his willowy brunette receptionist, a cute redhead, a petite Japanese
woman in a miniskirt, and a —

*A man in a ski mask?*

What the hell was *this?*

It was a dark, nighttime shot of Dennis
Sarafian handing over a briefcase to a man
with a ski mask covering his head. But the
ski mask man didn't have any weapons that I
could see, and it didn't really look like a
stickup. Apart from the unusual costume,
this transaction had the aura of a business
deal. It was the same sort of deal I'd seen recorded in that other photo of Sarafian,
Pierce, and the envelope of cash.

Speaking of envelopes, as I stared closely
at Ski Mask I noticed something in his left
hand that looked like a large clasp envelope.
He seemed in the process of handing it over
to Sarafian. Were the two men exchanging
the briefcase for the envelope?

The next two photos in the file confirmed
that impression. They showed the men
walking away from each other, but now
Sarafian had Ski Mask's envelope and Ski
Mask had Sarafian's briefcase.

Who was that masked man? Pierce again?
No, the guy was about as tall as Sarafian,
which made him way too tall to be Pierce —

And then all at once I knew *exactly* who

that masked man was.

Okay, maybe I was jumping to conclusions — but they were the only conclusions that fit all the facts. Yancy Huggins and Hack Sr. had been right all along: Hack Jr. did have dirt on Ducky Medwick. This was the dirt, right here. The man in this photograph was Ducky.

And the briefcase had to be full of dough. Sarafian was bribing Ducky, probably on behalf of Global Electronics. But unfortunately for Ducky, Zzyp had been spying on Sarafian's whoopee-making, and he'd stumbled upon this payoff. Zzyp managed to identify the masked man as Ducky, and then sold this newfound dirt to the Hack.

Everything was clicking into place. The Hack, thus armed, blackmailed Ducky into endorsing him for Congress. But then Ducky discovered the Hack was sleeping with his wife. To add insult to injury, maybe the Hack was also planning to double-cross Ducky and reveal the bribe during the radio debate. But Ducky found out. So finally he snapped. He couldn't take being blackmailed, cuckolded, and betrayed by some worthless two-bit politico. In a moment of fury he grabbed his gun and headed for the radio station to put an end to his own misery and the Hack's life.

With that taken care of, Ducky proceeded to eliminate the other major threat to his safety: Zzyp. I realized with a guilty start that I was the one who'd informed him of Zzyp's existence. That made me, in a way, responsible for Zzyp's death.

Not a pleasant thought, so I shook it off and started rifling through the rest of Sarafian's file. But then someone from the front room called out, "Hello?"

I stuffed the photos of Sarafian and Ducky down my shirt. Then I shoved "Wilson, Kate" back in the file cabinet and went to the front room. "Oh, hi," I greeted Freshly Scrubbed, faking nonchalance. "Has it been a half hour already?"

"Just about," he said brightly. "So what do you think?"

"No go," I answered sadly. "Wrong vibes."

He wrinkled his forehead. "Are you sure? Because if there's something you want changed, or moved around . . ."

I got an irresistible urge to mess with Freshly Scrubbed's narrow capitalist mind. He was probably a perfectly nice guy, but salesmen tend to bring out the worst in me. "It's the music," I said.

He threw me a puzzled look. "But that's no problem. You can always just shut the door and close the music out —"

"Too late," I declared. "Aural contamination."

"What?"

"That Muzak version of 'Eleanor Rigby' has already seeped through the walls and fatally infected this office," I explained. "Just like nuclear radiation. Before any true creative work can be done here, the building needs to be defumigated, possibly even bombed. But thank you anyway for letting me check it out," I said, giving him a firm manly handshake as he stared at me in befuddlement. "I appreciate it."

Freshly Scrubbed found his voice. "No problem," he said. "Why don't we come on out of the office, and I'll lock the door."

He seemed in a hurry to get rid of me. I couldn't imagine why.

Actually, I was in a hurry to go, too. It was 3:30, time to hook up with Will at Madeline's and hustle him for that big Washington job.

And after I got done with the Shmuck, I'd go after the Duck.

When I stepped into the espresso bar, the Shmuck-man was standing at the front counter, but I could barely see him. He was surrounded by fawning customers and employees. Amazing. For months, whenever he came into Madeline's with me, people would greet him with a nervous "Good luck" and then sort of sidle away from him. They didn't want to be stuck listening to his hopeless delusions about getting elected.

But now that it looked like Will would actually *win*, people just couldn't get enough of him. He'd taken that quantum leap from glasses-wearing nerd to BMOC. I had a sneaking suspicion I wasn't the only one asking him for a job that day.

I waved hello to him over the crowd, then ordered some coffee and found a table. After several minutes, Will tore himself away from his admirers and came over.

My first good gander at him threw me for a loop. Gone was that haunted, coffee-addled, lone-liberal-in-the-conservative-wilderness look I'd seen in his eyes ever since he started the campaign. He was transformed. He was positively beaming.

"Hey, Shmuck-man," I said, "you look great."

"I feel great. Listen, I only have a minute, it's incredible what's happening, Jake. I've got an interview with the *Saratogian*, then a photo session with the *Times Union*, then a meeting at City Hall, then drinks with the Rotary Club, which is actually going to endorse me if you can believe that —"

"I can't."

"Neither can I, but it's true — Hey, thanks. Don't forget to vote," he said to a gorgeous young woman who had come up to wish him luck.

"Now that you're famous, does that mean I can't call you Shmuck-man any more?"

"Damn straight. From now on, you have to call me The One and Only Shmuck-man."

"Okay, Mr. One and Only, I got something to say. I want to be your legislative aide down in Washington."

Will smacked his palm against his forehead in a show of mock irritation. "Oh, God, not you, too," he said, but then broke into a grin. "Just kidding. Consider it done. We'll put your writing talent to good use."

"Excellent, that's just what I was thinking."

"Shmuckler and Burns, together again." He clapped me on the shoulder and stood up. "Listen, I'm running late for the *Saratogian*, I gotta roll on out of here —"

"One more thing. Check this." Feeling like a magician pulling rabbits out of his hat, I pulled the photographs from my pocket and spread them out on the table.

He stared at them and frowned. "What

the hell is this about?" he said.

"Guess who the guy in the ski mask is?"

"Who?"

"Ducky Medwick."

He sat down, stunned. "You're kidding."

"Nope." Then I told Will about my growing conviction that Hack Sr.'s confession was false and the real killer was Ducky.

"Awfully far-fetched," Will pronounced doubtfully.

"Not when you really think about it. These photos gave Ducky all the murder motive he needed. He was covering up something that would've wrecked his career and landed him in jail."

"But I can't believe Hack Sr. would falsely confess to murder to protect somebody. Does he really like Susan that much?"

*You have no idea,* I thought, but said nothing. Meanwhile Will asked, "And how can you be sure this guy in the mask is Ducky? If you show that photograph to Chief Walsh, he'll laugh in your face."

Will had a point. "Here's what I'll do," I told him. "First I'll go to Sarafian, get him to admit this is Ducky. *Then* I'll go to Walsh."

"I don't like it," Will said.

"Why not?"

"Look, my campaign is going great now,

with everybody thinking Susan's father-in-law committed the murders. Why muddy the waters?"

"You really want to let Ducky Medwick get away with killing people?"

He put up his hands. "I'm just saying go easy until Wednesday, when the election's over. That's only four days away. It won't hurt your investigation to wait that long."

Before I could make a snappy rejoinder, Judy Demarest walked up. "Afternoon, gents," she said. "Thought I might find you here."

Will stood and shook her hand. "Thank you for all your coverage, Judy. That story you wrote really shook this district up."

"My pleasure," she said. "Sure beats writing about the county fair. Guess what?"

"What?"

"Our editorial board just voted to endorse you."

"Wow, that's terrific," Will said, beaming.

"It sure is," I agreed, then patted him on the shoulder and got up. "I'll go leave you two important public figures alone. Time to head home and take care of the kids."

"What are you up to later?" Will asked. "Wanna come by the Parting Glass tonight, hang out with the Rotary Club?"

"Sounds like a wild party. But we're hitting Grandma's for dinner tonight. Gonna sleep over and do some leaf peeping tomorrow."

At the time, that was my intention. But as I drove home, I changed my plans. It hit me that we might not get back from Grandma's until late tomorrow night, and I couldn't bear the thought of waiting that long before confronting Sarafian.

But I also couldn't bear the thought of telling Andrea and the kids I was back to work on the murder cases. I didn't want to ruin our family's newly acquired calm. So I made up a little white lie — actually, a medium-sized white lie.

"Honey, I'm so sorry," I greeted Andrea when she came home, "but I can't make it to your Mom's house until later."

She stared at me, not sure if she should be worried or angry. "But —"

"I know, I know, I promised. But I forgot I have a tournament game with Dima tonight."

Dima — short for Dmitri — is an old Russian guy who's in the Saratoga Knights Chess Club with me. We were in the middle of a long-running club tournament.

"Since when do you play your tournament games on Friday nights?" Andrea demanded. Anger had won out.

"We had to schedule a special makeup day. Don't worry, Dima will probably beat me in no time flat. I'll be at your mom's in time for dessert."

In truth, Dima usually does beat me in no time flat. For a seventy-nine-year-old codger who barely made it out of World War Two alive — he claims the only thing that saved him from freezing to death at the Battle of Leningrad was a bottle of home-made vodka he'd stashed in his gun belt — Dima packs a mean wallop in his King's Gambit Opening.

But tonight I wouldn't be facing that killer gambit. Instead I waited until Andrea and the kids were safely on their way, then stopped off at Madeline's for a quick prosciutto and brie on a bagel. This was my third time at Madeline's in one day, I noted; I was getting awfully predictable.

After my sandwich met its destiny, I headed out the door to my car. As I got in, I noticed Chief Walsh walking into Madeline's. I was surprised to see that; Walsh wasn't an espresso bar kind of guy. I wondered briefly if he was looking for me. But I had no desire to speak to him until I had firmer evidence against Ducky in my pocket. I started up the car and headed for Sarafian's place.

It was already past seven by the time I got there. I was hoping he'd be in his apartment upstairs, and not out on a date with one of the bevy of beauties he liked to surround himself with. At this hour on a Friday night I never expected to find him still in his office. But that's where he was. I guess when you're a shill for Global Electronics, you lose not only your soul but also your weekends. I could see Sarafian through the window, talking on the phone and gesticulating. There didn't seem to be anyone else there.

I got out of my car. The sky was a dark twilight blue and a couple of stars were already out. The street was quiet except for the lonesome sound of one chirping cricket. I guess he didn't realize that spring and summer had already come and gone and his chances of finding a mate were pretty non-existent. Well, you couldn't fault him for trying. I walked into the building without knocking, entered the deserted reception area, and observed my quarry through the gauzy curtains.

"Listen," Sarafian was saying, "forget this Pierce business. We've got something much more important going on. We're putting it out next week. I can't give you the details just yet, but it's gonna make the EPA and all the rest of them shit in their pants. So if I were you, I'd just sit tight for a while and not run any anti–Global El editorials — unless you want to end up with egg on your face."

Egg on your face, shit in their pants . . . Sarafian was making some pretty messy threats here. But maybe he was just pissing in the wind. He got off the phone just as I walked in. He eyed me, startled. Then his face reddened with outrage.

"The hell are you doing here? How many times do I gotta tell you people: Robert Pierce and I did nothing wrong! Jesus, I've got the cops hounding me, the media, now Global El is getting on my case —"

"I'm not here about Pierce."

He raised his eyes to the heavens in mock prayer. "Well, hallelujah."

"I'm here about Ducky."

He stared at me. "Ducky Medwick? Why?"

"Why do you think?"

"I don't have a clue."

"Maybe this will refresh your memory," I said sarcastically, and threw the photos of Sarafian and the masked man on his desk.

He picked up the photos, then gave me a strange look. He opened his bottom desk drawer and reached inside.

And like a cold cream pie in the shnoz, it

hit me: what if I got this all wrong?

What if the man who killed two people to cover up his bribes was none other than Dennis Sarafian?

And what if he has a gun in that drawer?

My veins turned to ice. But all Sarafian took out of his drawer was a cigarette. He lit it. Then he asked, "What makes you so sure it's Ducky Medwick inside that ski mask?"

I'd anticipated this question, so I had a lie all ready for him. "Because I have Zzyp's surveillance notes. He followed Ducky home from the meeting."

"He did, huh? That's very funny." Then, as if to show just how hilarious it truly was, he threw his head back and burst into laughter. His mouth was open so wide, I could have dropped a baseball in there.

"I'm glad you're amused," I said pleasantly, then got up, reached across the desk, and grabbed a fistful of Sarafian's tie. He stopped laughing in a hurry. I shoved him back against his chair. A part of me stood back and watched myself in amazement. The rest of me was having a ball.

"Listen, wise ass," I said, "you better can the bullshit or I go to the cops and the media all over again. Wait 'til I tell them about you bribing Ducky. Global El will drop your ass like a hot potato. So will all your other accounts. When I'm through with you, you'll be on food stamps."

Sarafian regarded me with surprising calm. "I suggest you don't tell anyone I was bribing Ducky."

I narrowed my eyes. "Are you threatening me?"

"No, just suggesting. I'll let you in on a secret. That's not Ducky in those photographs."

"Like hell it's not."

His lips curled into a cheerfully vicious sneer. "You sure you want to know who that masked man really is?"

I nodded uncertainly but tried to keep my voice tough. "Yeah," I growled.

"It's your pal. Will Shmuckler."

I sat back down without even realizing it. "What?"

His lips curled even further as he pointed at one of my photographs. "You see that big envelope the masked man is giving me? I had a friend of mine from the FBI take fingerprints off that envelope and run them through the computer. They matched up with Shmuckler's prints from twenty years ago, when he was arrested at an anti-nuke demonstration."

Maybe this was all some elaborate lie. But I didn't think so. I remembered that demonstration. Hell, they would have busted me, too, but the police wagon was too full.

"I don't understand," I said, in a voice that had suddenly turned very small. "What was in the envelope?"

Sarafian took a puff of his cigarette, enjoying my discomfort immensely. "Information."

"What kind of information?"

He made a big show of thinking it over, then gave a magnanimous shrug. "Oh, I guess I can tell you, since we're releasing it to the press next week, anyway." He opened his drawer and handed me a bound copy of some kind of long, official-looking report, about a hundred pages thick. It looked strangely familiar. Then I read the title — *On the Efficacy of Dredging Major Waterways for Settled PCB Contamination* — and realized where I'd seen this report before.

I'd seen it in that box of the Hack's personal effects.

"Look pretty dry, doesn't it?" Sarafian said. "But trust me. It's dynamite."

"How?"

He put his feet up on the desk, drawing out the moment. "This is a scientific study, commissioned by the Hudson-Adirondack Preservation Society. The outfit Will works for," he added.

I nodded, my head feeling almost too heavy to move, and Sarafian continued. "They thought it would help them prove that Global El should pay to dredge the Hudson. Imagine their shock when their own study showed that in reality, dredging the Hudson is the absolute worst thing to do, environmentally speaking. When you dredge, you stir up the sludge and release all the chemicals. It's much better for the river if you let the PCBs just lie there undisturbed and gradually disintegrate.

"But the problem is, the Hudson-Adirondack Preservation Society has been fighting for four years now to get the river dredged. That's the main thing they harp on in all their fundraising letters. So they couldn't afford to suddenly change their position — it would ruin them. They decided to hush up the study and just file it away.

"The only reason I ever found out about it was because someone called me anonymously one night last May. He told me the highlights of the study and offered to sell it to me. Very cloak and dagger — midnight rendezvous, lonely spot, no witnesses, all that. Global El gave me the money and the okay, so I went ahead and met with the guy." He pointed to the photographs. "That's what you're looking at right there."

337

My heart was sinking, but I kept going. "So what did you do with this study when you got it?"

He shifted his feet on the desk. "Soon as we realized how powerful it was, we thought about the best way to publicize it. We decided to give it to some friendly politician. That way he'd get lots of good press, and we'd get the word out."

*Oh, God.* I would've given anything not to have to ask this question, but . . . "Who was the friendly politician — Jack Tamarack?"

"Yeah, he was gonna break the story at that radio debate. To spice it up, I even told him who I got the study from."

I could hardly breathe. "Did it ever occur to you that Will might've killed Jack Tamarack over that study?"

For the first time Sarafian looked troubled, and stubbed out his cigarette. "I wondered about that. But I didn't want to get into any big controversy, so I kept my mouth shut. And then it turned out the Hack's father killed him. So it doesn't matter anymore, right?"

I just sat there. "Right?" Sarafian repeated, eyeing me with growing concern.

I picked up the photographs and stuck them inside the study. "You mind if I keep this?" I asked, but didn't wait for a reply. Instead I walked out the door, revved up my Camry, and headed home.

I gripped the steering wheel tight and tried to reign in my racing emotions and think logically and impersonally. The first thing I should do was call Chief Walsh at the station. If he wasn't there, I'd try him at home. If that didn't work, I'd call Lieutenant Foxwell.

I hurried up the stairs to my front door. I put my key in the lock —

"Hey, Jake!" someone called out.

I turned.

It was Will Shmuckler.

# 19

I instinctively hid that Hudson-Adirondack Preservation Society study behind my back. If Will spotted it, then he would figure out what I'd been up to. Luckily our front porch light was turned off.

"Hi, Shmuck-man," I said, and was relieved to hear that my voice cracked only slightly. *Keep calm, he doesn't know that you know.* "How come you're not out drinking Guinness with the Rotary Club paparazzi?"

"That's not 'til nine. Thought I'd drop by and see if you were still around. I called your mother-in-law, she said you were playing chess tonight."

"Yeah, I forgot my chess clock. Came back to get it."

"You mind if I come in and chill out for a while? Seeing as I got some time to kill."

"Sure, come on in." Holding the study close to my side with my left hand, I unlocked the door. "I'm gonna grab the chess clock and go, but you can stick around if you want."

We went in. I left the hall light off. Will

was a step ahead of me, and my eyes darted around desperately, looking for someplace to stash that study. I found the perfect hiding spot, behind the radiator in the hall. I took a quick half-step over there and was about to drop the study in when Will turned. I put it behind my back again.

"So have you given any more thought to that whole Ducky Medwick thing you were telling me about?" he asked casually.

Hoping to keep my tone just as casual, I said, "I did, actually. I talked it over with Andrea."

If I hadn't been looking for it, I might not have seen his eyes suddenly turn hard. "Oh, yeah? What did she say?"

I gave a shrug, then regretted it immediately, afraid the movement might call attention to the fact I was holding my left hand behind my back. But Will didn't seem to notice.

"She agreed with you, that I should just let well enough alone," I said. "She's got a point. It's really not good for the kids if I keep doing this silly Colombo stuff. I mean, the fact is, George Tamarack confessed. He's the guy that did it."

Will's eyes aimed at me like poisoned arrows. "So you're gonna take Andrea's advice and let this whole thing go?"

"Yeah, screw it. No sense looking for trouble, right?"

"Right." Suddenly Will's eyes relaxed. All the hardness went out of them, and my old college roommate and best friend was standing before me once again. "Man, I'm glad to hear you say this. I'm really glad."

So was I. Now if I could just get Will the hell out of here and call the cops, I'd be home free.

"Okay, I gotta take off," Will was saying. "Yo, next year. You and me, bro. D.C." He put up his hand to slap me five. I put up my right hand.

We slapped.

And the slap jarred loose one of the masked-man photographs that I'd stuck inside the Hudson-Adirondack Preservation Society study. The photo fell to the floor.

"You dropped something," Will said helpfully. He stooped down to pick it up, and saw what it was. He frowned, then straightened back up.

"I was just about to throw those photos away, since I don't need them anymore," I said nervously.

But Will was eyeing my left arm. "You got something behind your back?" he asked.

"No, of course not," I answered. I could feel a foolish grin spreading on my face.

He held out his hand. "Let me see."

I didn't move. There had to be some brilliant trick I could pull here —

"Let me see," Will repeated harshly.

If there was a trick, it eluded me. I slowly brought my left hand out from behind my back.

It only took Will one quick glance to recognize the study. Then he looked up at my face. "You lied to me," he said.

"I can explain," I said.

"Go ahead."

"Well . . ." I began, but then drew a total blank.

Will didn't draw a blank. He drew a gun. *"Explain."*

We were facing each other in my front hallway, less than three feet apart. I was so petrified with fear that my mental synapses misfired. I found myself flashing back to a September day twenty-four years ago, my first day of college, when I first met Will in the hallway outside our dorm room.

But now my old roomie brought me back to the present by bashing my right temple — hard — with the barrel of his gun. Dizzy with pain, I stumbled backward into the living room. My legs somehow found a chair, and I sank into it.

Will turned on the light, then stood in

front of me and peered into my eyes. "You went to Sarafian, didn't you?"

I nodded weakly.

"And he told you all about me and that PCB study."

I finally found my tongue. "I don't get it, Will. Why did you sell it to him?"

"Why the hell not?" he snapped angrily. "It was a damn good study. Showed the best way to deal with PCBs. It was wrong for the Preservation Society to hush it up!"

"But still, I mean, *selling* it?" I said disapprovingly, and instantly felt like an incredible idiot. What was I trying to do, make him even angrier?

But Will seemed to have a need to justify himself. "Hey, selling it didn't hurt anybody, and I made fifty grand. I needed that money for my campaign! Jesus, Jake, what's the matter with you? Come on, you know how hard it is to run as a Democrat in this country, with the Republicans always getting all the money. I just wanted to even the playing field a little, that's all. Like Clinton and Gore did with the Chinese."

The way Will was talking to me now, like I was a friend and confidante, I felt a ray of hope. Maybe when push came to shove, my old pal wouldn't find it in him to kill me.

But Will extinguished that ray pretty

quickly. "I wish I didn't have to kill you," he said.

"You don't, Will," I whispered.

"Sure I do, you're too damn conscientious. You'll tell the cops on me — even if I *am* a Democrat."

I couldn't tell if he was joking or serious when he threw in that Democrat line. This man with the gun in his hand was a mystery to me. Politics had twisted Will beyond recognition.

"If you kill me, Sarafian will figure out what happened," I said. "He'll know you did it."

"I already thought of that."

"So why don't you just put down the gun —"

He shook his head, exasperated. "After I kill you, I'll have to go kill him, too. Goddamn it, Jake, why'd you make me have to do this?"

"Will, you are out of your fucking mind! I can't believe you're going around killing people. You're against the death penalty, for God's sake!"

A guilty look flitted across his face. "Hey, I didn't plan on doing all this, it just *happened*. I'm sitting in that stupid green room and the Hack comes in waving that photograph. Fucking sadist, says he knows all about the fifty grand and he's gonna kill me with it in the debate. Plus he's got friends in the D.A.'s office that'll make sure I do five years in prison for illegal contributions, tax evasion, all kinds of shit. He's trying to get me all rattled before the debate starts, like I'm not rattled enough already. I mean, I didn't sleep for a week, getting ready for that goddamn debate."

Will's eyes were begging me for understanding. "I got so mad I couldn't think. I had this gun in my backpack — I'd just come back from a gun show, and I bought it off some guy in a stairwell. I was gonna use it for a prop when I talked about gun control, like I told you. So this bastard Tamarack is gloating about how he's gonna send me to jail while he's up in Washington hobnobbing, and he's going on and on and laughing and laughing and all I wanna do is just shut him up, so I reach in my pack and before I know it . . . I'm shooting him." He paused. "I mean, I knew the gun had bullets in it, 'cause the guy told me, but somehow I just didn't believe it would really work."

Will looked like a lost little boy. He was holding his gun loosely at his side. Now was my chance to spring up out of my chair and bumrush him —

But he brought his gun back up again and pointed it at my face. "Don't try it."

"I wasn't trying anything," I said innocently, and quickly added, "So then what happened?"

I was hoping the gun would go down to his side again if he kept talking. But no such luck; he kept it aimed at me as he said sadly, with an air of wonderment, "Then the Hack falls down dead. And I'm staring at him, but then I get hold of myself. I wipe the gun on my shirt real quick to get rid of fingerprints. Then I rip the photograph into pieces and flush it down the toilet. And then when it turns out I have to kill Zzypowski, I just do it. And now it looks like I have to kill you, too. I'm sorry, Jake."

I could see his finger starting to squeeze the trigger. "Wait!" I shouted.

His finger backed off a fraction of an inch. "What?" he said, annoyed at the interruption.

"There's something I have to tell you," I said, then stopped.

"Yeah, what?"

I sat there groping for words. To this day, I have no idea what I would have said next if the doorbell hadn't rung.

But it did. Will, startled, shifted his gun and pointed it at the door.

This was the only chance I'd get. I leapt out of my chair and threw a hard forearm at

Will's gun. He fired. The shot went through the ceiling.

Then Chief Walsh suddenly burst into the room, bringing his gun out of its holster.

Will aimed his gun at the chief's head. I aimed a right jab at Will's face. It hit him just as he pulled the trigger. His shot missed the chief's head by about two inches.

Meanwhile the chief was aiming his gun at Will — and at me, since I was only about a foot away from him. If the chief fired now, there was a good chance he'd hit me.

As I dove to the floor, the chief fired.

Will gasped. Then he fell down in a heap right next to me and lay flat. His arms and legs splayed in odd directions, and blood poured out of a hole in his chest.

I lay where I was and watched him for a few moments. I guess I still wasn't totally convinced that he was harmless. Then I crawled over to him and took his hand.

He died pretty quickly without any famous last words. I held his hand till the very end. That was all I could do for my old buddy now.

After a while I stood up and nodded to the chief. He nodded back.

"Hey, thanks for not shooting me," I said.

"Don't think it didn't cross my mind," he replied.

# 20

The following Tuesday, Will got two percent of the votes in the election. Not a bad showing for a dead guy. He managed to beat out Yancy Huggins for third place. Robert Pierce finished second with a mere twenty-six. Susan Tamarack won in a landslide.

As for George Tamarack, he was released from prison and stayed alive long enough to see his daughter-in-law and lover get elected. He died the very next morning, at home, with Susan and Sean by his bedside.

My family stayed at Grandma's house until we got a new living room rug — one that didn't have bloodstains all over it. We were fearful that if Derek Jeter and Bernie Williams found out about Daddy almost getting himself killed again, they might get a tad disturbed.

It wouldn't surprise me if, despite all our precautions, the kids still found out somehow about my latest brush with death. After all, they do have elephant ears. And when we moved back home, we had a tough week of bedwetting and sleepwalking.

But the kids never talked to me about it.

And fortunately, in the excitement of the major league pennant race, they pretty much forgot about everything else. Why worry about minor details like murders, when their beloved Yankees had a shot at winning yet another World Series?

Meanwhile Andrea's tenure prospects at Northwoods Community College were looking solid again. Sometimes she'd catch Jeremy Wartheimer eyeing her strangely, but he never said anything.

I gave Judy Demarest at the *Saratogian* an exclusive about the murders, and she sold an extra twenty thousand newspapers that day. She had me and Chief Walsh pose together for a front page photo, and you could never tell by looking at us, arm-in-arm and smiling, that we hated each other's guts. It turned out, by the way, that the chief had come looking for me that night because Freshly Scrubbed called the cops about some crazy writer who was poking around the scene where Zzyp was murdered.

In other news, Ducky and Linda Medwick got back together again. Don't ask me for more details on that. I really don't want to know. Like they say, politics makes strange bedfellows.

Winter came. I decided to buy that HUD foreclosure down the street and begin the long process of tearing things down and building them back up again. Late one night in February, after a strenuous day of sheet-rocking, I grabbed a midnight snack and turned on the television. As I channel surfed, I happened upon Congresswoman Tamarack on the local cable access station. They had a tape of her giving a speech to some PTA group in Ballston Spa. I took my hand off the remote control and listened.

I was so surprised by what she was saying, and the way she said it, that I spilled potato chips all over the rug. Four months of politics, and being out from under her husband's thumb, had changed the woman. Her woodenness had disappeared. She was actually quite moving. She told her audience that after seeing her father-in-law falsely accused of murder, she could no longer support the death penalty. And after seeing her husband killed, she had changed her mind on gun control.

It hit me that Susan Tamarack was turning into a pretty good congressperson — maybe even better than my old pal Will Shmuckler would have been. Maybe I should ask *her* for a legislative aide job. But then she started explaining piously why raising the minimum wage would be just plain bad for poor people. I guess I wouldn't be voting to put her on Mt. Rushmore just yet. I sighed, turned off the tube, and went upstairs.

Derek and Bernie had fallen asleep with Andrea in our big queen-size bed. I got into bed, too. If I rearranged the boys' bodies a little, and wiggled my own body just right, there'd be room for all four of us. Of course, Bernie might pee in the bed . . . but I'd take that chance.

We private dicks are pretty tough.